DRAGON OF DESTINY

LEGENDS REBORN SERIES #3

EVA CHASE

To the dragons you refuse to tame

I

A frantic voice pierced through the blankness in my head. "Em? Em!"

Normally I wouldn't have objected to waking up with my head cradled in the lap of the guy I'd been in love with for fifteen hundred years. It might actually have been a plus. The trouble was, as soon as I opened my eyes to Darton's whitened face staring down at me, I remembered why I'd been knocked out in the first place.

The images rushed up: The ear-splitting *crack*. The shudder of breaking earth beneath my feet. The itchy pull of the binding spell tearing away from my body. The wave of darkness sweeping from the cave as the Darkest One charged forth.

I'd failed. Sodding hell. Despite all my efforts, the most powerful of the dark fae had broken free from the prison my half-fae magic had kept her trapped in for the last fifteen centuries. No doubt she was very peeved. And who was she going to want to inflict her rage on first? Me, the wizard who'd sealed her away, and the current incarnation of my king, whose soul she'd been determined to twist to her malicious purposes all those years ago.

I'd used the last bit of my exhausted magic to apparate us away from her, but I'd been too panicked to give the spell much focus. Where exactly had I gotten us *to*?

I pushed myself into a sitting position. My hands pressed down into soft, cool grass. Darton kept one hand by my elbow, as if he thought I might need further steadying. A reasonable concern. A rush of dizziness sent my thoughts spinning. I closed my eyes until the sensation subsided.

We were sitting in an open field. The breeze that licked past us smelled like autumn, damp and earthy. Across the field, the sunlight glimmered off the surface of a small pond. Weeping willow trees lined its bank. I blinked.

Oh. Not exactly the place I'd have chosen if I'd been thinking straight, but I guessed this was fitting.

"Do you know where we are?" Darton asked. The rising wind ruffled his gold-blond hair.

I nodded as I heaved myself onto my feet. "This is a park not too far from my parents' house. I played here a lot when I was a kid. We're just outside Boston." Apparently I still associated my most recent childhood home with safety. At least it was plenty far from Britain and the Darkest One. For the time being.

Darton stood up too. He bent to grasp the hilt of his sword. He'd been clutching Excalibur when I'd grabbed him to whisk us away. At least we still had that enchanted weapon, after all the trouble we'd gone through to retrieve it.

"Boston?" he said. "What do we do now? What exactly *happened* back there?"

I winced. Right. He didn't know yet. The knowledge sat heavy in my chest. I'd failed a lot of people by not stopping the Darkest One, but no one more than my king.

"Rhedyn offered herself up to the lightning at the last second," I said. "She sacrificed herself. To free her master. The Darkest One snapped my spell, the one that was keeping her bound. She's out now."

Darton went still. "Out? Then..."

"Then she'll be coming after you. Which is why I got us out of there." I rubbed my hand over my face. I'd lost my purse and my bag of supplies in the chaos. I had no phone, no wallet. Nothing but the now rather muddy sweater and jeans I was wearing. I glanced at Darton. "What do you have on you?"

He shook himself out of his daze and reached for his pockets. His phone's screen stayed dark when he tapped the buttons. He grimaced. "It had a little power an hour ago."

"Lightning plus magic might not have been a good combo for the battery. If we're lucky, it's not completely fried."

He patted his other pocket, and his frown deepened. "My wallet's gone. It must have fallen out—maybe during that landslide. Damn."

"So we've got no money and no means of communication. Perfect!" I reached my awareness out into the air, testing my magical sensitivity. Every nerve in my body ached in protest. No way was I hopping us to the other side of the country, to our house and all the supplies I had stashed nearby, by my power alone.

Which meant there was only one reasonable course of action, as much as I balked at it. "I guess we'd better drop in on my parents. Their place is about a twenty-minute walk from here."

Darton looked down at himself. In the middle of the battle, Rhedyn had sent a landslide over us. It had left as much dirt smeared all over his sweatshirt and jeans as I had on my clothes. "This isn't exactly how I'd have wanted to meet your mom and dad for the first time, but it sounds like we don't have much choice."

"Yeah." I wanted to say they'd seen worse, but for all my childhood weirdness, I was pretty sure showing up out of the blue and caked with mud—as a grown adult of twenty, no less—was going to make the top of the list. "Come on, Art."

Little shivers traveled up my legs as we started walking. My breath started to catch in my lungs before we'd made it to the road that ran alongside the park. That last apparating spell had really drained me, and my brief "sleep" had hardly left me recovered. All I wanted was to curl up in a bed and really sleep, for at least a week.

But I wasn't sure I could afford to sleep at all with the Darkest One on the loose. How long would it take her to figure out where we'd gone? What was she going to do to all the people who stood between her and us?

A sharper shiver raced down my back. We definitely weren't going to stay at my parents' house long enough to find out. I'd already gotten them into enough trouble. Just a few days ago, one of the Darkest One's fae minions had gotten my mom into a minor car accident, meant as a threat to me.

Darton held the sword close at his side when a car cruised by. "I feel kind of conspicuous. How much do your parents know about... all of this, Merlin and King Arthur and the rest?"

"Nothing," I said. "And we're going to keep it that

way. All they know is their daughter Emmaline is a little odd and sometimes knows more about things than it totally makes sense that she should. It's basically never a good time to tell your mom and dad that you're not their kid but the reincarnation of a legendary wizard they probably don't even believe really existed."

"Ah. I can see how that would be tricky." He gave me a wry smile that looked slightly pained. "So, just so I'm prepared, what's our story?"

Good question. "Hmm... We can say it's some kind of college club hazing ceremony. The ringleaders drop people off in pairs, and then we have to use our wits to get back to campus. As long as we sound like we're fine with it, my parents won't ask too many questions. We just won't stick around too long."

It might be good to stop by anyway, just to look for any lingering dark fae influence in the area. As far as I knew, the Darkest One's minions had left our families alone after we'd ignored their threats and headed overseas. The fae hunter we'd gotten to know, Jagger, had called up a few of his colleagues to keep an eye on things here just in case. But I'd feel better checking with my own senses.

The road swerved to the left, meandering past a few blocks of well-spaced suburban houses. The yards and driveways grew steeper with the rising hill. I scanned the lawns ahead of us as we came up on my parents' home, a two-story colonial in pale peach-toned brick. Thanks to the time difference between here and Britain, it was still early morning on this side of the ocean. Late enough that Mom and Dad should be up, but not so late that they'd have left for work yet.

A rental car was parked at the top of their steep

driveway—theirs must not be back from getting repaired after Mom's accident. No one stirred around the house. This late in the fall, there wasn't much to do in the gardens anyway. I didn't see any sign of the fae hunters either. Of course, they'd know better than to be totally obvious in their surveillance.

I showed Darton where he could stash Excalibur in the depths of the hedge, since I had no idea how we could explain why we were carrying around an ancient sword on top of everything else. Then I walked up the front steps and rang the doorbell. It felt strange, requesting entrance like a stranger. My keys had gotten lost with the rest of my stuff back in Britain.

Dad answered the door. His thinning hair, the same dark brown as mine, lay damp from his shower. His eyes widened at the sight of me.

"Emma! We weren't expecting you. Are you all right?" He paused, the corners of his mouth creasing with worry as he took me in. "You look as if you've had a rough time." His gaze slid farther, to Darton. "And who's this?"

"Emmaline is here?" Mom's voice carried from deeper in the house. She hustled over, bringing her cup of tea with her. A thick neck brace held her heart-shaped face stiffly straight. "My goodness, honey. I'd say this is a wonderful surprise, but if there's been some sort of trouble—"

"No, no," I said quickly, with a faked laugh and a casual wave of my hand. "We're fine. Just a crazy club activity that got a little out of hand. You know how college adventures can end up. This is my friend Darton, who was my partner for the weekend. We're kind of cheating by showing up here, but as long as you don't tell anyone..."

As I'd expected, my lack of distress put my parents at ease. And they'd always fretted a bit about whether I was making friends. The idea of me being in some kind of adventurous college club would probably make their day. Yeah, Dad's lips had already curled into a little smirk. He and Mom had gotten into way crazier escapades when they were my age.

"Come on in, then," he said. "Do you need something to eat? We just finished breakfast."

The tension wound around my stomach pinched too tight for the thought of eating to be appealing. But I wasn't going to get my energy back by starving myself. "That would be great," I said. "First I think we should get cleaned up, though. I wanted to grab a change of clothes and a few things from my old room. Dad, would you mind lending Darton a pair of pants and a shirt?" Dad was a little shorter and a little broader, but we couldn't afford to be picky.

"We can put your things through the wash," Mom offered. "I'm taking the day off, but even if I wasn't, you could stay as long as you like."

"Oh, no, we'll have to get going to make sure we don't get caught out." I winked at her, burying my guilt over the lies. They were safer the sooner we were out of here.

"Well, come on then, young man," Dad said, clapping Darton on the back.

I hurried up to my childhood bedroom, which my parents had left intact for summers and holiday visits. The pickings in my dresser and closet were pretty sparse, but anything clean was better than the muddy stuff I currently had on. I grabbed an old, faded pair of jeans and a sweater that had developed a hole in the sleeve. After a quick stop in the bathroom, my bladder was relieved and the dirt streaks gone from my face. I shoved my messy hair into its usual ponytail. A shower would have been amazing, but I wasn't sure we had time for that.

Back in my bedroom, I dug into a box I'd left tucked in the back of my closet. An emergency stash for circumstances like this—not that I'd ever really thought I'd be having a showdown with the Darkest One in this life. When you've gone through dozens without your biggest fear becoming a reality, it starts to feel a little less real.

I grabbed a purse I hadn't used since high school and stuffed in the few wands and baggies of herbs and salt I'd left here, as well as my spare credit card. There. Now I wasn't totally helpless.

As if a few handfuls of herbs and the wave of a wand would do much good against all the Darkest One's coiled power.

The floor creaked as I was straightening up. Darton stopped in the doorway, looking a little comical in the baggy khakis that bared his ankles and the checkered button-up shirt he'd borrowed from my dad. But still handsome. You could deck that guy out in a garbage bag and he'd make my heart flutter anyway.

There definitely wasn't time for thinking about *that*. Anyway, he knew how I felt now, how much I'd always felt, and I knew it wasn't the same for him. Better that we'd put the whole subject to rest.

"So this is where you grew up," he said.

"This time," I couldn't help saying.

He arched an eyebrow at me before taking a step

inside. "It's hard to imagine you being a kid. I guess I never knew you as one."

His gaze swept through the room. I felt suddenly exposed, even though my king already knew me better than anyone else in the world.

My duvet had a deep green vine pattern that had appealed to the sensibilities of my light fae side. The books I'd left behind on my now-dusty shelves included a bunch of science-y nonfiction, which was odd for teen reading but not embarrassing, and several historical romances, which were *definitely* embarrassing. An herbal, slightly smoky smell still clung to the walls from all the incantations I'd cast over the years, hoping to provoke the vision that would lead me to my king. A black smear marked the floorboards where I'd once dropped a lit candle.

Darton nodded to one of the band posters tacked over my bed. "Justin Bieber fan, huh?"

I made a face at him. "Past tense. I *was* an actual teenager along with everything else, you know."

He gave me a teasing smile, and sod it if my heart didn't flutter all over again.

Enough nostalgia. We had bigger problems to tackle.

We walked downstairs to the smell of frying eggs and fresh toast. "Mom," I said. "You really didn't have to. Are you even feeling okay?"

"I'm perfectly all right!" she insisted, waving the spatula. "I'm not sure I even need the neck brace, but I wasn't going to argue with the doctor. It's not as if I was in some huge crash—I was barely out of the driveway."

"Right," I said skeptically, and paused. "You haven't seen anyone suspicious around here since then, have you?

Dad said some weird guy made a strange comment to him."

"Nothing suspicious at all," she said. "And the mechanic told us it was a random system failure—unusual but not impossible."

Definitely not impossible when magic was involved. But when she shoved the plate of eggs and buttered toast into my hands, I reached for the fork automatically. I'd barely eaten anything all day—and by British time we'd have been well past due for lunch now.

"This is wonderful," Darton said to my mother. Mom beamed. Dramatic music and a serious news reporter voice trickled from the living room. I ambled over to find my Dad sitting in front of the TV.

He motioned to the screen. "Quite the storm."

What appeared to be an atmospheric pressure display was showing on the TV, but I'd never seen colors quite that stark. The broadcast cut back to the reporter. "After several days of stormy weather all across England," he said, staring solemnly at the camera, "winds are building to unprecedented levels. Some areas are already experiencing hurricane-like conditions. Residents have been advised to follow local alerts, but hospitals are already filling with injured civilians."

My stomach dropped. I put down my plate on the side table. Darton had come in behind me. He lowered his fork, his face paling, and caught my eye. I gave him a slight nod.

The Darkest One was already making her presence felt. How many more people was she going to hurt along the way?

2

A battle raged around us, but the heaving bodies were little more than a blur. The shouts and clatter bled together into a shapeless din. The taste of iron lay on my tongue, and a chill coated my skin. The blue sky darkened above us. And a figure shifted across the field like a traveling shadow.

The Darkest One. I reached for my king's arm, but Arthur was suddenly across the battle from me. The clamor rose. The blur of bodies churned between us. I threw myself into it, but the dark fae lady loomed over him already. Gray mists curled around her tall, slender body. Her arms shot out so quickly he didn't even have time to move. She dug her thumbs through his chainmail into his chest and wrenched him apart.

His body split open with a burst of shadow. His head lolled, bloodlessly pale. A scream of protest jarred in my throat. I raised my hand—

"Em." Darton's voice, like my king of old's but not quite the same, broke through my sleep. He gripped my shoulder with a quick shake. My eyes popped open. A narrow, gray space came into focus around me.

The plane. We were in the same stuffy plane cabin we'd entered a few hours ago, stiffly padded seat beneath me, recycled air filling my lungs.

Darton was eyeing me closely. "We just landed. And you... seemed like you weren't all that happy being asleep. You were jerking your head back and forth like you were fighting with something."

A flicker of the nightmare rose in the back of my head. "Don't worry about it," I said, waving him off. "Just a bad dream. Have to expect a few of those, these days." But my chest still felt tight.

It hadn't been only a nightmare. The images had come from a vision. The vision I'd had of my king's death, fifteen hundred years ago, five years before the Darkest One had nearly made it come true. It had been the first warning I'd gotten. I'd tried to heed it. And still, here we were.

The second we were allowed off the plane, Darton pulled out his phone. My dad had lent us a charging cable, and the battery had proven to be in working order. Darton skimmed through the news feeds as we made our way through the terminal in the state I'd called home for the last few months.

I patted my pocket to make sure the twigs I'd stashed for quick access were still there. I'd been able to present a couple of slips of paper as our ID cards when we'd gotten on the plane, but the illusion would have worn off shortly after we'd gotten into the air. It hadn't been worth wasting my still-limited energy to maintain that magic if I didn't have to. In my current state, casting the spell to make sure everyone ignored Darton's sword, which we couldn't exactly check, had been exhausting enough.

"The storms in Britain are still building," Darton said. "They've totally shut down the London subway system. They're evacuating a bunch of towns and cities along the coast." He shook his head, his jaw tight. "The news articles are already reporting six deaths they attribute to the storm."

"She could have done a lot worse already, if all she cared about was killing lots of people, and fast," I said, keeping my voice low. This wasn't the sort of conversation I wanted anyone overhearing.

"So what do you think she does want?"

"I have no idea. I've never been able to understand how dark fae minds work. From what we're seeing, I'd say for now she's just playing around. Collecting energy from people's fear and pain. It's been a long time since she's been able to affect anything in the world. She's stretching her muscles."

Darton shoved his phone back in his pocket. "And what happens when she's done stretching?"

I hesitated. "Probably she comes looking for us. So we've got to get ready."

A jittery itch crawled up my arms under my skin. I rubbed them through the sleeves of my sweater. I'd dozed a little on the plane, but it wasn't that long a flight. Apparently my body still hadn't recovered from this morning's jump across the ocean.

"We can grab a rental car to get home," I said, pointing Darton toward the sign. The drive would only take an hour from here. Then I'd know Darton was at least somewhat protected before I got on with other business.

The guy at the rental car desk gave us a bit of an odd look, I guessed for our lack of luggage, but he led us to a car quickly enough. "I'll drive," Darton said after the guy had left us. He set Excalibur in the back seat. "You should rest as much as you can after everything we've just been through."

I had the urge to argue. I should have been looking after him, not the other way around. But if I'd learned anything during our adventures around Britain, it was that Darton could protect himself a whole lot better when he held on to his confidence. And he could do *that* a whole lot better when I showed I trusted him to handle whatever our current situation threw at us. So I made myself simply say, "Thank you," and settled into the passenger seat.

I really *did* need that rest, after all.

As Darton maneuvered the car out of the lot, I leaned my head against the cool glass of the window and closed my eyes. I was tired enough that my mind started to drift without any effort. But the little twitches running through my body kept jolting me back into consciousness. My fingers curled of their own accord, as if needing something to grasp.

I had those few wands in my purse, but that didn't feel right. Was my body responding to some instinct I didn't quite understand?

The muscles in my arms coiled tighter with each minute. I found myself gritting my teeth. Okay, this was definitely not restful. I tried to inhale and exhale slow and deep, but the tension didn't ease.

Something was wrong. Something I couldn't ignore.

I opened my eyes in time to see a sign for an upcoming rest area off the highway. I pointed to it. "Let's pull off there. Something feels... off. I don't want to go any farther until I figure out what."

Darton took the next exit. "Do you need me to do anything?"

"Grab some food from the vending machines?" I

suggested. "I'm just going to search around with my magic."

He parked at the edge of the lot near the squat dun building that held bathrooms and a small seating area. I stayed in the car when he got out. Less likely to draw attention that way. I pulled one of the wands from my purse and sat with it resting on my palms in my lap. I didn't want to draw much energy from it, but it'd be good to have it on hand.

Closing my eyes again, I let my awareness seep out into the world around us. My fae-enhanced senses swept over the rest area and across the highway and the landscape beyond.

The itch in my muscles had already started to subside. Maybe my instincts had been responding to something we'd been heading toward? I stretched my senses west, watching for any hint of dark power. The Darkest One might be playing around in Britain at the moment, but she had plenty of underlings on this side of the pond.

A shiver ran over my skin. A small but steady stream of glooms were heading our way from various directions. The scraps of dark fae vermin were still more concentrated than usual around our state thanks to the fae mercenary who'd sent them on a hunt after us just a few weeks ago. And now they were on a new hunt. A few had already nearly reached the rest area.

Glooms weren't much to worry about on their own, but in large enough numbers they could do plenty of damage. I'd cast a protective shield around Darton before we'd left the country, but it must have worn off with all the magic we'd encountered since. And the soul of my king inside him was certainly a lot more woken up than it'd been before.

Not much I could do about that, but I could cast a new shielding spell on him. It'd be an awful irony if glooms got him before the Darkest One even showed her face on this side of the ocean.

I got out of the car and ambled over to a sapling near the edge of the paved walk. By the time I'd collected several twigs from it, Darton had rejoined me. "Do you need to work some more magic?" he asked.

"I want to redo that spell I put on you in the hotel room a while back." A fresh jitter ran through my limbs. Yeah, stopping here definitely hadn't solved the problem. "The glooms are reacting to your presence again. Come here. We don't want someone calling the cops on a couple of weirdos playing with blood."

Darton grimaced, but he followed me into the single-stall handicapped bathroom. A dank, sour smell filled my nose. Muddy footsteps and a puddle of what I hopped was water marked the floor. Not exactly ideal spell-casting circumstances, but I couldn't afford to be picky.

I scattered the twigs around us on the floor and murmured a quick incantation to sever a lock of Darton's hair. He slung his hands in his pockets and inclined his head as I broke open the skin on my palm. Seeing me do blood work always made him squeamish.

Apparently it made me squeamish today too. My nerves were twitching even harder now. The glooms weren't *that* close, were they? I tensed my arms to keep them still as I pressed the lock of hair against the cut. A murmur in my first language spilled over my lips. I drew the power from my life's liquid and the green pulse of the twigs. Then I brought the tip of my wand to my hand, circled it against my palm, and waved it in another circle around Darton.

A tingle raced over my scalp as the magical barrier formed around him. At the same time, my hands started to shake. They wanted to move—to fling out? To reach for something? My tongue quavered too, attempting to reject the words of my casting. What the hell was going on?

I barreled on through my discomfort. "*Like mist conceal, and never reveal.*" The spell wouldn't be enough to hide him from the Darkest One when she decided to look for him—it wouldn't even discourage a particularly determined regular fae, as we'd discovered not long ago—but it'd divert the lesser creatures at least temporarily.

Darton closed his eyes when I pressed my bloody palm to his forehead. The threads of my magic pulled tighter around him. There. That would do for now, at least. I could do a more thorough job of the spell once I had more supplies on hand. Assuming we had the chance before the Darkest One and whatever she had planned came calling.

"Okay," I said. "All done. Wash up." I let him go to the sink first while I tucked away my wand. The twigs had disintegrated into a circle of dust around the stall. I smeared it with my foot. No need to advertise that magic had happened here.

That strange, itchy energy kept wriggling through my bones. Whatever my body was worried about, casting this spell hadn't reassured it. I frowned as I switched places with Darton at the sink. My hand flinched away from the soap dispenser for a second before I got it under control. Hog's balls, this was annoying.

Well, I'd done what I could. I dragged in a breath,

willing myself to relax, and turned around. Darton moved to open the door. And my body suddenly sprang into motion without consulting my mind at all.

My arms snapped through the air toward Darton's back, my hands jerking up so my palms pointed toward the area behind his heart. Power pulsed from my soul and onto my tongue. "*Seize and—*"

I had to bite my tongue to cut off the spell before I finished it. A chill flooded me. Darton glanced back at me the second before I wrenched my hands down. He looked at them and then my face.

"Are you okay? Was there something else you needed to do?"

I swallowed hard. *Yes*, the urge echoing through my limbs said in answer to that second question. *Yes, yes, yes.*

Oh, light have mercy. I'd forgotten. Before we'd gone to strike down the Darkest One's allies in the hope of keeping her contained, I'd struck a deal with the light fae enclave that used to be home to my father—and me, fifteen centuries ago. In exchange for their help summoning a lightning storm, I'd sworn an oath to the elders.

If the Darkest One walks free, I will sever Arthur's soul before she can.

"It's nothing," I said quickly. I crossed my arms over my chest, jamming my hands under my elbows. "Let's get out of here."

The Darkest One was walking free all right. And the oath bound me whether I was thinking about it or not. I hadn't given an exact timeline, but clearly the threat was already great enough for the power of that binding to try to force me to act.

If I didn't figure out how to control the oath, *I* would kill Darton before the any of the dark fae did.

3

We reached our house in the middle of its lonely concrete yard in the late afternoon. The shadows of the trees along the country road were already stretching long, but the boxy structure we currently called home cast no shadows at all, thanks to the flood lights that had automatically turned on with the fading sunlight.

"Looks like everything's still in working order," I said with forced cheerfulness. "I guess nobody saw any need to mess with our house while we weren't in it."

Despite the reassurance of the lights, I kept one of my wands in my hand on the way past the door. Motioning for Darton to stay close, I walked through each of the rooms.

The furniture we'd bought less than a month ago stood exactly where we'd left it. The faint smell of oil and garlic from the last meal I'd cooked here lingered in the kitchen. No signs of any dark fae presence or anything else worrying appeared. Other than the continued jumping of my nerves whenever Darton moved closer to me.

Sodding hell. I should never have made that oath. Of

course, if I hadn't, then we might have had both the Darkest One *and* her most loyal lieutenant still to deal with... Argh.

The safer I made Darton, the less I'd feel the impulse. If the Darkest One couldn't kill him, then I didn't need to. No one could argue with that strategy. But if I was going to make this house any safer than it already was, I needed more supplies. I'd already emptied this place in our dash out of the country a few days ago.

I came to a stop in the living room after my search of the house was done. "All right. I need to go out to my storage locker to bring back some more magical materials." And maybe some of my journals too—had I ever written about dealing with oaths? I couldn't remember anything like this coming up before, but then, my memories of all but my first life were awfully hazy.

"Sure," Darton said. He headed to the front door.

I shook my head. "No, I want you to stay here. The house has way more protections than the car. The sun trap stopped a full dark fae before. And I'll only be gone a few hours."

Darton frowned. "I trust *you* more than I trust a building. Half the stuff here only works because of your magic."

"Well, you've got your nifty magic sword to defend yourself now too." I nodded to Excalibur, which he'd been carrying from room to room with us.

His frown deepened. "Do you really think we'll be in that much danger here? We just got back. How quickly can the Darkest One follow us?"

I bit my lip. "Not instantly. She doesn't have any connections here to make the leap by magic. But she's not the only thing we have to watch out for."

"If any dark fae things attack, I'm sure I'll be safer if I'm with you."

I'm not, I thought but didn't let myself say. I looked down at my hands. The hands that had moved to stop Darton's heart less than an hour ago.

That was what my feelings came down to, wasn't it? I was more afraid of the oath that was riding me than of the dark rabble or any other of the dark kind. What if the impulse to kill Darton hit me more strongly next time? What if I *couldn't* control it?

The spell that had bound my and my king's lives together, kept us reincarnating after each successive death, had been broken in the Darkest One's escape. If he died, by anyone's hand, there was no returning.

Darton was watching me, his expression puzzled and determined. "*You'll* be safer too," he added. "The dark fae are afraid of Excalibur. We took them down so much easier when we could work with both your magic and the sword."

"It might not be enough," I started, but that line of argument wasn't going to be enough either. He was right. We were both safer from dark powers with our own powers combined. And to explain why that wasn't enough, I'd have to tell him about the oath. How much would he trust me then?

I trusted myself, didn't I? I'd caught myself in the bathroom before I'd hurt him. And now I understood what was happening inside my body, so I could stay more aware of it. The only reason the oath had worked on me as far as it had was that I hadn't known what I had to defend against. It couldn't take me by surprise like that again.

"All right," I said, as breezily as I could manage. "Have it your way. But prepare for extreme boredom."

* * *

The bland beige building of the storage facility made a gloomy picture in the deepening evening. We stepped out of the rental car—I'd insisted on doing the driving this time, to keep my hands busy—and I led the way up to the main doors.

A gloom glided toward us along the edge of the building. The thicker patch of darkness amid the shadows was moving fast enough to catch even Darton's eye. His head jerked around a second before I waved my wand at it. "*Darkness begone.*"

The dark vermin shuddered out of existence. If only I could tackle the actual fae and their queen that easily.

I tapped in the code, and the door unlocked with a beep. The inner hall always smelled strangely like stale bread. I hurried past the rows of garage-style doors to the one I'd moved my stash to after a vision had brought me to this part of the country looking for my king. My keys might be lost somewhere back in Britain, but it only took a tiny twig and a few murmured words to open the padlock.

I pushed the door halfway up and ducked under. Darton followed. His eyebrows rose as I shoved the door back down to give us privacy.

"Wow. You really do like to stay well-prepared, don't you?"

"I've had a lot of time to collect supplies and not too much need of them until recently," I said. "I'll try to make this quick."

I grabbed a couple of the duffel bags I kept there for purposes like this and started stuffing them full of pre-enchanted wands, bags of dried herbs and flowers, various types of salt, incense and candles, various semi-precious stones that might come in handy, and a knife to replace the light fae dagger we'd also lost somewhere in our battle with Rhedyn. Like that one, its handle was made of magic-sealed living wood. But it didn't come close to the craftsmanship the full fae were capable of when they bothered.

My life would really be a lot easier if they bothered more often.

Here and there I paused with an instinctive urge to leave some behind. For next time. My hands balled, and I shoved more into the bags.

There wasn't going to be a "next time." No more rebirths. No certainty that no matter what happened, I'd find my king again. This was the last life we were going to get, however little might remain of it.

Darton meandered amid the shelves, stopping to finger a folded cloth, to sniff a bunch of herbs dangling from the top of one shelf. He wrinkled his nose. "It reminds me of the apothecary shop. At least, as well as I remember that at all."

"I don't suppose you've had any other incredibly helpful memories?" I said. His recollection of visiting the apothecary in our first lives had led us to the brainstorm of using lenses to amplify the power of sunlight. That idea had allowed us to destroy the dark fae mercenary who'd attempted to grab Darton for his own purposes, and powered the sun trap in our house.

"Not so far." Darton rubbed his mouth. "I still can't even remember why I was looking into the dark fae without talking to you about it. I mean, it's one thing to want to help on my own, but having seen what I have now, I'm pretty sure I was smart enough to realize I'd accomplish more with your knowledge on my side."

"You grew up back then knowing you'd be king," I said. "You weren't used to having to hold yourself back for anyone else. Besides, knowing *me*, you might have asked and I just told you to leave it alone and let me handle everything."

Although I didn't actually recall Arthur ever coming to me asking what strategies I'd looked into for defeating the dark fae. He'd listened well enough when I'd talked about them, but he'd seemed willing to leave that conflict to me while he dealt with his many totally human opponents. I'd never realized he'd wanted to tackle that part of our problem himself.

"Hmm," Darton said, sounding unconvinced. "I'm sure I could have pressed you into talking if I'd tried hard enough."

That was also true. I'd always had trouble denying my king anything.

I moved to my stacks of musty journals, some dating back hundreds of years. A pang ran through me at the thought of the different set of better-cared-for journals I'd left behind on the other side of the ocean. My father's friend Cormag—the elder who'd insisted on the damned oath—had given me a set of my father's journals that detailed his observations and thoughts on the dark fae influence on Arthur's family line. It hadn't made sense to bring them to our confrontation with Rhedyn. I'd left them with two of Jagger's fae-hunter colleagues for safe-keeping, thinking I could come back for them.

I hadn't expected to be making *quite* such a huge or

hasty exit.

It would have been good to pour over those more thoroughly right now, but the truth was that nostalgia and family ties aside, they hadn't offered me much useful information in the skim I had been able to give them. If my father had figured out anything that could definitely have changed Arthur's fate, I'd have known about it.

Darton crushed a few leaves of the herb between his thumb and forefinger. A sharp, bittersweet smell drifted through the air. His gaze had gone distant.

"You said Rhedyn let us kill her. That she sacrificed herself so that she could free the Darkest One. Right?"

"Yep. A sneaky trick. We were going to kill her anyway, but she stopped fighting at the last moment. Giving herself over so she could tap into that magic." I made a face and opened up one of my journals to check the contents.

"So she could just make that choice in the moment, because she wanted to? Did she need any magical materials for that? Or is it something the fae can just naturally do?"

"Sacrificial magic is completely internal," I said. "It's about the shape of your will and the strength of your intention." I paused, glancing up. "Why are you asking?"

Darton shrugged. "I just wondered. Obviously it's not something we'd want the fae using against us again."

It wasn't something I wanted *him* thinking about either. Darton could be a little too eager to prove himself a hero sometimes. You'd think years of princely and then kingly valor would have satisfied that urge. It wasn't as if a twenty-year-old college guy could match that kind of past. But so far that fact hadn't stopped him from trying.

Which was why I loved him, wasn't it?

That was another line of thinking it wasn't wise to go down. I bit my lip, poked through the rest of the stacked journals, and finally grabbed a couple to add to my bags. I wasn't sure they'd be useful, but they seemed like the most likely.

The duffels weighed heavily on my shoulders now. "Okay," I said. "I think we're done here."

Darton held out his hand in an offer. I let him take one of the bags off me. I swung the other behind me and heaved up the storage room door. The bag bumped against my hip with each step as we walked down the hall. Fifteen hundred years of stockpiling and experimenting... and it still didn't feel like anywhere near enough to sustain us through the battle ahead.

4

The newscaster's solemn voice carried from our TV.

"This catastrophic storm shows no sign of abating. Many coastal areas have completely flooded, but the intense winds are making further evacuation difficult both by land and by sea. Rescue teams are doing as much as they can under these extreme conditions. Still no agreement from meteorologists on what might have caused this truly bizarre and horrific weather over the United Kingdom."

The five of us huddled on the couch and loveseat winced together at the video footage of telephone poles toppling in the gale. On the TV screen, shingles flew away off a nearby house's roof. The pelting rain colored the entire image in shades of gray.

No lightning, of course. The Darkest One wanted her torment to be as grim and gloomy as possible.

"So all that was stirred up by just *one* of these faeries?" Keevan said, his eyebrows high.

"The oldest and most powerful of all of them," I said. And probably not quite at her full power yet. She was just warming up. My stomach listed queasily. "Plus she'll have all the lesser dark fae in the country pitching in."

"Man." He rubbed his hand over his dark face. "That's just— Shouldn't you be over there, like, fighting her or something? Isn't that what wizards do?"

"I'm the only wizard I know, and I can't match that." I waved at the TV. "If we're going to stop her, or at least contain her, we're going to have to be incredibly smart about it. She'll show more of her hand soon." I hoped... and also dreaded. I couldn't imagine she'd wait much longer before coming after me and Darton.

"But all those people..." Izzy shuddered where she was perched next to Keevan, her pale auburn waves drifting over her shoulders. "What about the light fae? Those enclaves you talked about, here and over there. Can't they do anything?"

I made a face. "The light fae generally don't care about anything they don't have to care about. The ones affected in Britain will be doing what they can to protect themselves—and not wanting to expend any additional energy trying to get into some sort of fae war. The ones here won't see any reason to get involved, since it isn't affecting them. They're not exactly philanthropists."

Beside me, Priya twisted her hands in her lap. "My old enclave might be willing to do *something*. They did help monitor what the dark fae were up to around here last week." My former roommate had grown up with the light fae as a sort of changeling, until they'd brought her back to the human world to be adopted. And to be fair, her bunch *had* stepped up when we'd needed them. But keeping an eye on things and waging war were pretty different requests.

"I'll keep that in mind, when I have a better idea of

our best strategy," I said. "The other enclave I'm familiar with around here wasn't even willing to keep us protected on their own territory, so they're definitely not getting involved in some huge conflict off of it."

The news broadcast moved on to the next big story. "With the International Peace Summit approaching in just one week, the Windy City's hotels have already started to fill with citizens from all around the world, eager to have a voice in their leaders' conversations. The summit is scheduled to be hosted at Chicago's Fairning Convention Center in—"

Darton switched off the TV and stood up. "We'll do what we can, when we can. Let's get the table set. The food should be here any minute."

The rest of us ambled with him to the kitchen. He'd texted his best friends last night to let them know we'd gotten back in one piece, for now, and I'd reached out to Priya. After all the five of us had already been through together, I guessed I shouldn't be surprised that they'd all insisted on coming right over after classes to confirm the whole "in one piece" part in person. But all their visit was leading to was a whole bunch of uncomfortable conversations.

"Wouldn't it be better if you were at least closer to where the dark fae are casting their magic?" Izzy said, grabbing glasses out of the cupboards. "I mean, so that when you know what to do, you can act right away."

I turned away from her to place a stack of plates on the table. "I don't think there *is* any safe way of getting into Britain at the moment." Maybe flights were diverting around the storm to land in France or other countries closer than we were right now... but the closer we were to the Darkest One, the more I'd feel that impulse to fulfill my oath. Even now, the itch scrabbled faintly under my fingernails. Darton hadn't let me go off to my storage locker on my own—he sure as hell wasn't hanging back here while I flew across the ocean.

Thankfully my king was also quick to defend my reasoning, even if he didn't know all of it. "Em jumped us back here in five seconds flat," he said, handing Keevan another Coke from the fridge. "If we need to get somewhere, distance isn't going to be a problem."

"Is there anything *we* can do?" Keevan asked. "I mean, I'm still not cool with evil faeries and crazy magic and all that, but you know if you need someone to have your backs, we're here."

Izzy and Priya nodded. My heart squeezed. I'd never really had friends in any of my lives before—no one except my king. I'd never been able to let anyone else in on the secret of who I was. It was scary... but also kind of wonderful.

"If anything comes up that I can delegate to you guys, I'll let you know," I said, and I meant it. We wouldn't still be here at all if it weren't for them.

For a moment, the room went quiet except for the faint clink of Priya setting cutlery around the table. I suspected we were all trying to think of something less dire to talk about. And apparently failing, because when Keevan cleared his throat, what came out was, "Are you two staying holed up in here again for the time being, then? No classes, no football practice..."

"At this point, I'd probably be putting everyone else at college in danger by showing up there," Darton said. "I don't like it, but that's just the way it is." He caught my eyes with a meaningful look.

We'd argued over the last couple weeks about how much of his regular life he'd have to leave behind for his safety. How much he didn't want to leave it behind. But that had been before the dark fae had threatened his sister and nearly blasted us into pieces.

"Well, we'll keep our eyes open around campus," Izzy said. "If I see anything strange, I'll let you two know right away." She'd proven especially sensitive to glooms and other dark vermin that normally passed beneath human awareness.

"The campus crusaders!" Keevan announced, slinging an arm around Izzy's shoulders to give her a quick hug. She laughed and elbowed him. He let go of her sooner than I'd bet he wanted to, given the puppy dog look on his face as she turned away. I wasn't the only one around here who had it bad.

A cool prickling ran over my skin. I froze and focused on my senses. The feeling wasn't the same as the oath's itch—I could still feel that too. This was an impression wafting in from beyond the house's walls. Something was present out there that I didn't like. I knew I didn't like it very, very definitely, even without knowing what it was.

The prickling didn't have the pungent flavor I'd have expected if the Darkest One herself had suddenly vaulted to our doorstep, impossible as that was anyway, but my heart started pounding. "Something's outside," I said.

The others fell silent. "The Chinese delivery guy?" Keevan ventured with a weakly hopeful smile.

I shook my head. Whatever it was, I didn't get the sense it was *moving*. It was just there. Waiting. Somehow that unnerved me even more. It almost felt as if the presence *wanted* me to notice it.

Priya shivered. "I, uh, suddenly don't feel so well either." She rubbed her arms. "What's going on, Emmaline?"

The house's protective systems hadn't tripped. The baggie of salt I'd replenished and returned to my pocket wasn't trembling in warning of a dark creature crossing the boundary I'd drawn around the house. Whatever was causing that sensation, it was keeping a healthy distance. For now.

I swallowed hard. "I'm not sure, but I think I'd better check. The rest of you stay in here. Keep the door closed until I'm back."

"Em," Darton protested. I walked past him to the wand I'd left in the basket by the coat rack for exactly this sort of situation. My fingers curled around the warm wood. The pulse of life and magic inside it soothed my nerves just slightly.

"I don't know what kind of danger we might be facing yet," I said. I'd spent all day putting down every protection I could think of around the house, but some of them were untested. They might not be enough to hold an attacker at bay, depending on what was out there.

Darton jogged down the hall to his bedroom and emerged a second later with Excalibur in his hands. Held upright, ready to strike, it glowed with its connection to his soul. I'd enchanted that sword for my king centuries ago in our first lives, and it still lit up for him like no one else.

"Holy shit," Keevan said, his eyes widening. "You didn't tell me you brought back souvenirs."

Darton's lips formed a crooked smile. "Everyone,

37

meet Excalibur. I'm pretty fond of it, mostly because the dark fae don't seem to like it very much."

That was an understatement. Okay, maybe I *was* better off with Darton out there with me. We had worked together, sword and magic, awfully well back in Britain.

"Fine, fine," I said. "But stay close to me and to the door. The lights aren't potent enough to completely repel a full dark fae, and I don't know if the rest of my spells were enough to do the trick."

He listened to me at least on that count. I eased open the door, stretching my awareness ahead of me. Nothing close. Nothing in motion. I slipped outside, and Darton joined me.

We stood shoulder to shoulder as I kicked the door shut behind us. He held the sword poised, his eyes intent on the darkness beyond the flood of the solar lamps. It was only mid-evening, but the contrast made the space beyond the ring of light nearly black.

But only nearly. My salt pouch shuddered a second before a shape shifted near the edge of the light. I tensed, my hand clenching around my wand. Words of a spell leapt to my tongue.

A face framed by tendrils of shadow swam into view at the edge of our protective light. Brown skin, pale eyes, a mocking smile. The salt's vibrations intensified. Another figure emerged, and another, standing several feet apart, all around the house. Not the Darkest One, no, but her minions. We were surrounded by a circle of dark fae.

They didn't move any closer. The sun-powered lights might not have been able to stop them completely, but they'd still drain the fae's power. Maybe my herbs and salt and the rest were enough to hold them in place. Or maybe they weren't here to take Darton quite yet anyway. Their master was still making her preparations, wasn't she?

"We see you, halfling wizard," a pale-faced woman sneered. "We know your weaknesses."

Another chuckled. "Consider this a reminder that we can take what we desire whenever we want."

"The Darkest One is rising, and when she arrives, you will crumble in front of her."

"How does it feel to know you've already failed?"

That last remark and the smirk that followed it cut deep. I swallowed hard and nudged Darton backward. "Stand around puffing yourselves up all you want," I called to them. "We've got better things to do than listen to your rambling."

They stayed where they were until I'd hauled the door open. Then I felt, like an exhaled breath, the pressure easing as they faded farther back into the shadows. But they didn't leave completely. No. They were still waiting along the fringes of the forest beyond the field.

I'd felt them like that before, hadn't I? So long ago the memory rose up like a mist in the back of my mind.

The horses' hooves clopped along the packed dirt road. A thick, piney scent carried on the breeze from the dense forests on either side. An autumn chill laced the air, but the voices of the soldiers around my king and I were light with pride and relief. Even Arthur was smiling, in a weary sort of way.

We'd won. We'd finally pressed the invaders back far enough, sent them fleeing, left them so wrecked that they shouldn't think it wise to return for a very, very long time. The country was safe. The people had been protected. What wasn't there to celebrate?

A prickle crawled across my back. I wasn't the only one who sensed it. My mare, who was calmer than most horses in the face of my half-fae nature, shied a few steps to the side. Arthur glanced at me with eyebrows raised, as if to question whether I'd managed to lose what little horsemanship I'd gained over the last several years at his side. He *couldn't feel that waft of unease.*

They were here. I tugged my mare back into the line, but my gaze searched the shadows between the close-spaced trees. Something cold and cruel was watching our procession, out of the reach of the setting sun. Something fae. And only one kind of fae would give me that impression, like the edge of a cool blade scraping down my spine.

My fingers clenched around the reins. Words clogged my throat. Let's race our way out of here, *I wanted to say.* Let the horses run until they're ragged. Until we've left the watchers far behind.

But as happy as our army was, it was exhausted too. I felt the dark fae marking our passage all down the road, too many to easily pass by. We'd beaten one enemy, but another one was still waiting to bring the battle to us.

And when they wanted to, there would be no outrunning them.

5

Darton and I stumbled into the house and shoved the door closed. The thump shook me completely out of my memory of that long ago ride.

Our three friends stood at the edge of the living room, staring at us. Darton lowered his sword, his knuckles white. "What do we do now?"

"To the fae?" I grimaced. "Nothing. Not yet, anyway. They'd probably like it if I started wearing myself out throwing spells at them. They're following the same M.O. as their master. Stirring up fear and pain. That was all they wanted—to taunt us."

To taunt *me*, mostly. The fae on both sides had always seen me as something of an abomination because of my father's light fae blood mingling with my mother's humanity, but the dark found it particularly repulsive. Totally contrary to the sense of order they were so fond of. And my soul's habit of leaping from one new human body to the next struck them as even more unruly.

Well, too bad. It wasn't as if I was looking for their approval.

"What the hell happened out there?" Keevan said.

"Dark fae," Darton said. "All around the house. They said a bunch of stuff, but they didn't come at us or anything." He froze up. "I need to call my sister."

He took out his phone and brought up his little sister's number. My arms twitched. I dropped my wand into the basket. Too much dark power, too close. The oath's hold was tingling through me more sharply than before.

"Hey, Audrey! How's it going? Ah, come on, can't I check in on my little sister now and then? Yeah, yeah. So everything's been fine there? Okay, good. Good. I know. I'll see you at Thanksgiving."

Darton lowered the phone looking only partly relieved. He was more protective of his sister than just about anyone. Maybe because he'd already had to save her life once, though not for fae-related reasons. When we'd first been getting to know each other, he'd told me the story of how he'd had to drag her out of a pool when he was twelve and do CPR to restart her breathing. A moment like that stayed with you.

But all the moments he and I had shared weren't enough to calm the oath's demands. I stepped away from him, toward the kitchen. Distance. If I could just get a little distance from him, let the sense of the threat fade...

"I don't think the fae will bother us while we're in here," I said to our friends, fighting to keep the strain out of my voice. "But if you all want to leave... or if you want to stay the night so you don't have to go out there while they're lurking around, it's up to you. We can put you up."

"Yeah, it's no problem," Darton said. To my dismay, he followed me over to the kitchen island. The closer he

42

was, the more my nerves jittered through my limbs. Urging me to turn on him, to snap out a spell or slash the knife in my back pocket across his neck. To end his life before the Darkest One could use it for her own ends.

I grabbed a glass and kept my hands busy filling it with water. What if we weren't safe even tonight? I didn't think the Darkest One had started the journey from England across the ocean yet—did she really have enough power to keep that storm raging without being present? But I could be wrong. The dark fae might be expecting her to make her appearance before the sun rose.

What in light's name would I do then? Swine crud and cattle sod. I wasn't ready. I didn't have any idea how to become ready.

My hands started to shake. "Emmaline?" Priya said gently.

"I'm okay," I said. "Just thinking it through." I gulped the water and set the glass down before I could spill it. The cold liquid pooled in my stomach.

I had my wands, my knife, and all my other supplies. Every magical protection I'd ever used or imagined was in place around and inside the house. There was no building more secure in the universe.

If we had to make a last stand, there was nowhere better to do it.

The thought of the Darkest One appearing in a gust of magic on our doorstep sent another tremble through me. "Em," Darton said. He stepped closer and touched my shoulder.

My lungs seized. My hand leapt to my knife. The urging of the oath ran through my muscles and closed my fingers around the hilt. It whipped my arm back in front of me, my hand clutching the weapon.

No. I clamped my teeth together and wrenched myself to the side, fighting for control. Every nerve in my body was screaming at me to spin back toward Darton, to let the knife do the work I'd promised Cormag.

No, no, no!

"Em, what's going on?" Darton said, oblivious. He started to move around me—toward the sodding knife. My hand jerked. I gasped, and my arm shot out.

I could only think of one way to interrupt the compulsion. With a heave of my muscles, I yanked the knife out of its arc toward Darton's throat—and into the palm of my other hand.

The magic-enhanced blade sliced right through skin and sinews and out the other side. Pain lanced through my hand and up my arm in a sharp, searing bolt. It left my body shuddering, but it washed away the oath's frantic itch. All I felt was that flare of agony.

"Emma!" Izzy yelped. Priya darted over. Darton had already caught me, his arms around my shoulders as I staggered. My head had started to spin. Possibly because of the blood streaming from my punctured hand to patter across the kitchen floor.

"What can I do?" he said, low and rough by my ear. "What do you need?"

"Is it really *her*?" Keevan asked. "Did one of those evil faeries get in her head like that one did to Priya before?"

"It's me," I mumbled. "I'm sorry. I need to clean this up. Come with me, Art?"

I cradled my arm against my sweater, the blood soaking into the wool fabric, as Darton ushered me to the main bathroom. There, I rested my wrist on the edge of the sink so I'd bleed into the drain. I eyed the knife warily. The pain had started to dull into a throbbing burn. But the blade needed to come out. That wasn't going to be fun.

"Is there anything I can get from your rooms—all those supplies we brought back—" Darton said.

I shook my head. "Just hand me a towel. Whichever one you like the least."

He laughed hoarsely and opened the cabinet. I took the towel he passed me and laid it under my hand. Gritting my teeth, I grasped the knife's hilt and jerked it out.

A fresh spasm of pain clouded my vision. Darton flinched. I tossed the bloody blade in the sink with a clatter and tugged the towel tightly around my palm to stifle the flow of blood. Then I snatched a few twigs from my pocket and murmured a quick incantation.

"*Seal the skin and flesh beneath. Stopper the blood that flows.*"

I didn't have the concentration to do a perfect job of it. I could feel even as the muscles knit back together that they weren't perfectly aligned. This hand wasn't going to work the same unless I redid the healing at some later time, with a clearer head. But at least it wasn't emptying all the fluid out of my body anymore.

I could have said a few more words to numb the pain, but I wanted it to keep hurting. As long as it was hurting, I had control. I'd really prefer not to have to stab myself all over again.

"Are you going to tell me what happened back there?" Darton said quietly. He rested his hand on the small of my back.

I closed my eyes for a second. The dizziness and the

pulse of pain set off jagged sparks behind my eyes.

If it had gotten this bad, I had to tell him. He had to know, so he could protect himself from *me*.

I inhaled shakily and looked up at him. "There's something I didn't tell you before. I thought I could keep it under control—I didn't want you to worry."

Darton's brow knit. "What are you talking about?"

It hurt almost as much as my hand admitting this. "When I went to my father's old light fae enclave to ask if they'd summon the lightning for us... They didn't want to. They were upset that we were even still in the country. They know that the Darkest One is particularly keen to get her hands on you, and they were worried... that you being here, her having the chance to kill you, might make things even worse."

I still hadn't told him about my father's suspicions, about the hint of darkness even I had sensed woven into his soul. He'd had enough trouble keeping his confidence steady without having to worry about danger lurking inside himself.

"And?" Darton prompted.

"And so I swore an oath to them, in exchange for their help. I gave my word, with a magical bond, that if the Darkest One got free despite our efforts... I'd kill you before she could."

I winced as I said it. How could he see my actions as anything other than a betrayal?

Darton stared at me. "I didn't think we had a chance otherwise," I barreled on. "I figured if we didn't manage to contain her, we'd both be dead anyway. But we didn't and we aren't, and the oath... It isn't happy that I'm ignoring it. Especially when the situation we're in starts to feels particularly risky."

"Like right now," Darton said.

"With the dark fae. Yeah. The oath almost took over. But I figured out a way to cut off the impulse." I held up my roughly bandaged hand with a crooked smile.

Darton leaned back against the sink counter, his head bowing. He rubbed his forehead. "You should have told me."

Guilt pinched my gut. "Like I said, I didn't think it mattered. I figured we'd either keep the Darkest One imprisoned and the oath would be moot, or she'd get out and kill us immediately. It's not something I'm *proud* of. I didn't want you thinking about it, about what I'd said I'd do, while we were fighting Rhedyn."

"And after?"

I dropped my gaze. "And after I felt like swine crud for having taken the oath in the first place. I thought I could keep overcoming the urge. I didn't realize it was going to get this bad with her not even nearby." I paused. My throat closed up. "I'm really sorry. You know the last thing I want to do is—"

"Of course I know," Darton said. He motioned to my bloody hand. "You'd always jump in front of a blow coming for me. Even if you were the one dealing it." He didn't sound all that happy about the fact. "I even understand why you didn't want to talk about it, especially considering all the trouble I was having just getting that damned sword to work with me..."

Yeah. And the shamed look on his face right now was exactly why I didn't want to burden him with any more troubles than I'd needed to. "Well, you know now. And I know... to be more careful." My stomach twisted. I didn't really think that was going to be enough.

My king must have seen that too. "Where do we go from here?" he asked.

My stomach twisted. I'd wanted to pretend the oath had never happened. To squash it down and keep going. But that didn't seem like such a wise approach anymore. How could I *ever* confront the Darkest One if a little taunting from her minions could make me attack Darton?

If I was going to save my king, I had to tackle the oath's sway first.

"There has to be a way to break the oath," I said. "I'll figure that out, whatever I have to do, and then we'll be ready to take on the Darkest One." Ha. Sure, it'd be that easy. But Darton's stance relaxed slightly, as if he believed we could do it.

Maybe I could use some more confidence too.

"For now," I added, "I think we'd better go out there and find a decent explanation to give to our friends, before they start to think I must have bled to death in here."

Darton nodded. "Better not to tell them about the oath?"

"Maybe not in excruciating detail..."

He touched my face, tracing his thumb over my cheekbone. The intentness in his eyes washed away the lingering pain. My breath caught.

"I know we can get through this," he said. "I know you'll be right here beside me, and I'll be right here with you."

I leaned into his touch, allowing myself that brief moment of comfort. Wishing I didn't feel even more terrified of what lay ahead of us than I had just ten minutes ago.

6

For the first hour of the drive to Priya's former enclave, Priya cranked bouncy pop music in the car. I was grateful to let it fill the space between us. There were too many things I didn't want to talk about. She hummed along with it, tapping her fingers against the steering wheel. But not far from Seattle, she turned the radio down a few degrees and glanced over at me.

"So how does a person, or a fae, usually undo a magical oath?"

Not a question I wanted to contemplate. "They usually *don't*. Generally speaking, the only way to get out of fulfilling a magically charged oath is to die before you have to."

"Oh." Priya's eyebrows leapt up.

"I'm hoping to find a different strategy," I said dryly. "With a little luck, your light fae friends will have some other ideas. I've actually never been bound by an oath before, so I haven't done a whole lot of research into that area." And the human databases of the present day? Pretty sparse on legitimate magical theory.

After a long night spent pouring over those internet resources, I'd decided visiting the fae was my best course of action, at least as a first attempt. They'd know more than anyone about how the oaths of their kind worked. And the trip would put a little distance between Darton and me if the compulsion hit me hard again.

Not that I liked leaving him on his own. But the dark fae hadn't made the slightest move against us all night, so it seemed unlikely they'd try to breach the house now with the sun shining bright in the cloudless sky. Whatever the Darkest One had planned, if she'd even made a real plan yet, she was taking her time.

"How's your hand?" Priya asked.

I ran my thumb over my palm. I hadn't healed it well enough to avoid scabbing. A mottled line marked the center of my hand, front and back, where the knife had pierced through.

I couldn't blame the knife, of course. I'd put it back in my pocket this morning.

"I've felt better," I said. "But it's only a little painful now."

"I know what it's like, having some other force take over your body. Making you do things you don't really mean to do. If you want to really talk about it, not just that hand wave-y explanation you gave us last night, I'm happy to listen."

I grimaced at the windshield. "It's complicated. But I can promise you it's got nothing at all to do with the dark fae." Other than as a trigger. "The light fae can be just as cruel sometimes in their own way."

Priya shrugged. "I don't love all of the ones I've met, but I've never seen one call up a catastrophic storm over an entire country either."

"Fair point." I tipped my head back against the seat.

"Generally speaking, the dark fae don't do that either. This one's just 'special.'"

She drove in silence for a few minutes before she said, "You really don't know if you can beat her, do you? Even if you figure out what she wants. Even if you're really smart about it."

My pulse stuttered. "No," I made myself answer. "I don't. Maybe I can't."

"Do you have to fight her at all? Can't you just... I don't know, find some really good hiding spot and hang out there?"

I had to laugh at that. "No. I don't even like that I'm hiding away right now, just letting her get away with everything she's doing. Standing back while she's hurting all those people. If I thought I had *any* chance of stopping her right this moment... It's my fault. I wasn't fast enough dealing with Rhedyn. I didn't stop the Darkest One from getting free."

Priya shook her head sharply. "But you were the one who managed to shut her away in the first place! It's not like you made her go around and do horrible things. She was already being awful back then, and you came along and gave the world, like, a fifteen hundred year respite. As far as I can tell, you've done more than your share."

"She'd probably be a lot less angry right now if I hadn't shut her away," I pointed out. "Anyway, who else is going to step up? The light fae over there clearly can't, if they've even bothered to try. Regular people don't stand a chance. So that leaves me. And Darton with his magic sword. It started with us and her, so it only makes sense it's going to finish that way."

Priya sucked in her lower lip. Her voice came out

quiet. "What happens if she just kills you two?"

I hugged myself. "I don't know. I'm trying not to think about that."

"Well, I'll ask the elders here to help you any way they can. I don't know how much they'll listen to me, but I've got a little sway. Ohanko will be there. He'll speak for us."

She pulled off onto a grassy patch by the side of the road. Ancient trees loomed over us. Like every enclave I've visited, Priya's adoptive one lay deep in a wild patch of countryside. The better to keep humans away without being too obvious in their repelling.

I could smell the light fae presence in the air as I got out of the car, like a faint sweetness lingering several hours after cookies have come out of the oven. Priya set off through the forest, picking her way over tree roots and around the underbrush. After just a minute, the canopy of evergreen pines and cedars closed overhead, leaving us in only dim, filtered sunlight.

Winter was nibbling at the edges of the atmosphere. I tugged my jacket tighter around me. The dark fae loved the coldest season. Shorter, darker days. Life gone dormant. So much of the world still and orderly. Nothing like the chaos of new spring growth. Maybe the Darkest One was holding off on her grand catastrophe until then.

"We're almost there," Priya said, motioning to a tree that must have been a landmark for her. Several steps farther, the tingle of the enclave's protective boundary washed over me. It would have repelled most regular human beings, but it didn't appear to affect Priya. The fae must have adjusted their magic to make her a welcome visitor despite her biology.

A lean, long-haired young man stepped out of a

sunbeam to meet us. A faint gleam shone in his bronze skin. He bowed to me with the same respect he'd shown when we'd first met last week.

"Hey, Ohanko," Priya said. "Thanks for coming out to meet us. Are the elders ready to talk?"

He made a pained expression that didn't offer much hope. "They have agreed to meet with Merlin. They were hesitant to discuss how we might get involved."

Well, they figured we were coming to ask them to battle the Darkest One. They might be overjoyed when I told them I was here on a much simpler errand. "That's fine," I said. "I'd actually like to talk to them alone, at least to start."

"Are you sure?" Priya said.

At the same time, Ohanko gave me another deep bow. "But of course, Daughter of Eóghan. Should you need any assistance, just call on me."

I bumped Priya's arm with my knuckles. "I'll be fine. I've been talking to light fae types for hundreds of years longer than you have, remember?"

Ohanko motioned for me to follow him. The trees within the enclave were spaced more sparsely, so warm streaks of sunlight dappled the ground. I drank it into my body as I walked behind the fae man. I might not light up like they did, but I still felt and welcomed the sun's power.

Ohanko led me to a large clearing. A dozen stones the height of stools stood in a ring at its center. Most of them were already occupied by light fae so translucent I knew immediately they were the elders. Ohanko directed me to one of the free stones. I sank down onto its hard, smooth surface, and the younger fae faded back into the trees.

The elders peered at me from around their circle. Their bodies were so filmy it was hard to make out much difference between their features. Their hair and skin faded into the light beaming down from above. If I tried to focus on any one of their faces for more than a second, my eyes started to sting.

They'd been part of this world for an awfully long time. I wasn't sure if that was to my benefit or not. Obviously this enclave hadn't seen much disruption over the years. That might have fortified them—or made them even more wary of conflict.

"Welcome, daughter of Eóghan," the woman nearest me said with a voice like a tinkling bell. "We understand that you come to us with a request for help."

That was as straightforward a statement as I could hope for from a light fae. "Yes," I said. "And thank you so much for agreeing to hear me out. I'm sure you'd like to keep out of this mess around the Darkest One as much as possible. I promise I'm not going to ask you to do anything that involves her, at least not today. I'm hoping you can advise me on a different matter."

One of the elder men bobbed his head, his silky hair drifting around his face. "There are many paths that may lead to the same destination," he said. "We cannot see the end without the beginning."

Yeah, that was more the kind of conversation I expected from these types.

"Right," I said. "So here's the thing: I swore an oath to a few light fae in Britain. I promised to do something that I didn't think I'd ever be in a position to have to do. But... things worked out differently than I expected. Circumstances changed. And now doing that thing, it wouldn't actually make things better. It would make them so much worse, for everyone."

"That is unfortunate," the first woman said. "The winds of life are always shifting."

I nodded as if that remark was in any way helpful. "Yeah. So, I'd rather not follow through and cause even more problems. Since it's light fae magic that went into the oath bond, I thought maybe you all would have some idea how to dissolve it."

The elders exchanged a glance around the circle. They didn't try to hide their discomfort at my suggestion. It flickered through their glow like a passing shadow.

The elder man who'd spoken before turned to face me again. "To give one's sacred word, it is a root dug deep. Cutting it off can only do harm."

"Well, that's not necessarily true," I hedged. "I mean, what if that root had a sickness take to it? And then if you cut off the root, you're actually saving the rest of the tree from dying. That's the kind of situation we're talking about here."

My adapting of his metaphor seemed to impress him at least a little. He pursed his lips, but he'd tilted his head in consideration. A couple of the others leaned closer to murmur to him and the elder woman who'd spoken first. I waited, trying to look responsible and deserving. Not like someone who made oaths willy nilly without consideration of the consequences.

I was trying to save the world from having the Darkest One inflicted on it, I thought, biting back the urge to say it out loud. *If your kind weren't so bloody self-absorbed, I wouldn't have had to make wretched oaths like that one just to get some help.*

The woman shook back her shimmering hair and met

my eyes. "It is not something any of us has ever attempted," she said. "But we will examine you and make a decision then."

"Sure," I said, my spirits lifting. They were actually going to try. "What do you need me to do?"

They consulted each other a few minutes longer. Then the man gestured to the middle of the ring. "Sit in the midst of our energies, and we will see from all angles."

Fair enough. I walked to the center of the stone circle and hunkered down on the soft grass. The combined presence of the light fae warmed the air enough that the ground here wasn't even cold.

Several pairs of glowing eyes honed in on me. I closed my own, a quiver passing over my skin. Exactly how much were they going to see?

A wash of light passed over me, flashing softly behind my eyelids. Then another, and another, as if it were the ocean's surf sending its waves toward me. A warmth bloomed throughout my body. A honeyed scent trickled into my lungs as I inhaled. The quivering spread across my scalp and into my head. It tingled through my thoughts.

Were they releasing me even now? Wearing down the tie between me and Cormag? I could almost taste the release on the tip of my tongue.

Then a faint cry split the air. I looked up, startled. Another fae woman was staring at me, the glow around her body dimmed and shivering. The man who'd asked me to sit there turned his head away with a jerk. His neighbor shook his head over and over, muttering something to himself. The waves of light and warmth fell away. Abruptly, I felt chilled.

"What?" I said. "What's wrong?"

The woman who'd addressed me before held out her hand. I let her help me to my feet. As I sat back on my stone, she looked down at her lap, her brilliant face creasing before she found the words.

"I am still not sure if we could touch the cord that binds you," she said. "But we do not want to. We fear more what would happen if the oath is broken than if it remains in place."

What? I bit my tongue before I could snap the question at her. "How can you say that? You don't even know—"

"We know," she said, even and solemn. "We saw. The one you serve has a sickness of a sort in him, yes, but it's not because of your oath. It's already in the core of him. You swore to defend the world from it. Can you not see that doing so may be the right thing after all?"

She looked at me, her eyes pleading. My throat closed up. My hands clenched, but I couldn't summon any real anger, not when her expression was so distraught. She didn't like saying this to me. She was only saying it because she couldn't bear not to.

She believed my king was meant to die.

"How can you condone it?" I said. "Killing an innocent person..."

"He has lived more than his fair share of lives already, has he not?" she said. "And how many other innocents might be swept up in the tide of darkness if the one you fear takes him first?"

"I don't know! I don't know what she did to him."

"Perhaps that is the answer you should seek then," she said. They all stood up to leave, not one giving me another glance.

7

The warm, salty water of the bath lapped at my arms. I lowered them deeper into the bathtub, breathing in the tang that wasn't quite like the ocean. Too much chlorine in the tap water for it to be an exact imitation. But it was real sea salt I'd laced the tub with, along with a sprinkling of burnt frankincense.

It didn't matter what the light fae had said. I'd learned something from them anyway. The oath was a thing they could see inside me, a thing they'd felt in my mind. If they could grasp hold of it and comprehend it, then I could grab it too. Grab it and hopefully snap it, if I'd picked my tools right.

The purifying bath had seemed like a reasonable first step. I'd cleanse myself as much as possible from any outside influence. Let nothing remain but me and the oath. Maybe the immersion would even wear it down a little before I got to the real work.

I'd been soaking long enough that my fingertips had pruned. I rubbed my thumb against them, grimaced, and climbed out of the tub. I pulled on my undyed cotton bathrobe and ambled out to the supplies I'd laid on the floor in my bedroom. I'd ordered Darton not to disturb me unless there was a total emergency. After seeing my face when I'd gotten back from the enclave, he hadn't even tried to argue.

I whispered to the sticks of copal incense set around my circle of twigs. They started smoking. The crisp, woody scent curled into the air. I set a black onyx stone on both of my knees to strength my will and resolve. A pile of bay leaves waited in front of my crossed legs, ready to accept the energy I planned to shed.

I brushed my hands over the stones and inhaled deep. The copal smoke seeped into my lungs. I exhaled it and scooped the bay leaves into my cupped hands. Closing my eyes, I turned my awareness inward. Deep, deep into my head, where the oath wound through my thoughts.

There. I couldn't see it, but I could almost hear it. Like a faint humming just a little too distant to pinpoint. But the itch beneath my fingernails shifted when the humming did, in time with the beat of my heart. If I could just find the threads of it, pick them apart...

"*Let me see what I seek,*" I murmured in the old tongue. "*Bring distant ties to visibility.*" Keeping my focus inward, I reached out to the life energy in the twigs at the same time. It thrummed into me. My nerves jittered alongside it. The tug of the oath's compulsion rippled through my muscles and squeezed at my lungs.

"No," I said. "*Let me find it. Let me grasp it. Let me—*"

I hauled at the energy around me even harder, slamming it against the magic twined through my head. That was the wrong move.

The burst of energy hit me like a punch. My thoughts spun, and the oath's power lashed back. My hands jerked, the bay leaves scattering. A flood of light seared behind my eyes. My body listed. I tumbled over, and the world went dark.

Everything was dark. I couldn't feel my body, not even my breath. I was floating, still and numb, in a blackness that might have been as vast as the universe or as shallow as my bathtub. I tried to turn, to feel, but there was nothing to move. Nowhere to move it to.

I'd knocked myself out into some kind of vision. But usually my visions hurtled me toward whatever they wanted me to see. They didn't just toss me into a random void. What was the point of this?

How did I get *out* of it?

Cold tendrils started to wrap around my consciousness like trickles of frigid water. I would have shivered if I'd had a body to shiver with. I still couldn't see anything, but a drifting sensation crept over me, as if I were gliding very slowly downward. Down and down and down, without any impression of what was slipping past me.

Was this some kind of trap the light fae had worked into their oath, to punish me if I tried to break it? It didn't *feel* like light fae work, but Cormag had struck me as being a little on the sadistic side. The only thing I knew was I didn't care for this situation at all. Was there some way to knock myself free?

I stretched and pushed my awareness, but that didn't seem to get me anywhere. I just kept drifting on. To where?

A thin crackle of laughter sliced through the darkness. The chill deepened, twisting around my mind. I sensed without seeing a gaze fixed on me. A gaze even more icy than the tendrils that tangled around my thoughts.

The presence expanded until it loomed over me, until it filled the blackness all around me, as if it had swallowed me up. I was pinned in place by it. My entire being strained to get away.

It was *her*. I'd know her essence anywhere.

"There you are, little wizard," said a voice that was both low and crisp. It echoed all around me. "Did you think you could run from me? Such a pathetic specimen of both fae and humanity. I've been waiting a long time to have you in my grasp. Don't worry. It won't be much longer until I'm there in the flesh to fully enjoy your torment."

The tendrils sharpened into frigid claws. They scraped through my mind, severing thoughts and sparking panic. I tried to cry out with a mouth I couldn't find. Some part of my will remained, an unbroken thread in the midst of the Darkest One's game. I held onto it tight. It was only a vision. I could endure this. She couldn't break me with an ocean between us.

Only I wasn't completely sure of that.

"Do you think you can defy me again?" she said. "Oh, halfling abomination, you know how many years I've had to contemplate the many ways I can take my revenge. Your death will be slow, slow and horrible. That's a promise. Your king's, though? You don't need to worry about him. That life I intend to snap fast. The better to unwrap that beautiful present inside."

Her laugh carried through the darkness again. *No*, I thought. *No, no, no, no, no.* I wouldn't let her. I'd make it through. I couldn't think any farther than that, not with her icy fingers digging deeper and deeper into my consciousness. *No, no, no, no—*

"No!" The shout broke from my lips. I flinched awake, my elbows smacking out against arms that held me in place.

Darton's arms. His solid football player frame was wrapped around me. His warmth and his citrusy, earthy smell washed over me.

I blinked at the scene around me. Most of my twigs had disintegrated into dust, and that dust was smeared in violent streaks all across my pale floorboards. Bay leaves scattered the room as far as I could see, as if a gale had whipped through the room. The onyx stones had both shattered. Dark shards speckled the floor around me like shiny black teardrops.

"Hey," Darton said. "Hey. I'm here. You're back. It's okay."

My mind tripped back to the memory of the Darkest One's presence swallowing me up, and my throat constricted. No, it wasn't. Nothing about this was remotely okay. I *had* failed, so badly. I couldn't even make *myself* safe for my king, let alone anything or anyone else. Even as my body came back into focus, that sodding itch was tickling up my arms. Reminding me of the oath I hadn't fulfilled.

I'm not going to, I thought at it, with a defiance that was more like a teenager sticking her tongue out at her parents behind their backs than anything really convincing. *You can't make me.*

Other than it probably could, if I let it go on long enough. If I didn't sever it soon. Not that I had any clue how, despite my best efforts.

Darton's arms shifted around me, tugging me closer. I let my head tip against his chest. My bathrobe had loosened during... whatever had happened while I was lost in that vision. The soft fabric gaped to the swells of my breasts and bared my legs halfway up my thighs. His hands rested so close to that naked skin...

A different sort of heat swept over me, embarrassment and longing mixed. "I told you not to come in," I muttered.

Darton sputtered a laugh. "Unless it was an emergency. Believe me, it sounded like one. You were yelling out stuff I couldn't even understand, other than I think I heard my name in there at least once, and when I came in you were shaking on the floor. You couldn't seem to hear me at all. You wouldn't open your eyes. It's been—I don't know, but a long time, since I came in. Where *were* you?"

"A vision," I said, the irritation draining out of me. Light help me, I must have terrified him. "I'm sorry. I had no idea what was going on outside my head. It didn't give me anything useful. The Darkest One showed up personally to add in a few more taunts."

Darton's body tensed against mine. "Oh." He lowered his head, his cheek brushing my temple. "Are you all right? Did she hurt you?"

"No. Not really." A splinter of a headache was working its way through my skull, but that might be my own fault for messing with the oath. "She said she'd make her way here soon. At least that means we can be sure she's not here *yet*." What was her idea of "soon," though? She might mean tomorrow or a year from now for all I knew.

I started to push away, but Darton's embrace tightened. "No," he said. "You stay right here a little longer. Lord knows you need more than five minutes to recover before you go charging off in some other direction."

I made a muted sound of protest. "I still have that wretched oath to break."

"I'm just asking for five more minutes. I don't want my wizard completely run ragged. How are you going to come to my rescue then?"

He said the last sentence jokingly, but I heard the hint of bitterness in it too. "Seems like you're the one coming to my rescue," I said. That earned me a chuckle that sounded a little less strained.

"I try." He shifted me against him so we were almost facing. His fingers stroked over my hair. Then they dropped to cup my cheek. His lips brushed against my forehead. Almost a kiss. My pulse kicked up for reasons that had nothing to do with the enemy whose grip I'd just been in.

"Art."

"I know." His mouth grazed my skin again as it moved. A delicate, teasing heat. Almost begging me to lift my head so my lips could meet his. "I'm sorry. I know we can't— You have no idea how hard it is not to even be able to kiss you."

My heart fluttered. I set my jaw. I had to say it. "To kiss *Emma*."

He swallowed audibly. "I'm not sure I know how to tell one part of you from the other anymore."

Maybe he couldn't, but I could. I could tell the part he'd never have wanted to kiss back when we'd been only ourselves. My soul had been in a body that didn't suit him. Just because that had changed didn't mean I didn't remember. And conditional affection... No.

I'd learned over and over how much that hurt. He understood now. I'd been honest with him. *I have loved you utterly always*, I'd told him a few nights ago, after he'd accused me of rejecting him, of not caring enough. *And you have only loved me sometimes.*

That was the crux of the problem, wasn't it? I'd never even known whether his affection and attraction meant anything at all or whether they'd only been conjured by the spell that bound us together, the closeness it created.

Of course, *that* bond was broken now. And he still wanted to hold me, to touch me like this. But it had only been a few days. Maybe this was only habit, an echo that would fade with the magic over time.

I'd let myself hope too many times. Even all the way back then, when I should have known there wasn't a chance. A memory swam up, as if I needed the reminder.

"There's nothing wrong with taking advice from others, Your Highness. I'd never suggest as much. Gods, I hope you listen to my advice now."

"Then what exactly are you suggesting?" Arthur's voice rang *cold from the private alcove where one of the local lords had stopped him for this little chat. It was just down the hall from the king's chambers, which was where I'd been heading when my fae-sharpened hearing had caught their conversation from down the castle hall. I stood now with my back braced against the hard plaster of the wall and my stomach twisting.*

"He always *has your ear. He's always at your side. I've seen you change your mind after a few words from him—"*

"Because I trust him," Arthur interrupted. *"Because he has proven himself right time and time again. He's earned that trust."*

"My point is only that the extent of his influence... it's

concerning. You want to be seen as a king who rules with his own mind first."

"And I do," Arthur said, his voice absolutely icy now. "My mind tells me that my rule can only be stronger with Merlin's support. If you have proof that he's caused any harm, by all means, bring that to me. But all I'm hearing at the moment are vague and baseless assumptions."

The lord muttered something else, but I could tell he'd been dismissed. I murmured a hasty distraction spell. He stalked past me down the hall without a glance in my direction, totally oblivious to my presence. Arthur strode into his chambers, shutting the door a little harder than necessary behind him.

My heart had squeezed. It wasn't as if I didn't know my king trusted me, valued my assistance. But hearing him defend me so firmly and absolutely left me a little short of breath. I gathered myself and continued my own walk to his chambers.

"Good afternoon, my liege," I said breezily as I ambled in. No need to remind him of that troublesome conversation.

Unfortunately, my king knew me far too well now that I'd spent more than a dozen years in his service. He turned where he'd been standing by the chair near the door, and the second he caught my expression, he grimaced.

"You heard," he said.

"Heard what?" I said. He cocked a skeptical eyebrow at me. "Oh, well, there might have been some lordly blathering carrying down the hall, but it didn't sound like anything I should worry myself about."

Arthur shook his head. "It really isn't. If they could see everything you can do..."

"Hmm, let's not push things too far. I spent most of my first year here afraid you might decide to send me to the chopping block for sorcery."

He winced. Then he reached out to grasp my arm, just below the elbow. Not an intimate touch by any means, but these days, even a faint brush of one of those capable hands was enough to make my pulse leap. I steeled myself against my internal reactions. I couldn't let them show. He couldn't know that.

But he stepped closer, until there was less than a foot of space between us. His voice dropped low, making my heart thump even faster. "You do *know you never have to worry, don't you? I'd rather have you at my side than twenty of those preening lords. How can they understand loyalty when they barely know how to demonstrate it themselves?"*

"I know," I said. The words came out quiet. My king smiled. His gaze held mine. The rattle of my pulse echoed in my ears. For one instant of insanity, I almost thought his hand would rise from my arm to stroke my cheek, to draw me closer, to—

He stepped back, his eyes jerking away. "Well, maybe if you played the fool a little *less, they'd see why I respect you."*

My head reeled for a second before I caught myself. "Ah, but then you'd be even more bored during those bloody conferences."

"That's true. Forget I said that." He smiled again, with a distance that was only friendly. Damn my sodding overactive imagination.

That was all it'd ever been. Hope feeding my imagination. Wanting to read more into a kind word, a warm look. We'd been best friends, or as close to it as liege and subject could be. I hadn't *needed* more.

Darton tipped my head so he could tuck it under his chin. I let out my breath, the twist of longing and tension in my chest relaxing now that his mouth was no longer quite so close to mine.

"I don't want to hurt you," he said. "I've done that too many times already without meaning to."

"I know," I said. "This is enough, Art. It really is. As long as you're by my side, I'm happy."

I'd be a whole lot happier if I could count on keeping him there.

And I still had an awful lot of work to do toward that end. I started to straighten up, and this time Darton let me.

I'd just eased off of his lap when a pounding on the front door resonated through the house.

8

"You weren't expecting anyone to stop by, were you?" I said, yanking open my closet. I grabbed a sweatshirt and jeans at random and tugged them on, modesty be damned. Darton was enough of a gentleman to avert his eyes anyway.

The knocking rang through the house again. "No," Darton said. "Keevan and Izzy had exams to study for. They'd have called or texted if something important came up. And it's not like I'm talking to anyone else about what we're up to here."

"Right. Well, let's see who's hassling us tonight. I'd have hoped we were too far off the beaten track for door-to-door solicitors to bother." At least we could assume a dark fae army here to make good on the Darkest One's promise wouldn't have bothered with knocking. I was pretty sure of that.

Darton followed me into the living room. I was about to wave him back, to keep his distance while I opened the door, when a voice carried through it with the next knock. "Emma. Darton. If you're in there, don't leave an old friend hanging."

It was Jagger's voice. I hadn't known the grizzled fae hunter very long, really, but considering he'd blown up his house to save the bunch of us not that long ago, I figured he'd earned the right to call himself an "old friend." A smile leapt to my face as I hurried the rest of the way to the front hall.

Jagger was just turning away from the door when I opened it. His head jerked back around, his face lighting up under its spider web of pale scars. He grinned. "Good. I figured the car meant you were around."

He hadn't come alone. An even more recent friend stood beside him. Eric, the young fae hunter who'd come with his mother to give Darton and me a hand when we'd arrived in Britain, ran his hand through his dark hair. He gave me a sheepish smile. "We meet again."

My eyebrows shot up. "Oh. Hey. When did you get here? *How* did you get here?" With the tantrum the Darkest One was throwing over his country, it couldn't have been easy to get out.

I stepped back to let them in. Eric shrugged, gripping the strap of his shoulder bag. "The network can create opportunities most people don't have. I made it over to France and got a flight from there."

"And I'd just made it back in town," Jagger put in. "One of my buddies reported he'd seen you stopping by your parents' place, so I knew you'd made it home relatively safely." He gave me a questioning look.

The fae hunters had been invaluable allies, but I hadn't given them the full story of my identity, or Darton's. They didn't know why the dark fae were so interested in us, only that the fae's determination in coming after us obviously wasn't good for anyone. So far it had seemed simpler not to complicate things by getting into legends and so on. Talking through the explanation with Keevan and Izzy had been hard enough.

"We made it back by the skin of our teeth." I motioned for them to sit in the living room. Darton was still standing by the sofa, his expression hesitant. He'd gotten along with Jagger okay, but he and Eric... There'd been a bit of a clash. "You should have told us you were coming."

"I tried," Jagger said. "But it seems your old numbers aren't doing me any good."

Oh. Right. Which was the exact same reason I hadn't reached out to him or Eric earlier. I'd gotten their phone numbers, but they'd been in the phone that was now being thoroughly rained on and wind-blasted back in Britain.

"Sorry about that," I said with a grimace. "It's been... kind of a chaotic few days. What's going on?" My gaze shifted to Eric. "Why did you come all the way over here? Have you seen any activity from the dark fae—I mean, other than the obvious storm? Is your mother all right?"

He nodded. "She sends her best. We were pretty worried about you for a while there. But then Jagger mentioned you'd turned up back on this side of the pond... It sounded like this dark fae queen has a particular bone to pick with you. I figured she'd be heading this way before too long, so maybe you could use some extra help."

It seemed like a long way to come when he hadn't been able to help all *that* much with the actual fae-fighting even on his home turf. Maybe he simply hadn't been able to tolerate sitting around in the middle of that storm, not knowing what was going on. But it was a generous gesture anyway.

"You're probably right about her intended direction," I said. "As, er, you may have figured out, we didn't quite succeed in our plan the other day. We stopped the dark fae who was trying to free the Darkest One, but not soon enough. She's totally free now. We've just been regrouping, observing, deciding on our best steps for trying to contain her again. I... I'm really sorry." The country she was tearing through had once been my home, but it was currently Eric's.

"Please. I've seen what a force of nature you are when you put your mind to something." Eric gave me one of his flirty smiles. "I'm sure you gave it your all. I can only imagine matters would be much worse if you hadn't intervened."

"Well, that might be true." I glanced at Darton, but his gaze was focused on me, not Eric. His expression had relaxed. A little jealousy had reared its head thanks to Eric's flirtatious nature before, but that was also before I'd confessed my eternal love to my king. I guessed he felt a little more secure in my affections after that.

Jagger leaned forward, resting his sinewy elbows on his knees. "The whole fae hunter network is on high alert. The second we can act against the dark fae, we will—in any way we can. But the folks over in the U.K. have been pretty much overwhelmed. They haven't even been able to determine what part of the country your dark fae menace is throwing her magic from, there's so much of it whirling around in the atmosphere."

"And the atmosphere is doing plenty of whirling of its own on top of that," Eric said.

"I think the storm should let up before much longer," I said. "Unfortunately that'll be when she heads this way.

I've laid all the protections I could think of around this house. A bunch of really determined dark fae, or a really powerful one, could still break through, but we're about as safe as we can get. Beyond that... I'm still working on a solid plan."

"If you need to put your head together with anyone..." Eric said, his smile returning. I managed not to roll my eyes. To my surprise, he turned to Darton next. "And you have that fancy magic sword of yours. Is that here? There was something I wanted to discuss with you about it. Maybe better as a private conversation to start, man to man."

One of Darton's eyebrows arched. "You want to have a private talk about my sword?" he said, not quite suppressing a note of snark.

Eric looked unfazed. "Unless that's a problem."

Darton glanced at me. I shrugged. I might have insisted on being in the loop, but they were only going to walk to the other room. If it was important, Darton would fill me in when they were done talking. He wouldn't enjoy me babysitting the conversation. Anyway, it might be good if they put *their* heads together a little, in a constructive sort of way, after all the knocking heads they'd done last week.

"All right then." Darton got up. He led the other guy into his bedroom, where he'd stashed Excalibur.

What could Eric possibly have found out about the sword *I'd* commissioned and enchanted that we didn't already know? And that he felt he needed to talk to Darton about privately? I looked to Jagger, but he spread his hands.

"First I'm hearing about it," he said. "I thought you'd want to know, though, that my guys didn't see anything worrisome around your parents house while you two were away."

I'd already guessed as much, but it was still a relief to have it confirmed. "Give them my thanks for keeping watch. And thank *you*. I'm sure I've set some kind of record for amount of trouble caused in under a month."

Jagger laughed. "Ah, it's worth it. After chasing after the occasional stray shadow varmints here and there most of my life, I'm finally getting to take on the big guns, if only from the sidelines. I'm glad to be involved at all."

"Well, your help is more than appreciated."

"Let me get that new number of yours," he said. "I don't want to be left out again."

I took his phone and typed in the number for the disposable I'd picked up. "I'd guess the people in your network who monitor all those dark energies have noticed more fae activity stirring all over the place, not just in Britain."

"You'd be right. Lots more activity. Lots more partial sightings. Nothing extremely intrusive, but it's clear this dark fae lady's influence has a wide range."

"That'll all end if we can deal with her," I said. "I was wondering—"

A *crack* rang out, so loud and sharp it seemed to snap my eardrums. A... gunshot?

From Darton's bedroom.

I threw myself to my feet. There was a thump. Someone shouted. And with a few murmured words, I apparated across the entire house to appear at the foot of Darton's bed.

9

My feet hit the floor with a jolt. Darton and Eric were tussling by the door, Excalibur on the floor near their feet. Eric had a pistol clasped in one hand. He tried to swing it toward Darton. Darton shoved his arm to the side, but his own arm faltered. Blood was seeping through the fabric of his shirt over his shoulder.

I didn't have time to find a wand or even a twig. Wrenching at the life energy inside my body, I spat out a phrase. "*Melt it, meld it.*"

A bolt of energy hit the gun. The pistol's barrel warped in on itself, the opening collapsing. Eric stared at it in shock. Then he swung its blunt surface at Darton's head.

I dashed forward to catch his wrist. Jagger burst in the door at the same moment. He shoved Eric against the wall by his shoulders. "What the hell are you doing, kid?"

I turned to Darton. His mouth was twisted, his hand clamped to his bleeding shoulder. Beyond him, a dark circle showed where the bullet had dug into the wall.

"Let me see," I said.

He shifted his hand. Blood smeared his fingers. "I

don't want you using any more of your own energy to heal me," he said through partly gritted teeth. "I can wait long enough for you to get a wand."

I eased back the torn fabric of his shirt. The bullet had grazed him, taking a chunk of flesh with it, about a quarter of an inch deep and an inch across. The wound was bloody and painful, but nowhere near fatal. Easier to patch up than what I'd done to my hand yesterday.

"It's the right thing to do," Eric said raggedly. He grunted as he struggled against Jagger's hold. "We have to think about protecting *every*one."

"What in light's name are you *talking* about?" I snapped. Patting myself down, I found a spare twig in my pocket. I gripped it and murmured to seal the skin over Darton's wound. The twig crumpled in my hand. "What happened?" I asked my king. After what Eric had done, I didn't trust *his* account of the situation.

"I turned around to pick up the sword," Darton said. "He must have had the gun in his bag. I looked back just as he was about to shoot." He glanced down at Excalibur with a slanted smile. "I should probably be thanking that fencing training. I managed to smack his arm to the side with a quick block. Didn't even realize what I was doing or why until after instinct kicked in."

"As long as he's alive, he's a danger to the entire world," Eric said. His words rippled into me, setting off the itch in my muscles. The itch of the oath. I stepped toward him, my eyes narrowing and my arms crossing over my chest to hold the urge in check.

"Where did you get that idea from?"

He stopped struggling, evidently realizing that fit as he might be, Jagger had at least fifty pounds, most of it muscle, on him. Instead he just glowered at me.

"You left behind those journals," he said.

Journals. My father's journals. The ones where he'd written out all his observations and fears about Arthur and his family. A chill raced down my back. It hadn't occurred to me that the people I'd left them with might read them. It hadn't occurred to me that they *could*.

"How much did you even understand what's written in those?" I said. "It's Old English—it makes *my* head hurt going through it." And I'd grown up on the language, as distant as that first growing up now was.

"There are skills it's useful to know if you want to be effective in our line of work," Eric said. "I've got a passable grasp, and my mom's nearly fluent. When I got the gist, I brought them to her to confirm."

I thought of Mavis with her kind smile. My gut knotted. "Did she know you came out here to kill Darton?"

For the first time since I'd appeared in the room, a hint of uncertainty crossed Eric's face. He scowled. "No," he admitted. "She has no idea. She thought it was for you to figure out. But you obviously aren't willing to do what's necessary. You care more about him and the time bomb lodged inside him than whether the rest of us have a chance."

My father's journals had been all about Arthur and his family. But he'd made notes in the last one about the cycle of rebirth I'd gotten me and my king wrapped up in. Notes to me, warning me that he believed the darkness would have clung on to Arthur's soul no matter how many reincarnations it went through. After everything Eric had seen me do, the way he'd heard us talk to each other, he must have put those pieces together too.

"Em," Darton said behind me. "What does he mean?"

Sodding hell. This was not how I'd wanted to have this conversation. "I don't think I want to discuss it with *him* still here," I said, matching Eric's glower. "You can count yourself no longer welcome on our property. You have no idea what you're messing with, and I do. You could have asked a few questions before you came charging in."

"And maybe I'd have tipped you off. I didn't even manage to get the job done as it was." Eric's head sagged.

Jagger scowled at him and then glanced back at me. "I'm sorry I brought this delinquent into your home, Emma," he said. "Let me do the honors of taking out the trash. I'll give you a shout when he's well away from here."

Keeping a tight grip on Eric's arm, he walked the younger man out of the room. My shoulders didn't sink back down until the front door thudded shut behind them. Then the breath rushed out of me. I sagged onto the bed.

Darton rubbed his mouth. "A time bomb?" he said, his voice hesitant.

The knot in my gut came back, twice as large.

"Sit down. This is going to take a while."

Darton eased himself down on the bed, wincing as his wounded arm bumped it. My hasty healing spell hadn't fixed him completely. He tipped onto his back to stare up at the ceiling. His jaw had tightened.

"Okay," he said. "Hit me with it. The whole story this time, if you don't mind."

I bit my lip and looked away. "This isn't something new I've been keeping from you. I mean, I didn't tell you about it, but... I've always not told you about it."

I thought he'd already been lying still, but his body went even more motionless at that. "Since how long ago?"

My chest clenched. "Since always," I admitted. "Since..." My head bowed. "Art, I never told you the whole reason why I came looking to serve you in the first place."

"Oh." He paused. "But you didn't do anything wrong while you were with me. You always *did* serve me. How bad can it be?"

"Well, I... I had a lot of arguments with my father about my methods. Working with you changed my mind about what was really important. I hadn't had a chance to form my own opinions before. All I'd had was what he said and the knowledge of the enclave to go by. I was always honest with you about how *I* saw things. Just not about how my father wanted me to."

"Your father who was a light fae."

"Yeah." I pressed my hand to my forehead. "You know I was always worried about the dark fae hanging around. That they would try to talk to you, or just watch... You aren't the first in your family that they've taken an interest in. My father had observed their interactions with your ancestors going back several generations."

Darton frowned. "He thought we were colluding with them?"

I laughed shortly. "Oh, no. That wouldn't even have occurred to him. A dark fae would never lower themselves to align with human beings. But he was sure they were planning to use one or more of you for some purpose. He noted signs of magical ceremonies being carried out. Saw them lurking around the castle. Noticed a faint energy that seemed to grow across each generation..."

"What kind of 'energy'?"

"I—I don't have all the details. *He* wasn't even sure exactly what they were doing, and I didn't have time to read through all of his notes after I got his journals. But he believed the dark fae had placed some sort of dark enchantment on your family line. Something that was passed on with each generation and that grew in strength as it did. And the signs he saw made him believe that you were the culmination of whatever they were planning."

Darton was silent for a long moment. "That's why she came for me. The Darkest One. The dark fae hadn't ever attacked the kingdom like that before, had they?"

I shook my head. "A direct assault isn't their usual strategy. But I think she had something larger planned. Something she wanted to... release from your soul."

He set his hand on his chest. "That dark enchantment your father thinks they were casting. It was inside me—it's still inside me?"

"I've caught glimpses of it when I've worked other magic on you," I admitted. "Not enough that I thought I needed to worry. I mean, as far as I knew, whatever it was, she's the only one who could activate it. So as long as she was bound, it didn't affect us anyway."

"But that's why your enclave was so nervous around me. Obviously. That's why they made you swear that oath." His gaze slid back to me. "That's why even part of you wants to kill me. Before the Darkest One can get to me and set off... whatever this 'bomb' inside me is."

"No part of me wants to," I said firmly. "We've managed to stay ahead of her for fifteen hundred years and we'll—we'll find some way of fighting back now. I'm not giving up. I'm not giving up on *you*."

Another silence settled over us. Darton's brow furrowed. "Some of the things I've remembered from back then make a little more sense now. There've been a couple of people I had the feeling must have been dark fae—the way they looked at me, talked to me... Like there was something in me that they wanted."

I couldn't help perking up. "Did they say anything about what they expected from you?"

"No, nothing like that. If I'd known I should wonder, maybe I could have prodded. If you'd told me there was something to prod about."

A lump rose in my throat. "I thought you'd cast me out if you knew why I'd come. I was meant to be, well, a spy more than anything else, for my father's research. And a plant within your castle to try to prevent the Darkest One's plan from coming to fruition, of course. It seemed more important that I was there with you than that I was completely honest." My voice dropped. "That's the only thing I ever kept from you. Well, that and... the exact nature of all my feelings for you."

"All right. And what do we do about it now?"

"I don't know."

He stirred, swiping his arm across his forehead. "I need to think a little. On my own."

I probably didn't deserve even that polite a dismissal after what I'd just admitted. I bobbed my head and slipped out of the room. In my own bedroom, I leaned back against the wall. A burn filled my eyes. I dragged in a breath and swallowed the beginnings of a sob.

Of course he was upset. That was why I hadn't told him about the dark fae's doings over all this time. I had to allow him those feelings. If my omissions ruined things between us, well... our friendship had always been living on borrowed time, hadn't it?

The sense of loss rolled over me, bringing an ache between my ribs, but one clear thought came with it. I hadn't been completely truthful even just now. I *did* know what I had to do.

I'd been going about this all wrong, trying to combat the oath instead of the reason for it. I'd never wanted to look at the darkness inside my king too closely. It was the work of the Darkest One and her underlings, built up over hundreds of years. There might be no hope at all of me even pricking at it.

But I had to try. If I could untangle her fingerprints from his soul and wrench her enchantment out of him, the oath wouldn't matter. Her power wouldn't matter. We could take her on directly, magic and sword, without needing to fear what she might do with my king.

Between me and her and Eric and everyone else who might come calling... Tackling that dark curse was the only way Darton was going to make it through this catastrophe alive.

IO

I put the kid on a plane back to France, Jagger told me by text. *That seemed like the safest option for all involved. Have you and Darton sorted things out between you?*

He didn't ask any questions about who we were, or how we'd come to be this way, or anything like that. Had Eric told him what he'd figured out about our past lives? I guessed if he had, Jagger had decided it wasn't really his business. Or at the very least, that he trusted me to work my way out of this mess more than he trusted Eric's preferred strategy.

For the most part, I typed back. *No permanent harm done.* Physically, anyway.

A knock sounded on my bedroom door. I pushed myself upright. "Come in."

Darton eased the door open. He stepped over the threshold and stopped there. His striking blue eyes were shadowed.

"There's nothing else you haven't told me?" he said.

Guilt jabbed me in the gut again. "Nothing," I said. "I swear it. *May the light strike me down if I lie.*"

He caught the gist of the old language enough to

glance at the ceiling as if to check for a lightning bolt about to take me up on the request. When none appeared, he sank into the chair at my desk and swiveled it to face me.

"So this dark fae magic," he said. "It's been in me all this time?"

"I'm sorry," I said. "So sorry. I gave you a bunch of excuses earlier, but none of them are enough. I should have tried to deal with it sooner. I wanted to think it wouldn't matter... but obviously I should have known it would."

I hadn't wanted to deal with the possibility that once I looked at my king's soul that closely, I'd realize I couldn't do anything to fix it. I was *still* scared of that.

"Can you get it out of me?" Darton asked, getting right to that point.

I gave him a pained smile. "I can't answer that without knowing exactly what it is. The magic is buried deep. The Darkest One and her underlings didn't want anyone seeing it, let alone poking at it. But I'll do my best. Come here?"

For a second, my breath caught with the fear that he was too upset with me to want to even sit next to me. But he got up and settled on the edge of the bed. I turned, taking his hand in mine.

"We don't need some big magical ceremony for this?" Darton said without looking at me.

"Not for an initial look around. My soul knows yours pretty well by now." All of it except the part the Darkest One had touched, anyway.

I palmed a few twigs in my other hand and closed my eyes, focusing my awareness on the skin-to-skin contact of his hand in mine. The pulse of life flowing through his body. The warm earthy smell of him that filled my nose, tugging at me to lean closer. I ignored that impulse and the rising itch running through my fingers.

His pulse turned into a glow. A glow with a tremor of darkness running through it. I reached my mind toward that shadow. *"Delve deep, delve clear,"* I murmured.

The hint of it flickered away from me. I stretched my awareness farther into the glow. Glimpses of Darton's memories and Arthur's shimmered past me. For several minutes, I waited. Finally, the shadow surfaced again. It seemed to catch sight of me and flinch away, flitting as fast as a minnow in a stream.

"Come forth to be seen," I crooned to it. It only slipped away faster. In a second I couldn't see it at all. I hesitated, watching, as Darton's heart beat on. The tremor of darkness stayed hidden this time.

I drew myself out of my meditative state with a sharp inhale. Darton was looking at me now, studying my expression. "Did you see it? What *is* it?"

"I don't know," I said. "I couldn't get close enough to—"

My hands jerked. I shoved them back into my lap, ramming my thumb against the palm I'd stabbed yesterday. A bolt of pain shot up my arm, and the oath's urge faded. Darton looked down at my hands warily, but to give him proper credit for bravery, he stayed where he was.

"It wasn't good, though, obviously," he said.

"I think we could have been sure of that already." I took another steadying breath and folded my arms over my chest to better restrain the itch. "My magic hardly touched it. Actually, it seemed to *repel* it, if anything... Whatever they've conjured, it knows that it should only show itself to dark sorts. My own nature is probably repelling it. Which means my usual tricks aren't going to work."

"So you can't do anything?"

"No." I paused. *My own nature.* So how could I overcome that? What else? "Maybe I can make it believe I'm a dark fae." I glanced around the room. "But for that, I'm going to need a different sort of supplies than I've usually collected..."

* * *

The crisp autumn leaves crunched under our feet as Izzy and I strode along the narrow forest path. The branches were all but bare now, just a few browning strays clinging on. Though the breeze that brushed over us was dry, a damp tang of rot was starting to creep into it already. Soon all those leaves would be mulch for next year's growing.

"I swear there are a bunch of willows out here somewhere," Izzy said, shoving her pale auburn hair behind her ears. "It was last year the hiking club came out here, so I don't remember *exactly* how far along they are..."

"It's okay," I said. "I'm just glad I already knew someone who had the scoop on the nearby forests."

She tucked her gloved hands into her pockets. "I'd have thought with all your magical senses, you could have tracked a tree by its vibes or something."

The corner of my lips quirked up. "Oh, I can. But only if it's alive." I'd already used that method to find a nice clump of the other plant I needed to add to my stockpile, aconite, in all its highly poisonous glory. "For my current purposes, I need to scrape bark from a willow that's dead—and has been dead for at least a few months."

"That sounds... ominous."

"Usually the best way of dealing with dark magic is to overwhelm it with light," I said. "But sometimes you need to be a little sneaky. Lull it into complacency with something familiar." Izzy's eyes widened, and I gave her a tense grin. "Don't worry, I'm not planning anything horrifying."

I was still keeping the darkness in my king's soul a secret from everyone except Darton. After he'd told me about Izzy's hiking club inclinations, he'd paused and asked if I could avoid telling her exactly why I needed these new materials. *I know it's not my fault the dark fae did this to me,* he said. *But the thought of my friends knowing... I wish you'd told me sooner, but I guess I can see why it wasn't a subject you wanted to discuss.*

He'd still been a little awkward with me before I'd left. An ache spread through my chest at the memory. We'd come so far, learning to trust each other. I hoped I hadn't broken that trust too much.

Izzy pushed aside the branch of a sapling that had sprouted across the path. "Honestly, I don't know if I even mind horrifying if it means you can take care of this 'Darkest One.' The way she's practically tearing apart all of England... It's awful. Sometimes you have to fight fire with fire?"

"Something like that," I said.

We hopped stones over a shallow creek. "This looks familiar," Izzy said. "I'm pretty sure the big stretch of willows wasn't too far from here. There were enough of them that I think there's got to be at least one fallen."

"One is all I need."

A gloom drifted by, following the shadows along the

edge of the stream. Izzy tensed an instant after I saw it. She'd always been the most sensitive of Darton's crowd, but for her to notice it that quickly, it was obviously a lot more potent than usual. The Darkest One's influence was spreading far and fast.

I snapped a twig off a nearby shrub. *"Darkness begone."* The gloom wisped away, and Izzy exhaled.

"There've been more of them again," she said. "Floating around campus. They're even more visible than they were the first time, when you said that mercenary was giving them extra energy. I've seen people getting freaked out by them. Not that they have any idea what they're seeing, but moving shadows is going to creep anyone out."

"Maybe I'll have to go do another cleanup of the grounds," I said, but I didn't really believe I'd have time for that. The glooms weren't likely to hurt any regular human beings. Unless the Darkest One started commanding them to. Now that was a horrifying thought.

Izzy fell silent for a moment, studying the forest and the path ahead. When she sucked in her breath, I could tell from the sound she was nervous about the question she was about to ask.

"I've been thinking," she said, in an even softer voice than usual, "about the Darkest One, and everything you've told us about her... You knew she was a threat all the way back in your first life, right? You knew she wanted Darton—Arthur... You know what I mean."

"I knew the dark fae were keeping an eye on him." My thoughts dart back to that long-ago vision of the Darkest One ripping into Arthur's body. "And I was worried about her in particular, yeah."

"But even with that... I'm not saying this to criticize

or anything, really. It's not as if I'd stand half a chance at stopping her. But when she did come, back then, if you *could* have just destroyed her instead of the whole binding spell, you would have, wouldn't you? You sealed her away because that was the best you could do."

My throat tightened. "That's a fair read of the situation. The direction I took was also partly due to how quickly the attack happened and how little time I had to think." But I'd had plenty of time to think about how I'd defend my king from the Darkest One before she'd arrived, and I hadn't come up with a definite solution any of those times either.

"Mostly she was too powerful," I added. "She's the most powerful dark fae there is, and I'm only half-fae myself. Creative strategy can get you a long way, but..." I shrugged, my heart heavy.

Izzy bit her lip. "So... If that was the case back then, and you haven't had as much time to prepare now..."

Ah. It wasn't hard to figure out what she was asking, as much as she obviously hated to. "I don't know if I'll be able to take her on properly this time, no," I said. "I just can't think about that. I have to try. Maybe I can at least seal her away again. Maybe I can find a way to get her attention off Darton, at least, so whatever she's planning that involves him, she won't be able to do." If I could rid him of his curse, that would throw a wrench in her schemes.

"And Darton will help fight her."

"Of course. In some ways he knows *more* than he did back then, so he'll be able to do more." I hadn't been enough to stop her on my own, but maybe the two of us together, both with a full understanding of the threat...

But how could I let him get close enough to the Darkest One to fight her while her influence was still tied to his soul? No. The spell I was going to attempt had to work. I had to release him from the darkness she'd woven into his soul, or we were screwed. It was that simple.

"Oh, look!" Izzy pointed ahead. The drifting branches of a weeping willow had come into view. We hurried along the path. The breeze passed through the grove with an eerie rustling. But as we ventured into the midst of the willows, my gaze caught on a prone trunk a short hike down the path. My spirits lifted, and a real smile crossed my face.

This was the first time I could think of that I'd been happy to see something dead, but I'd take my victories where I could.

II

"You went all that way to gather this stuff, and now you're going to burn it?" Darton said.

I poked at the shavings of dead willow bark I'd gathered in a small pile in our concrete yard. "Reduce it down to its most basic, orderly state. That's the whole point. Anyway, I've got more if I mess up the materials somehow."

I had to be careful not to add extra elements to the mix. That meant no matches and no chemical lighters. And no light fae magic.

I knelt down and struck the rocks I was using as flints against each other. One, two, three—there. I got a spark. It leapt onto the finer shreds of bark beneath my hands and caught. The flame sizzled over the pile as I straightened up. A thin, acrid scent drifted into the air.

"And this will convince the... whatever... inside me that you're a dark fae?"

"That's the idea." I glanced over at Darton. He was trying to keep his voice casual, but tension showed all through his posture. I was about to go digging deep into his soul. We both knew there wasn't any other option, but I couldn't help saying, "If you've changed your mind, we can just leave it. We can just make sure the Darkest One never gets the chance—"

"But we can't really make sure she won't." Darton shook his head. "It's fine. I want her magic out of me. You can't do that unless you know what *it* is."

The scraps of bark had been small enough that the fire had already consumed most of them. I stirred the ash with my poker. "I'll be done here soon. Why don't you go lie down where we decided and relax as well as you can. That'll make my job easier."

"Right." He turned to go with a jerky motion. It tugged at my heart.

"Art," I said. He looked back at me. "It's going to be okay. Whatever it is, we'll deal with it. Like always. Isn't that what you always say?"

His mouth twitched into a small smile. "I guess I should be glad you do listen to me every now and again."

The door thumped as he went in. I watched the flames crackle lower over the disintegrating bark. That little smile had warmed me more than the fire did.

When the fire had sputtered out completely, I took out my bag of dried aconite petals and scattered them in the ash. Then I scooped some of the mixture into a bowl. With a stone pestle, I ground petals and ash together into a fine powder. The scent that rose off it, tart and prickling, made my stomach turn.

There was darkness here, all right. My fae senses cringed at it. Well, they'd just have to tolerate it for a little while. I had work to do.

Inside, the cup of chervil tea I'd brewed had stopped

steaming. That herb was the only one I'd already had on hand that I thought might be useful, to thin out the light fae essence running through my veins. I drank it in slow gulps. The delicately sweet flavor seemed at odds with the smoky smell still clinging to my clothes.

I left those clothes on—the willow smoke could only help my cause—and carried my bowl of powder into the guest room.

We'd pushed the bed into the corner to leave as much open floor space as possible. Darton lay on the polished wood, shirt off, his arms resting at either side of his well-muscled chest and his eyes closed. He was breathing deep and even, but the twitch of his jaw as I came in told me he was far from sleeping.

I knelt beside him and rolled up my sleeves. The willow ash and aconite powder was faintly grainy and still warm under my fingers. I smeared it up my forearms to the elbows, rubbing it in until my skin looked darker than Keevan's. Then I coated my face with it, eyelids, nose, lips—everything. Next a ring around my neck and down past my collarbone to shield the energy of my heart. The only impression I wanted to give off during this exploration was that of the deathly darkness that characterized my opposite in fae kind.

The itch in my hands had faded. Maybe the oath thought all this work was going toward bringing death to Arthur's soul. Well, at least that'd be one less distraction.

I dragged in a breath and leaned forward to set my hands on Darton's bare chest. His heart beat against my palms from beneath those firm muscles. And all through his body, the energy of his soul quivered. I let my eyelids fall shut.

"*I travel in, I travel well. Darkness, come to meet me.*"

My sense of the energies inside Darton expanded. I glided on into them, as if into a vision.

A pulsing light filled the space around my awareness, forming the walls of a tunnel. I moved onward through it, my senses on high alert. Little traces of shadow flickered here and there amid the glow. I could see them more sharply now. They gleamed darker for me as if welcoming me.

Come to me, shadows, I thought without speaking. I had no real voice in this inner realm. *Let me see you in all your dark glory.*

I had the sense of something stirring, up ahead. A faint waft of cold cut through Darton's natural warmth. I was closer, far closer than I'd managed to get before.

The tunnel turned and twisted, as if someone had knotted it here. The speckles of shadow grew larger and seeped even deeper. I braced myself as I ventured on. Whatever dark curse the fae had conjured inside Arthur's soul might not be racing out to greet me, but it wasn't fleeing either. I could feel it hovering, waiting, with a quiver that was almost curious.

I turned another corner—and whatever breath I had in this strange space fell away. A shadowy shape sat coiled in the space ahead of me. The thrum reverberating off it gave me the same icy chill as the Darkest One's voice in my vision. I could almost feel her fingers reaching off of the thing to smear her frigid essence on my skin.

That was it. My king's curse. If I could touch it, scry out the purpose of it—

I took another step closer, and the thing raised its head. A wave of horror crashed over me, sweeping all my thoughts away. I froze, numbed with panic.

I didn't need to touch that thing to know what it was. The head that peered down at me was narrow and sharp, with puffs of smoke trailing from its two wide nostrils. Slanted eyes shone with a darkness so complete I couldn't focus on them for more than a moment. Scales gleamed all along its shadowy length as it uncoiled its sinewy body. Claws like obsidian cut into the glow of the soul around us. Folded wings stirred by the line of spikes running down its back.

A dragon. I was looking at a dragon. A dragon shaped entirely from dark fae magic, some two hundred years of it, all packed into this tiny gap in Arthur's soul.

But it wasn't tiny in essence. The power humming inside it was enough to leave my head ringing. Bottled up and waiting to explode—like the time bomb Eric had called it.

All the Darkest One had to do was rip Darton open and set this thing free, and it would unfurl its cruel shadows over humankind with a wallop that would put shame to the storm now raging over Britain.

The stories called Arthur "Pendragon." As if they'd known somehow. How absurd. Light help us, how the hell was I supposed to conquer *that*?

A hysterical giggle bubbled through my mind. The dragon shifted toward me with another wave of its cold, concentrated energy. It stabbed through my awareness as if I'd been splashed with liquid nitrogen. It barred its fangs, gathering its breath for whatever horrible sort of flame a creature like that could produce, and the last shreds of self-control holding me in place vanished.

I flinched away, tumbling away from the shadow,

through the glow, and back into my now-quaking body. The chill raced after me. No. No. I clenched my fingers as more shivers raked my body.

The Darkest One's laughter echoed in my ears. The ice of her energy ached under every inch of my skin. Not just a curse. A monster. A monster so vast I could hardly comprehend it.

A whimper crept from my throat. I clamped my mouth shut, but Darton's eyes had already blinked open. He sat up. "Em."

My arms shot out of their own accord. My hands clamped around his neck, thumbs poised to channel the killing energy straight into his throat. My lips parted, the oath's urge burning in my mouth.

No. I hadn't gone through that horrible journey just to give in now. I tried to wrench my arms away, but my muscles wouldn't obey. Air stuttered from my mouth. My tongue shifted. I couldn't even drag my thumb to the side to press it against my wounded palm. But I had to feel something, something other than this drive to snuff out the life in front of me—and the beast contained within it.

Darton stared at me. He gripped my forearms, but I already knew he couldn't have dislodged my grasp now, football player muscles or no. The warmth of his touch bled through my skin, and I did the only thing I could think of. I yanked him forward and pulled myself to him at the same time, catching his mouth with a kiss.

It had only been a few days since we'd last kissed. Since we'd last... almost everything. But somehow it felt as if I'd been waiting ages to feel his lips against mine again. As if I'd gone nearly mad with the lack of them. He kissed me back, hard and hot, setting off sparks all through my body. My hold on his neck loosened.

Darton cupped the back of my head, his fingertips tracing over my scalp. I tipped my head to angle the kiss even deeper. To drink up every drop of pleasure it could offer, before we had to stop.

Because we did. When the itch of the oath had completely dampened, I eased back. My body was still quivering, but for a very different reason. Darton let out a shaky breath. His hand slid away, but only as far as my shoulder. He ran his thumb over the peak, and that single contact was enough to leave me longing to throw myself back into his embrace.

"Em?" he said. I thought I heard the same longing in his voice, but there was confusion too. "Are you— Was that okay?"

Hadn't he noticed I was the one who'd initiated the embrace? I laughed, a little roughly. "A minor exception to my rules. I figured it was better to kiss you than to kill you."

He touched his neck. My fingers had clutched him hard enough that the skin there was mottled pink. Guilt knotted my stomach. "I'm sorry. I was overwhelmed, and the oath took over—"

"And you stopped it. Even then you stopped it." He let out a huff of breath that was almost a chuckle. "Even when you've got a magical oath compelling you to hurt me, I can trust you with my life."

The only urge I was fighting now was the urge to kiss him again, which had only gotten stronger with that comment. I took his hand from my shoulder into mine, twining my fingers through his. We were still in this together, my king and me.

He bowed his head toward me, and my heart skipped. His lips only brushed my cheek with the briefest of pecks. Then he tugged me to him so I was leaning against his solid frame. He looked down at our twined hands.

"You said you were overwhelmed. You found the dark magic inside me, then? I'm guessing it's pretty bad."

He was braced for the news. It still took me a few seconds to open my mouth, and another several to find the words.

"The dark fae conjured a dragon. Bit by bit, it must have been. Shaping it and feeding it more and more power. For now, it's just a ball of energy hidden in your soul. But if the Darkest One gets her hands on you..."

"She'll release it," Darton finished for me. "A dragon. A fucking *dragon*." He pressed his hand to his forehead. "I don't even know what that means. Is it going to burst out of me someday, all *Alien* style?"

I'd kept up with modern culture enough to understand the reference. "No. It's not a bodily thing. It's all dark energy pulled into a form. If she never gets the chance, it'll just stay there, dormant, until... well, until you die."

"But we can't count on staying ahead of her that long. So what do you do about a soul plagued with dragons?"

I hesitated. "I'm not sure. I've never dealt with a dragon before. It's not something light fae are inclined to construct."

Darton's fingers tightened around mine. "It scares you," he said.

"I'll try my best," I said quickly. "There has to be something—"

"Right." His voice had gone brisk and distant. "And

if there isn't, and the Darkest One comes—how bad exactly will it be if this dragon gets out?"

I wet my lips. "I can't know for sure. But... they were feeding it with power, all through your first life and the lives of your ancestors. The Darkest One wanted something that could rain more destruction down in an instant than even she can on her own."

"So it'll be *worse* than what she's already doing."

"A lot worse," I admitted. "From what I felt of the thing, it could lay waste to this entire state—people, animals, plants, everything destroyed—in a matter of minutes."

Darton sucked in a breath. I heard him swallow. Then he said, "Maybe you *should* kill me then."

I jerked away from his chest to stare at him. "*What?*"

His jaw set. He looked back at me steadily. "Maybe your old enclave was right. Maybe Eric was right. The Darkest One could decide to go through with her plans for me any minute now. As long as I'm alive with that thing in me, she can. But if I die, if my soul passes away, the dragon dies with me. Doesn't it?"

"Yes," I said, "but—"

"No but. I don't want to be responsible for millions of people dying. *I* don't want to die, but I'm not going to kid myself that I'm that important."

My chest clenched. My fingers curled around his, as if he might slip away from me right now, just by saying that. "You are to me."

"Em. Merlin." One side of his mouth slanted up, but the shape it made was too crooked to really call it a smile. He touched the side of my face, leaning in so our foreheads nearly touched. "You've done so much for me already. Kept me going all this time. Don't you think maybe it's time you let me go?"

"I'm really not good at that," I said. "As I think the last fifteen hundred years should prove. Art—Arthur. I don't want you to be turned into the Darkest One's weapon either. If it comes to that, if I know we don't have a chance... I'll do what I have to do. But I don't believe we're there yet. I *do* believe there's a chance. I swear to you, on all the years we've spent together, I'm not giving up on you yet. Don't give up on me?"

Darton made a choked sound. "Of course not. Don't say it like that. You know I—" He faltered. "What's next, then? Where do we go from here?"

12

"Dragons, huh?" Jagger turned the wheel of the fae hunter van he'd lent to us and now temporarily reclaimed. The wheels bumped over a pothole in the near-abandoned dirt road with a lurch and a squeal. "Just when I thought I'd seen everything. You do like to top yourself, don't you?"

"Believe me, I'd rather not have in this particular way," I muttered. Sunlight wavered over us from between the sparse trees along the side of the road. Its intermittent light wasn't enough to provide any comfort. "Thanks for coming back. I mean, after everything you must have heard from Eric..."

Jagger's mouth flattened into a grim line. "He's not a bad kid, but he could do with a little more thinking before he acts. If you are who he says you are, then I can't see how he or I are better equipped to handle the situation."

He left that statement between us like a question, for me to confirm or deny. I opted for the middle ground.

"I'm sure any ideas you have about that are highly distorted by time and imagination. The stories don't get a whole lot right."

Jagger gave a bark of a laugh. "Emma, I have spent more than a minute in your presence. You don't need to tell me *that*."

I braced myself for the sorts of questions Keevan and Izzy had asked when they'd found out—about what Arthur and I *had* been like, about our long series of lives and rebirths, about the spell that had thrown us into that cycle. But Jagger just left it at that. Maybe I'd been silly to keep it from him in the first place. He'd never been the dramatic type.

"I prefer not to shout it from the rooftops," I said. "As you've probably also already figured out. So with this expert of yours—"

"By all means," Jagger said. "But so there's no misunderstanding, I wouldn't exactly call Hugh an 'expert.' He, er, is mainly known in the network as a kook. The guy spends all his time obsessing over creatures the rest of us didn't have any reason to believe existed, despite all the things we had seen. I'm not sure anything he thinks he knows is any more true than those stories you mentioned."

"That's fine. I couldn't really expect anything better than that." How could I when *I* didn't even know what to do about a dragon? The Darkest One must have been amused with her cleverness, taking human nightmares and letting them guide her magic-making. I'd heard of dark fae-formed dragons in my first life, but those had been brief conjurings designed more to scare than do any real destruction. The dark lady had truly outdone herself.

Jagger turned down a drive even narrower and bumpier than the road we'd been on. A small stone house stood at the end, spotty forest all around it. One tree leaned over so far it nearly touched the mossy shingles on the roof.

My eyebrows rose. "Doesn't worry much about dark fae access, does he? No floodlights or solar panels?"

Jagger brought the van to a halt. "Like I said: a kook. From what he's said, he doesn't do any actual hunting, just 'observing.' So I suppose he's never pissed off a dark thing enough to find out what it's like when they follow you home for payback."

Like many times before, I had to bite back the question of how exactly Jagger had gotten those scars on his face. It'd been some kind of dark creature's doing—I had no doubt about that. I also suspected the creature that had done it had done worse to someone else, someone Jagger cared about, at the same time. But he'd never volunteered the information, despite my occasional vague prodding. If he wasn't going to make a fuss about my secrets, I could do him the same courtesy.

The house's door opened as we climbed out of the van. A short, pudgy man with wire-rimmed glasses peered at us from the front step. For a second I thought he was wary. Then he rubbed his hands together, and I caught the excited gleam in his deep-set eyes.

"Jagger," he said in a slightly raspy tenor. "And you must be Emma. I understand you've come dragon-hunting." He gave me a flash of a smile.

"That's one way of putting it." I glanced around. The terrain by the house was a mishmash of shadows. It made my skin crawl even without seeing anything definite crawling in it. "Should we go inside?"

"Yes, of course. Come on in."

Hugh swept back inside, leaving the door wide open. No, this guy clearly had no worries about dark vermin following him home. It was a damned good thing after a fair bit of waffling I'd decided to leave Darton at home, on the condition he kept his sword in arm's reach.

Besides, I didn't like the way Hugh was already sizing me up. Like I was a specimen rather than a person. It reminded me too much of the way the fae looked at me sometimes, as if they were trying to figure out how my half-fae soul could have come to be in this completely human body. I doubted he could have seen the dragon in Darton anyway—it'd been hard enough for me to reach it—but he no doubt would have tried, by light only knew what methods.

"I understand you're the dragon expert in the network," I said, matching Hugh's academic tone. "I was hoping to hear some of the results of your research. In particular, about how a person gets rid of a dragon."

"Hmm." He sat in one of the armchairs in the cramped living room and took off his glasses to rub them with the hem of his shirt. The place smelled of dusty leather, probably due to the stacks of old books on the shelves that filled one wall. I stayed standing, not trusting the wooden chairs that remained. The woven seat on one looked ready to unravel the next time anyone put their weight on it.

"Tell me a little more about this dragon," Hugh said, putting his glasses back on. He folded his hands in his lap. "General appearance? Behavior? Where did you happen to find it?"

He was taking this all very calmly. Exactly how many actual dragons had he run into before? Jagger had given me the impression Hugh's research was purely speculative.

"It was formed by dark fae energy," I said. "Like all

of the dragons I'm aware of, which to be fair isn't a large number. Long and scaly, beady eyes, fangs and sharp claws, wings. You know the deal. Based on the smoke it had coming from its nose, I'd say definitely some sort of fire-breathing. They've encouraged it to stay still and quiet for now, though. It's all burrowed down in my—my friend's soul."

"In their *soul*," Hugh repeated.

"Yes," I said. "It's complicated to explain, but the fae have basically twisted a little portion of his life energy into a sort of home for it. Fed it from their own energy somehow. And I'd like to get rid of it."

"Right." Hugh gave me an odd little smile. Then he glanced at Jagger. "I know the rest of the network doesn't think much of my work, but this is a bit much, isn't it? Haven't you got better things to do than resort to pranks?"

Oh. I bristled as the realization hit me. The kook thought my story was so ridiculous he'd decided *I* was a kook. Hog's balls. What, did he expect me to have brought the dragon with me on a leash so he could inspect it?

"Hugh," Jagger said in his gravelly voice, "I think you should listen to the girl. She knows what she's talking about. I thought you'd be happy to put all that research to use."

"I would be if you'd brought me something other than a farce."

I cracked my knuckles. At the sound, Hugh's head jerked toward me. I gave him an even smile. "What exactly would you need for you to believe I'm not joking around?"

He blinked at me. "Well, I— Some sort of evidence of your story, I suppose. A better explanation of how this dragon came to be. Honestly, dark fae conjuring dragons in people's souls is nothing I've ever—"

"Fine." He wasn't getting a full explanation, especially not when he'd just proven he wasn't likely to believe that either. The whole story wasn't any easier to swallow. But I could show him proof that he was dealing with someone who knew more about fae dealings than he ever would. I didn't like to have to show off my magic as if it were a parlor trick, and showing him what I needed to wasn't going to be *fun*, but I didn't have time for all this blathering.

I pulled a couple of twigs from my jacket pocket. "Take a close look," I said, "because I'm only going to draw this for you once." I clenched my fingers around the twigs and held out my arm, my hand turned toward the ceiling. "*Picture from memory, take shape, take form,*" I murmured, reaching back to my memory of Arthur's dragon.

The air above my hand shimmered. The energy I was drawing from the twigs balked at my command. I was asking that life to imitate a vision of death, which was the last thing it wanted to do.

"*Picture from memory, take shape, take form,*" I repeated. Sweat beaded on the back of my neck as I trained my will on those wisps of energy. They whirled, darkening with the sharpening of my attention. They were visible to my spectators now. Hugh inhaled with a hitch of breath.

I ignored him, training my mind even more closely on the image of the dragon. The memory sent a chill down my spine, but I ignored the discomfort. I wasn't going to stop until the kook was well and truly convinced.

The shadows rippled into a more detailed form. The illusionary dragon uncoiled its body over my hand the way the real one had moved when I'd encountered it. Its teeth even flashed when it opened its mouth. It shuffled its wings, peering at Hugh.

A prickling started to dig down into the roots of my teeth. I gritted them, holding the illusion for a few seconds longer. Then I snapped my fingers, and the shadows dispersed.

Hugh was frozen in his chair, his jaw slack. He looked from the spot where the dragon had hovered to me and back again. I decided to sit down in the slightly less ramshackle chair after all.

"That's what it looked like," I said. "Although I expect its actual size when not imprisoned will be a lot larger than this house. Now what can you tell me about it?"

"Well, I— How did you do that?"

"I know a few fae tricks," I said. "Enough to recognize a dragon when I see one. Enough to know my friend is in a whole lot of trouble if we don't get rid of it. And an awful lot of other people will be in trouble as well."

Hugh paused. His gaze turned thoughtful. "Is this at all connected to that strange storm that's been attacking Great Britain for the last few days?"

"Only so far as the fae causing that is the same one who orchestrated the creation of the dragon," I said. "We'd really rather it wasn't inside him when she comes to collect."

"All right. All right. In his *soul*." His chuckle sounded a little frantic. "Unfortunately I'd imagine the easiest way—"

"If you suggest anything that involves getting rid of

my friend to get rid of the dragon, I'll be very tempted to get rid of you," I said matter-of-factly.

Hugh paled. "N-no. Of course not. Let me see." He stood up and went to his wall of books. He pulled one leather-bound volume out, paged through it, considered a few of the pages, put it back, and repeated the process a few more times. I waited, tapping my fingers against the chair's wooden arms. Jagger leaned against the door frame, looking mildly amused by his colleague's distress.

"I don't believe I've ever heard of a dragon formed in someone's soul before," Hugh said after several minutes. "Not even in the more outlandish stories. I assume you don't want to simply *remove* it..."

"No. It's not going to do anyone any good out on the loose either. I need a way to destroy it without moving it—or to at least weaken it." Maybe the latter would help me get to the point where I could do the former on my own.

"All right. Well, my research *has* given me some insight into dragons formed by energy. In fact, I've always believed those reports sounded the most authentic." The academic's enthusiasm had come back into his voice and his eyes. "There are of course the traditional methods of dragon-slaying involving swords and other weaponry..." At my grimace, he nodded. "Obviously this would require more of a... metaphysical approach."

"That's what I was thinking," I said. "But I want to be careful that the methods I use do actually weaken it rather than simply annoying it. It didn't look like a very forgiving creature."

"Understandable, understandable." He wet his lips. "Unfortunately, as I said, this isn't a situation I've encountered before. But I can tell you what I have found out about dragons' general inclinations. They seem particularly drawn to flow—of an even, orderly sort, being dark creatures. Many modern sightings have taken place near trains, trolleys, and other vehicles that tend to move along a clear path at a steady pace. They also seem to enjoy rivers and streams."

"I'm not seeing how that's going to help Emma slay one," Jagger put in.

I waved him off. "Let me figure out how to piece it together." If I could piece anything together from what Hugh's questionable sources had taught him. I turned back to the scholar. "What else? Anything at all. There's no way to know what idea might at least point me in the right direction."

"Well, perhaps for that reason—the appeal of a steady flow—dragons also seem to be drawn to... blood. And respiration."

"Which flow through the body, in an orderly way—under ideal circumstances," I said. "Got it."

He nodded. "Dragons are almost like fish themselves, needing to be in continuous motion when they're active. Trying to restrain a dragon in any way tends to have unfortunate results. I assume yours is subdued rather than contained."

Lurking, waiting. "Yeah, that describes it pretty well."

"What else, what else..." He frowned, looking away. "There are some accounts that myrrh smoke can send them into a stupor, but I wouldn't rely on that. They're known to be fickle, shifting their attention easily, and difficult to tame. Their weakest point is generally thought to be either their throat or a particular point on their belly, which I suppose might hold true even in metaphysical terms..."

He fell into a silence. I waited a few minutes before I said, "Is that everything?"

"There's relatively few accounts of dragons at all," he said with an apologetic shrug, and waved toward his shelf. "I've spent more of my time on less impressive creatures. But I can say this." He paused, holding my gaze. "I've visited a site that was apparently the target of a dragon not much bigger than a sparrow. The destruction that creature wrought, if that is indeed what wrought it... If this one is as large as you say, I hope for all our sakes that something I've told you today is useful to you. Because the last thing I'd want to see is that creature getting loose."

13

Jagger kept his own council until we'd climbed back into the van. "Is any of that rambling going to do you any good?" he asked. "I can't promise his information is at all reliable."

"I know," I said. "It gives me a starting point at least. Would you mind—I think I'm going to... meditate for a little while, in the back. To see if I can connect what he said to any of my own observations."

"Be my guest," Jagger said with a sweep of his arm.

I squeezed between the two front seats and sat down on the carpeted floor between the shelves of fae-hunting equipment. Jagger started the engine. The van rocked as he turned it around to head back up the pocked driveway. My body swayed.

Maybe lying down was a safer bet. Especially seeing as I planned to slip far back into my memories, where I'd barely be aware of what was happening outside.

I sank back on the floor. The bristles of the carpet prickled against the back of my neck. I didn't need any magic to travel back into my memories—they were already in my head, after all. Concentration would do the trick just fine. I dragged in a slow, steady breath, trying not to think about how appealing a dragon might have found that sensation.

There'd been several times I'd witnessed the dark fae interacting with Arthur. My father would have seen many other encounters, and maybe he'd even written about them in his journals, but Eric hadn't done me the favor of bringing those back along with his murderous intentions. So I had to make do with what I had in my own memory.

I let my mind drift back toward the sensations of fifteen hundred years past. The chalky smell of the plaster in the castle halls. Roast meat sizzling over a spit for hundreds of royal dinners. Hoof beats as my prince and then king dragged me off on some new quest. The lilt of his voice, low and measured. Always trying to help his subjects in any way he could.

Always listening, patiently, even when he shouldn't.

The woman was standing by the side of the road, a basket covered with a scrap of cloth slung over one arm. Her face sagged with apparent weariness and her clothes were torn, but it was a feigned distress. Shadows licked higher on her feet and deeper into her eyes than was truly natural. When she looked at my prince riding up to her, they shivered in anticipation.

She had more power in her toenail than the average human did in their entire body.

"My liege!" I said, but as always Arthur was ahead of me. His horses never balked at his taps of his heel or tugs of the reins. He drew his current stallion to a stop in front of the woman.

"What brings you out here, good woman?" he asked. "It's a long journey from the nearest town."

"I don't mind the walk," she said in a thin voice. Shadows unfurled with it from her mouth, too dim for my prince's eyes to catch.

"Are you the prince? Arthur? I'm sure I'm no one important enough for you to trouble with."

I didn't believe for an instant that she hadn't known exactly who he was before we'd even come into view. She'd been waiting for him. And she couldn't have picked a better ploy to keep him there. At the suggestion that he might think himself too high to bother with a peasant, he immediately slid down from his saddle. He didn't see any threat, just a harmless peasant.

Swine crud. After a few jerks of his head, the gelding I was riding finally agreed to stop behind the prince's steed. I scrambled down after my prince. My feet hit the ground with a jarring thump. The gelding snorted as if mocking me.

"Every person in this kingdom is important to me," Arthur was saying. "If you have any concerns at all, I'd much rather you told me than didn't."

"Oh," the woman said, suddenly coy, "I don't have any troubles big enough to complain. It's enough just to know we matter to you."

She took his hand and bowed down over it, as if in a gesture of supplication.

I cleared my throat sharply. "My liege," I said. The prince looked over. I gave him that look, the look he really should have been familiar with by now. His shoulders tensed slightly, but he still smiled at the woman as she straightened up. Too sodding confident for his own good.

"I appreciate your kind words," Arthur said, warming up to an excuse, but the woman waved him off before he had to produce it.

"You have business to attend to, of course. Think nothing of it. Stay well, Your Highness."

The hint of sarcasm in her tone had nagged at me even then. But now, studying the memory, I focused more on her bow. The way she'd tipped her head over Arthur's hand. Her chest had contracted—I hadn't paid special attention to *that* detail in the moment back then.

She'd exhaled over his knuckles. Had she been passing energy into him that way? I hadn't seen the dark fae work exactly like that before, but then, I hadn't dealt with dark fae conjuring monsters in people's souls before. Hugh had said dragons responded well to the rhythmic, flowing bodily functions like breath, after all.

I inhaled deeply and sent my mind drifting back again. There'd been that one time we'd run into a whole group of fae...

A chill raced up my spine before we'd even reached the cluster of tents. There was no fire lit to provide light or heat for the "band of travelers" the local townspeople had complained to Arthur about, even though evening was settling in. Shadows drifted over the tents from the scattered trees, undulating before my eyes. My hands tightened around the reins.

"Those are dark fae, sire," I said. A flicker of that old vision, the one that had predicted his death at the Darkest One's hands, darted by behind my eyes. My chest tightened. "Maybe it would be better to leave them be. The townspeople didn't say they'd actually done anything wrong. Confronting them may cause more harm than letting them finish their business."

My king glanced back at me. "If they haven't been doing anything wrong, there's no reason to avoid them, is there? I have my sword and you have your magic. I'd like to know why they're venturing so far into human territory."

I couldn't think of any good reason for a bunch of dark fae to be hanging about here. But I also knew that Arthur wasn't a big fan of caution. "Stay on your horse, stay wary, and be ready to ride at the first sign of trouble, all right?"

"Don't worry, Merlin," he said with a grin. "I'll keep you

safe."

He turned back toward the camp, and I rolled my eyes at his back. He didn't even know half the times I'd saved his hide. For the sake of his pride, I didn't rub those moments in his face. But I wasn't keen to add to that number.

The chill deepened as we came up on the tents. I shivered, but my king didn't appear to be affected. Maybe because it was a cold that only touched my fae senses. The flavor of it brought back my vision of Arthur's death again. Was she here? I scanned the figures moving to greet us. Shadows clung to all of them, but none of them emanated the cool power of their great lady. I wasn't sure if I was glad of it or more wary. My nerves tingled.

She was nearby, I'd nearly bet on that guess. This glade didn't look like the place in my vision, but those visions weren't always completely literal. I eased my mare closer to Arthur's stallion.

"Your Highness," one of the assembled fae said. "What an unexpected visit."

"I got word of a camp that had settled here, and I wanted to discover what your aim is," Arthur said. "War is brewing. Many people are wary of strangers."

"Completely understandable," the young man said with a nod. "We apologize if we've caused any distress. We've been traveling for a long time, and merely stopped here for a few days to gather our bearings. We'll be moving on to our home in the south tomorrow."

Because they'd only stopped here in the hopes of gaining the king's attention, I suspected. The fae man doing the speaking cut his gaze briefly toward me, with a flash of a smirk. He knew I recognized what they were.

"Our loyalty is to you and this great country, of course," he said, turning back to Arthur. "We give you our utmost respects."

He bowed his head where he stood beside Arthur's horse, by Arthur's leg. The others gathered close, stepping up to Arthur and *bowing in turn. The first man stepped back, rubbing his thumb against the palm of his hand.*

The chill of that encounter followed me out of the memory. I stared up at the ceiling of the van. The hum of the engine did nothing to soothe my nerves.

They'd all exhaled by him, the same way the fae woman had. I hadn't put it together at the time because I hadn't thought to watch for their *breathing*. And that one man—that gesture with his palm—something about that felt familiar. Where had I seen that before? I closed my eyes.

The smells of straw and manure drifted down the town street from the stable where we'd left our mounts. My prince picked up the pace of his strides, no doubt eager to make it back to the castle before dinner. You'd think he was fifteen and not twenty-five the way he ate—like a bottomless pit. I hurried along behind him, debating whether the discomfort of the ride would cancel out the joy of feasting for me.

A horse-drawn cart rattled by and stopped with a clatter. One of the wheels had popped off the frame. Arthur leapt to help, catching one of the sacks of produce near the back of the cart before it could tumble out. I moved to join him, but I froze when the driver hopped down. He swept his hand over his dark hair, and wisps of shadow followed it. My back tensed.

"Bit of bad luck there," Arthur suggested. "I can help you get that wheel back on."

"Thank you kindly, sir," the dark fae-playing-farmer said. He knelt down to grasp the wheel. When he started to lift it, he gasped. It thumped to the ground, and he raised his hand. Blood streaked down the palm.

"Damn. You'd better bind that," my prince said. "I think I have a handkerchief that'll do the trick." He reached to his pockets.

"I'm sure he——" I started, but Arthur had already produced the cloth.

"You're too kind," the dark fae man said. He bowed his head and reached for the handkerchief with both hands. The wounded one twitched around Arthur's as if to brush against it.

"Hey!" I said, pushing closer. But the back of Arthur's hand was unmarked. The fae man mustn't have touched him. He was wrapping the cloth around his palm now. He tied it and bobbed his head again. His thumb rubbed against the wounded spot on his palm through the fabric, as if he were pressing the pain deeper in.

At the time I'd thought the strange gesture he'd made was some kind of tic, nothing important. But Hugh had mentioned dragons and blood too. Had the dark fae man smeared some onto Arthur's skin with a magic to send it straight through to feed the dragon? And his bow—I'd be willing to bet he'd exhaled over Arthur's hand at the same moment.

Had the fae man at the camp passed on blood to my king somehow too? That rubbing of the palm... It could be tied to their magic.

It had to be tied back to the Darkest One somehow. Had she ever approached him directly back then, before the last near-fatal time? I'd seen her. I'd spoken with her, unpleasant as that experience had been. I frowned, reaching back into my memories once more.

Cheerful voices and laughter carried across the fields outside the castle. The smells of fresh baking and cut fruit wafted through the air. Jangling music assaulted my ears from different directions. It seemed half the country had arrived to celebrate their new king.

Arthur sat on his temporary throne on the dais, nodding and saying a few words to every person who stopped to give their blessing. His smile was warm and his face bright, but I recognized the restrained weariness in the way he held his head. It was only one month since his father's death. Long enough for the festival not to seem insensitive. Not long enough for him to have completely recovered, as devotedly as he'd thrown himself into his new role.

I watched him from my little nook out of the way between two of the stalls selling sweets and breads. The first few months of his ascension felt the most dangerous to me. I had a wand tucked up my sleeve and another in the satchel slung over my shoulder. How many twigs were tucked into various corners of my clothing, I couldn't count.

A quiver passed over my scalp, a sensation like the sun disappearing behind an unexpected cloud, although the actual sun was still shining brightly. My gaze jerked away from my new king. It caught on a figure standing in the middle of the crowd, which thronged around her without touching her.

She stood there, still and unmoved, like a stone protruding from a frothing sea. The darkness of her bled into the shadows beneath the people's feet and between their bodies. A haze drifted over her face as if she wore a veil of shadow.

My stomach knotted. The chill of the fae woman's presence burrowed deep into the center of my body. But I couldn't just stand here. She could make everyone else avoid her, but she couldn't escape my notice.

I squared my shoulders and strode over. Her eyes slid toward me when I was a few steps away. She smiled thinly and looked back toward Arthur.

She was watching my king too. Of course she was.

"What are you doing here?" I said, in the boldest voice I could summon. "You're not welcome."

"No one else seems to mind," the dark fae lady replied. Her voice was shadow too, low and smoky. It licked my ears with its chill.

"No one else sees what you are. You don't let them."

"And how much do you let them see what you *are, halfling?"*

she said silkily. "Isn't this an occasion to pay our respects to our new king? Why can I not do the same?"

She kissed her palm and exhaled over it as if to blow the kiss to him. My arm shot up, the wand flying into my hand. But Arthur didn't so much as wince. The Darkest One let out a cool chuckle.

The din faded. The rush of bodies around us fell away. It was only me and her and darkness falling. My jaw dropped. The Darkest One loomed over me, her hair streaming from her head like black water, her eyes flaring with a blue flame.

"I see you, little wizard," she said. Her voice warbled, echoing into my ears as if from every direction at once. "I see you and I'm coming for you now."

I opened my eyes with a gasp. The van. I was still lying on my back in the van.

The suspension was jostling less now—Jagger must have gotten us off the back roads and onto the highway. I scrambled to the feet and peered out one of the windows, letting my fae senses solidify my sense of place.

We'd been on the highway for a while. We weren't far from my house now. Good. Because my heart was thudding away and a cold sweat was tingling over my skin.

That last part hadn't been a memory. The Darkest One had sensed my investigations into the past and broken straight into my mind.

I pulled myself between the front seats and dropped into the passenger one. Jagger had tuned the radio to a classical station, the volume low so it wouldn't distract me. I pushed the button to switch stations.

"Don't care for Bach?" the fae hunter said lightly.

"I want to check the news." Hip hop. Pop music. There. A reporter was speaking in a crisp voice. She finished commenting on the ongoing preparations for the

World Peace Summit in Chicago and started talking about a recent earthquake in San Francisco. I pressed my feet against the floor to hold back the urge to squirm in my seat.

Finally she got to the story I'd been waiting for. "Citizens of the United Kingdom may soon be able to breathe a sigh of relief," she said. "The unprecedented storm that has raged over the country for the last five days is finally showing signs of abating. Wind speeds have dropped by half in the last few hours, and rainfall has ceased over much of the country."

Jagger glanced at me. "What does that mean for us?"

I sagged back in my seat, setting my hand over my churning stomach. "The Darkest One is tired of playing games. She's on her way to find us."

14

I adjusted the position of the carved obsidian bowl for what was probably the hundredth time. The holly-handle knife lay where it should beside me. I'd drunk my chervil tea and smeared myself with dead willow ash and aconite again. I'd even wiped a small portion over my tongue, teeth, and the insides of my cheeks, careful not to swallow the semi-poisonous powder. My stomach churned with the feel of it anyway. My fae side was not pleased.

Everything was as it should be. Except I wasn't entirely sure about any of this.

"How exactly is this supposed to get rid of the dragon?" Darton asked. He was sitting up in the circle of twigs I'd laid around us, his arms folded over his bare chest. I wasn't even sure he needed to be shirtless for the spell I was about to attempt, but it made sense that having fewer barriers in the way would be better. It said something about my mental state that even his sculpted body in all its glory didn't hold much appeal at this particular moment.

"I don't think the ritual will be enough to fix everything all at once," I said. "But the process will weaken the dragon. I think. We'll just keep going until I feel it's stopped working, or it gets painful for one of us. And then, if it seems to have done some good, we can have another go after a little recovery period."

"And then the Darkest One won't be able to use the dragon?"

"If we can weaken it enough, it won't be able to do what she wants. And the oath will lose some of its grip on me."

"So it's a win-win situation then." He gave me his usual easy grin. The one that could still make my heart flutter, despite all the worries whirling in my head.

"As long as it works. And as long as we can reduce the dragon's strength enough before she arrives." Like all dark fae, the Darkest One should abhor the idea of plane travel, so close to the sun that could kill even her at the right intensity. Most likely she was traveling by boat, the fastest one she'd been able to hitch a ride on. Which gave us maybe two days before she showed her face on this side of the ocean.

Not anywhere near as long as I'd have liked, but I guessed I should just be glad she'd never bothered to travel over the ocean in her earlier life. Hopping from one place to another through magic, like I had done to get Darton and myself away from her, required an emotional connection to your destination. She couldn't care about someplace she'd never seen.

I picked up the knife. "Okay. Let's get started." Waiting around was only giving my worries more time to dig in their roots.

I pricked the skin of my palm where I'd stabbed myself the other night. The blade slid into my flesh easily, just half an inch. I wanted a steady but slow trickle of blood. Draining myself dry wouldn't do anyone any good.

Darton grimaced. "Are you sure that part is necessary? You said that in the memories you looked back on, you didn't actually see any of the fae using blood."

"No," I said, "but I saw enough to think it played a part. And even if *they* didn't use blood, dragons are supposed to respond to it, and it makes any magic more potent. Now be quiet and lie down."

"I thought it was the king who got to give the orders," he muttered, but he lay back as I'd asked. His chiseled chest rose and fell with his breaths. I shifted my weight over my knees and rested the heel of my bleeding hand on the edge of the bowl so the blood would collect there unhindered.

Flow, steady and orderly. Breath and blood. If the fae could cast their dark energies *into* Arthur that way, I should be able to dredge them out. It sounded reasonable in theory, at least.

The glow of my king's spirit ran all through Darton's body, but when I focused with my fae-touched sight, it shone brightest around his heart. So I'd aim my efforts in that area.

I leaned forward, dipping so low that my lips almost touched Darton's skin above his rib cage. My hair, bound in its usual ponytail, slid against my neck. The warmth of his body tickled over my cheeks. I closed my eyes, sending my awareness down into his soul. Into that bright space with its flecks of shadow, the traces showing where the dragon had passed.

"*Darkness, come to me, come through me,*" I murmured. The bitter flavor of the ash paste filled my mouth. I parted my lips and sucked in a long, steady breath, willing those thready shadows to creep from his soul toward me.

A wisp of darkness drifted into me. It prickled over my tongue like a shard of ice. I channeled it into my lungs with the air I inhaled, and pushed it on with the thump of my pulse, out through the dribble of blood seeping into the bowl.

Yes. Only a tiny shred of the dark power wound into Arthur's soul, but I'd taken it. Sucked it out of Darton like poison from a snake bite. I just had to keep going.

I eased my head an inch to the side and inhaled again, reaching out to the darkness. Another icy shard drew a frigid line over my tongue. It stung my lungs and then my veins as it traveled through me, but the pain disappeared with the flow of my blood into the bowl.

I smiled. The Darkest One thought I was helpless, did she? She had no idea what I was capable of when it came to protecting my king. I'd break down her dragon bit by bit, however long it took.

I continued breathing at a steady pace, careful not to lose my rhythm, shifting slightly with each new breath. Dragging the dark poison out of Darton one wisp at a time. When the fragments started to shudder and balk, I paused and repeated my spell. "*Darkness, come to me, come through me.*"

The speckles stirred again. Deep within the passages of my king's soul, I felt the dragon unwinding. My body tensed, but I kept my breath even as I sucked down another shot of dark fae power.

The beast stayed where it was. With my next inhale, the thread of darkness seemed to unravel straight from that sinewy form. My heart leapt with a rush of exhilaration as its energy streamed out of me through my blood.

I refocused, willing my body to relax. Steady, even flow. This only worked as long as I appealed to the dark energy's preferred state.

I leaned even closer to Darton, my lips grazing his chest, as near as I could get while still leaving room for breath. The more darkness I could pull out with each inhale, the better. The sting of the alien energy passing through me barely pained me now. All that mattered was watching the taint of darkness gradually release from his soul.

I crossed his heart and made my way down the other side of his rib cage. I'd just taken what might have been my hundredth breath when a faint groan escaped Darton's throat. I jerked my head up, my eyes popping open. Had I hurt him?

Darton was gazing up at the ceiling. His face was flushed, but he didn't appear to be in pain. "It's fine," he said without looking at me. His voice came out slightly ragged. "Don't worry about it. As long as it's working, don't stop."

Don't worry about it. I didn't understand what he was talking about until my gaze traveled down the length of his body—and stopped on the tented fabric of his khakis.

Oh. *Oh.* That hadn't been a groan of discomfort at all. I'd been so absorbed in the spell-casting, it hadn't even occurred to me what other sorts of effects the ritual might have on Darton. More concrete effects. I was practically kissing every inch of his naked chest. A spark of my own heat flared between my legs. Not that I intended to tackle *that* problem.

He'd told me not to stop. Maybe this was feeling like the worst kind of teasing to him, but that was better than the torments the Darkest One wanted to inflict on us.

I checked the bowl. It was only a third full from the red stream trickling down my fingers from my palm. I wasn't even a little lightheaded yet. I could dredge out a whole lot more darkness yet.

Darton kept his reactions under control as I steadied my breath and leaned in again. I shifted, breath by breath, down his rib cage to just above his belly button, and then back up the center of his chest. His musky smell seeped through the acrid scent of the powder that coated my face. I trained all my attention on the shine of his soul and the threads of shadow I was unwinding from it.

I hadn't seen the dragon, but now that I was aware of it, I could sense its movements. It wound itself tight and uncoiled itself more than once as I drained away those shreds of the energy collected in it.

Then, as I inhaled yet another time, it lashed out with a swipe of its tail.

The bolt of energy smacked me in the solar plexus. My pulse stuttered, and an ache swelled through my abdomen. I sat up, my breath gone shaky. My head swam. When I clutched the side of the obsidian bowl, my fingers dipped into what had to be nearly half a quart of blood.

Okay, maybe that was enough for one session.

Darton had closed his eyes. "Em," he muttered. "Gods, Merlin." A fresh wave of heat washed over me. I didn't know what he was responding to now, what we'd just been doing or some memory only he could see, but he was obviously still turned on. And he'd spoken to *me*, not just to Emma.

"My liege," I said cautiously. "I think we'd better take a breath from this. Your dragon isn't especially happy with me right now. And I could use that recovery time."

I said a few words to stop my palm's bleeding, but didn't seal the wound. No point in wasting the energy when I'd be reopening it before the end of the day. Darton pushed himself upright, adjusting his slacks, as I reached for the bandage I'd left just outside the circle. He coughed, still flushed. Still having some trouble meeting my eyes. "So, ah, did it work?"

"I captured some of the energy. I'm not sure how much of a dent I made, but at least the process accomplished something."

I patted the bandage in place and reached for the bowl. Darton's gaze followed the motion. He grimaced at the sight of its contents. "Are you sure *you're* okay after all that?"

"I've been studying human biology for centuries," I said. "I know exactly how much blood a body can stand to lose. Now if you'll excuse me, donation clinics recommend juice and cookies for a reason. I've got to stock up on fluids and energy for the next round."

"The next round," Darton murmured to himself, with a rough chuckle and a shake of his head. He scrambled to his feet to follow me. On his way out the door, he grabbed his shirt from where he'd draped it on the dresser. "I don't feel any different. Can you sense anything different with the oath?"

That was a good question. I paused, turning as he caught up. A glance downward told me his, er, enthusiasm for the situation had waned, and with that apparently his embarrassment. He looked at me questioningly when I raised my eyes. I tested the impulses running through my body.

Urge to grab the front of that shirt and yank his mouth to mine? Check. Urge to run my hands over *his* body until he was groaning my name again? Double check. Urge to snuff the life out of him...? Hmm. The now-familiar itch nagged faintly at my fingers, but without much oomph. I wasn't sure if that was because of all the other sensations running through me or because my king's soul had been downgraded in threat level, but I'd take it.

"I think it's a little better," I said. "I definitely don't seem inclined to kill you any time in the next hour or so."

Darton laughed. "Well, I guess I'll take that." He opened his mouth again as if to say something else, but he didn't get the chance. Because in the same moment, the ceiling over the kitchen collapsed with a hail of rushing shadows.

15

Darton leapt back, but a wave of dark magic was already crashing over us. It crackled cold over my skin and shrieked in my ears. I threw my arm toward Darton, groping for him, but my fingers only touched frigid air. I hurled myself in the direction I thought he'd gone, and finally my body collided with his.

His arms closed around me. "What's happening?" he shouted by my ear over the roar of the shadows.

"The dark fae," I said. "They've broken past my protections." I'd set aside my salt pouch so it didn't disrupt the ceremony, so I hadn't felt them cross the barrier outside.

They were coming for Darton. The Darkest One was on her way, and her minions had arrived to snatch up my king and deliver him to her. My heart thumped. "Where's your sword?"

"By the door."

"Then we run for it."

We dashed together, stumbling in the swirling darkness, toward the front of the house. My wand. Where was my wand? I'd set the one I'd been carrying on me aside for the ritual too, for the same reason. I should have picked it right back up when we'd finished. How could I have been so careless?

There. The energy in one called out to me like a beam of light through clouds. There was the wand I'd set in the basket near the door.

Excalibur gleamed as Darton grasped its hilt. I spun around.

Shadowy figures swept through the haze toward us: The dark fae, following the path their magical assault had broken open.

"*Darkness begone!*" I hollered, channeling all my intention through that wand. Light exploded through the room. The shadows splintered; the dark fae that had been running at us staggered backward. Only for a moment, but that was all I'd known I could hope for.

I grabbed Darton's elbow as the wand crumbled apart in my fingers. I'd used every shred of energy stored in it with that one spell, but it'd been worth it. "Come on!" I said, and yanked the door open. We hurtled out into the concrete yard.

The sky that had been clear and bright when I'd returned from my trip with Jagger now churned with dark gray clouds. They blotted out all but the faintest hint of sunlight. Dark creatures, filmy beings shaped like panthers and wolves, stalked along the edges of the yard, not strong enough to break through my protections.

Not *yet*. The Darkest One was coming, and her power was already sweeping over this country. My fingers dug into Darton's arm. I spun and tugged him toward the van Jagger had left in our possession.

If you can't fight 'em, flee from 'em.

A chant was ringing out from inside the house. I wrenched at some of my own bodily energy—goodbye, another three months of my life—and cast it out with a hasty spell. *"Shield us, save us, press back the darkness!"*

A quiver of energy shot up around us. It formed a gleaming ball of light, as if we were rodents in a giant, glowing hamster ball. And not a second too soon. A bolt of sizzling shadow smacked into its surface and burst apart. Icy fragments seared over my skin, but they didn't do half as much harm as if the bolt had hit me dead on.

Darton swung out his sword, shattering another bolt of magic streaming toward our shell. Then he turned and ran with me the last steps to the van. I hauled open the back doors, and we charged through to the front seats. I dropped into the driver's seat. A jolt of panic hit me.

"The keys. I didn't grab them from the basket." I'd been in too much of a hurry to get us out.

"You're a wizard, Em," Darton said. "You're *Merlin.* Can't you convince the engine to start some other way?"

Right. I didn't have a whole lot of practice with mechanical magic, but the principles were the same. And I couldn't have asked for more motivation.

The van rocked as some dark force struck it. The dark fae were almost on us. I hit the switch to turn on the flood lamps, hoping their sun-filled light would buy us an extra second or two, and shoved my hand into the cup holder between Darton and I. The twigs I'd stashed there during my drive with Jagger met my grasping fingers. I snatched a handful and pointed them toward the ignition.

"Spark and sing," I ordered the transmission. The engine roared on. Okay, that was a little more energy than

I'd intended, but I'd take it. I grabbed the steering wheel and slammed my foot on the gas.

The van peeled down the driveway with a screech that suggested we'd left a lot of tire on the concrete. We careened through the ring of dark creatures that had been stalking around the edges of the yard. All those nearby leapt at us in a rush. Their shadowy forms burst apart as the van's sun-powered lights hit them, but the wave of them was so forceful it rocked the vehicle anyway.

I jerked the wheel to follow the curve of the driveway toward the main road. A clot of darkness shot toward us in the rearview mirror. I braced myself half a second before the spell hit the van with a wallop.

Bulbs popped with a tinkle of cracking glass. The glow around the van dimmed. I had just enough time to mutter a curse before a pair of shadow creatures like giant eagles dove at us from above.

They slammed into the windshield at the same moment. The van's lights were still bright enough to shatter them, but not before the thrust of their energy had split a crack down the middle of the glass. Heart thudding, I swerved onto the highway, so fast we nearly spun.

My lips started to move of their own accord. A few words had spilled out before I caught myself—caught the spell they meant to cast. A choking enchantment to smack Darton in the throat. My stomach knotted. The itch dug into my hands even as I clenched the steering wheel with all my strength. My arm twitched. Another blast of dark magic hit the back window, blackening it.

I didn't know if we could make it. Maybe there wasn't anything I could do but grab Darton and think of some other place to apparate us to where the fae couldn't quickly follow. But the second I let myself reach toward him, I had the feeling I'd be driving magic into his heart, stealing the breath from his lungs—fulfilling that awful oath. They were right on our heels, and the urge didn't believe I could stop them from completing their mission.

My elbow jerked to the side. I gritted my teeth, biting down on my lip hard enough to draw blood. That sting wasn't enough. With every ounce of self control I had in me, I released my left hand from the wheel just long enough to press my thumb into the knife wound I hadn't bothered to seal.

I winced, but the jolt of pain that radiated up my arm was worth it. The oath's urge dulled enough that I could breathe. Darton looked over at me, his eyes widening.

"Em," he said. Then, without waiting for any response, he reached over and rested his hand on my leg.

A shaky laugh spilled out of me. He must have remembered the other way I'd tamed the oath's urge. His thumb traced a gentle line across the top of my thigh, and the heat of it flared up my leg to the core of me, despite everything going on around us. Maybe even because of it. Adrenalin could make quite the enhancer to physical attraction.

A slash of dark magic cut across the road in front of us—literally. The pavement snapped and gaped in a half-a-foot chasm. I jammed my foot harder against the gas, thinking maybe we could hop it.

Before I got the chance to find out, another dark bolt must have hit us from behind. The van jostled and listed to the side. One of the wheels gave a dull *thump thump thump* against the ground that told me the tire had blown out. We were coasting to a stop.

I pumped the gas pedal, hoping I could squeeze a little more speed out of our momentum. No such luck. I slammed my hand into the cup holder to grasp the last of my twigs.

A wave of shadow swept toward us and crashed into the side of the van. The vehicle swayed and skidded. With a screech, it tipped over into the ditch.

I clutched the wheel, but I still fell half out of my seat on the impact. The top of my head smacked the ceiling. I dropped down onto Darton, who'd had the smarts to put on his seatbelt during our mad rush away from the house. The passenger window shattered. Darton grunted as my hip hit him in the gut.

"Sorry," I mumbled. "Sorry." We had to get out of here. The dark fae and their creatures would be swarming us, getting closer every moment we lay here. I squirmed away from Darton as he fumbled to detach his seatbelt. My hand throbbed. My head ached.

There wasn't any other answer now. I had to use the magic, had to whisk us away from here, as far as I could. What were another few years of my life gone anyway? It wasn't as if I was going to live more than a few minutes if we stayed here.

Where to go? Not back to my parents. Campus was too close. Maybe the desert, near Jagger's former house. Could I summon enough connection to that place to port us out there? I grasped Darton's arm and closed my eyes, dragging up every impression I'd had of dry earth and blazing sun—

"That's far enough, you monsters!" someone hollered outside the van. My head jerked up.

"What?" Darton said, looking as startled as I felt. A

crackling, hissing sound that was almost familiar split the air.

No, it was completely familiar. I'd heard it when Eric and Mauve had taken on the dark vermin that had come for us at their house. It was the flare of flamethrowers spewing their fire. And another sound, too, that I definitely *didn't* recognize, but something about the warbling sizzle of it made my spirits lift.

I grasped the back of the driver's seat and hauled myself up to the door that was now above us. With a heave, I flung that door open. Darton gave me a leg up so I could poke my head out of the van.

Two rows of vehicles, all of them fitted with outer lamps like the van, had formed a blockade from one of the road's gravel shoulders to the other. Their passengers had streamed out of them to surround the van. Several of the men and women wore harnesses with flamethrowers attached. Others held devices I hadn't seen before, with a large spherical chamber at the back and a narrow rod at the front.

A bear-like dark creature charged at a young woman wielding one of the new weapons, and she pulled the trigger. A streak of electricity discharged from the rod. It zapped the bear right in the chest, and the creature exploded into fragments of shadow. Sodding hell, what was that thing?

Jagger stood at the front of the crowd, holding one of those electro-guns. He waved it at the surge of darkness that was swelling down the road toward us. The figures of at least two dozen dark fae glided toward us with strides hastened by their magic, flanked by a mass of dark vermin so dense I could barely tell where one creature ended and another began.

"Just try me!" Jagger shouted. It was his voice I'd heard earlier. But I'd never heard it like that before, so harsh and raw. He was angry—and terrified. Not that I could blame him.

I *could* get my act together and pitch in rather than sitting here like some damsel waiting to be rescued.

I hauled myself the rest of the way out of the van. "Pass me the sword," I called back to Darton. He held Excalibur up to me, hilt first. I hopped down with it to give him room to clamber out after me. My head swiveled, taking in the lay of the land.

The dark creatures had already nearly surrounded us. Jagger and the others—more of his fae hunter colleagues, I assumed—were torching or electrifying any that came within a few feet of their protective circle. Their chill carried on the breeze with a smell like slush mixed with rotted leaves.

My gaze snagged on a sapling at the edge of the forest on the other side of the ditch. Darton jumped down beside me, and I shoved his sword back into his hands. One of the fae hunters barbequed a snake-like creature that had just slithered past the sapling. I dashed over to her.

"Cover me?" I said, waiting only an instant for her nod. "*Darkness begone*," I yelled at the closest creatures and clamped my jaw against the jerk of my soul. At least I was only giving up a few weeks rather than the years I'd been looking at a couple minutes ago.

I leapt forward and snatched at the sapling's branches. With a murmured apology, I snapped two, and then another two, and another, dodging backward just as a hissing ball of dark magic whipped toward me. It vanished in the stream of the fae hunter's flamethrower.

Clutching my plunder between my hands, I hustled back to Darton. He'd joined the fae hunters facing the thickest onslaught, Excalibur gleaming in his hands.

"My liege!" I said. "A little assistance?"

He sliced through a snarling shadow fox and jogged backward to me. "The great wizard needs *my* help?" His grin was far too tight.

"Shut up, Art," I said. "Magic plus sword was a fruitful equation the last few times we tried it. I'm all for sticking with that strategy."

He glanced back toward the fray. The fae hunters were keeping the dark fae's magic and minions at bay, but the fae themselves looked unharmed, only frustrated. I felt the prickle of all those narrowed gazes seeking out me and my king.

"Can you kill them all?" Darton said, sounding uncertain. Which, fair enough, I'd had plenty of trouble simply killing *one* full fae not that long ago.

"Probably not," I said. "But in light of that fact, I figure we'll set our sights a little lower. Knock them unconscious and bind them up like I did on that hill near the overpass. That'll at least buy us some time."

What we were going to do with that time, I hadn't figured out yet, but that could come later.

I shoved all the branches I'd gathered under my left arm. My palm was bleeding all over them, but that was okay. A little extra life energy leaking into the magic would only give it more oomph.

The green energy pulsing within the just broken branches thrummed against my side. I breathed in deep and grasped Darton's shoulder by the crook of his neck, where my fingers could meet his bare skin. Waking up more memories hardly seemed like a reason for concern given everything else we were already facing, and I wanted as direct a connection as possible.

Darton readied himself without my needing to say anything. He raised his sword, his arms tensed, the muscles in his shoulder bunching under my grip.

"Three, two, one," I murmured. "Now! *Darkness begone, darkness fall! Light knock the sense from their darkened minds! Bind them to the ground they fall to.*"

As I shouted the words in the old tongue, Darton swung the enchanted sword. The power I was drawing from the fresh branches washed through me, into him, and blazed from Excalibur's blade. It seared across the landscape in every direction, whiting out my vision. Several of the fae hunters yelped or gasped.

I lowered my hand from Darton's shoulder, blinking the haze from my eyes. The remains of the branches fell in a shower of dust by my feet.

The road ahead of us, the forest on one side, and the field on the other were all washed clean of shadows— other than those cast naturally. And those still wisping around the dark fae that had collapsed in the wake of my spell. Their bodies dotted the pavement, the shoulder, and the grassy dip of the ditch. A line of glowing light arced over each of their unconscious bodies.

I didn't know how long my spell would hold them in place once they woke up and could put their own magic to work, but like I'd told Darton, it gave us time.

Jagger let out a rough chuckle. He strode through the group of his colleagues to greet us. "Looks like we showed up just in time."

I glanced around at the cluster of fae hunters. "Why *were* you on the way to our house?" They looked like they'd come prepared for full-out war.

Jagger shrugged. "After having that talk with the kid from overseas the other night, I thought we should provide whatever protection we could. Add a human factor to your security systems."

"Ah." I rubbed my forehead. The feel of the gritty paste of ash and aconite still smeared there made my nerves cringe. "Well, I think the house is a loss now. We're missing a pretty big chunk of our ceiling."

"Maybe not quite in time, then." Jagger grimaced. "I wish we'd made it here a little sooner."

"Better than not at all," I said. "We were practically goners." I nodded to the weapon he was holding. "Have you come up with some new gadgetry? It looked like those electric guns worked well."

"Oh, these?" He patted the rod by his side. "This idea I got thanks to your story about channeling lightning. You mentioned the shock had to be natural for it to affect the dark varmints. One of our more inventive members came up with a design that uses a slightly more sophisticated version of your fur and amber approach to create the current."

Huh. My attempts to combine physics with my magic had gotten us pretty far already. Maybe there were more possibilities to delve into there.

Jagger took another step closer, squinting at me. "What have you got on your face, Emma? Did the fae do that?"

I moved to swipe at the caked powder with my sleeve, which turned out to be a fruitless attempt. One sleeve was mottled with blood from my palm and the dust of the branches I'd sapped the life energy from. The other was flecked with slivers of glass from my scramble out of the van. I lowered both arms.

"I was doing a spell that needed me to suppress my innate energy," I said. "To give the impression I have a totally different nature."

And it had worked. Both times, the dragon had let me approach it, even though it had fled during my first attempt. I'd managed to convince it that I was a dark fae, an ally instead of an enemy, simply by covering myself with the right materials...

"Where do we go now?" Darton asked. He was eyeing the slumped fae warily. "Obviously we can't stay in the house anymore."

"No," I said. "But I think I have an idea about that, that should keep us under the radar for at least a little while. Long enough for us to come up with a longer-term plan. I think I'd better just grab a few things from the house before we abandon it completely."

16

"*Light and warm us, softly,*" I said, pinching my fingers against a twig. It burst into a glowing ball that floated toward the ceiling of the pitch-black room we'd come into. A thin heat took the edge off the stony chill.

The light revealed the smooth granite floor, the granite walls with their slabs of doors shutting away the mausoleum's silent inhabitants. The hairs on my arms were already standing on end, but my nerves jittered with a deeper shudder. The fae energy inside me did not like this place at all. But that was exactly why we needed to be here.

Beside me, Darton made a face. "It's definitely got a lot of atmosphere... Are you sure this is the best place for us to spend the night?"

He kept his hand tight around Excalibur's hilt, but I set down my duffel of supplies. I'd left some of what I'd scavenged from our ruined house with the fae hunters, but I didn't trust that we'd be safe here without some help.

"Death is the dark fae's arena," I said. "Stillness and silence and gradual decay. This whole cemetery stinks of it. With a little enhancement, it should mask our life energy from any dark fae looking to finish their attack. The same way my powder masked my light fae essence from your dragon."

"It's not *my* dragon," Darton muttered. He sat down in the middle of the room, as far from any of the individual tombs as he could get. His shoulders had tensed. He rubbed his hand against his chest as if a muscle there pained him.

My own muscles were still jumping, but not entirely because of the way my senses cringed away from all this evidence of death. The oath's itch had been creeping back through our entire journey here. Now it wriggled through my arms and nibbled at my fingers. I flexed them a few times, trying to work the impulse out of them. Then I grabbed my supplies to keep them busy in a preferable way.

The bitter smoky smell wafted from the bag of dead willow ash and aconite when I opened it. I dipped in my hand and sprinkled the powder along the edges of the room. If having this stuff smeared on my skin could convince a dragon filled with masses of dark fae energy that I was one of its kind up close, then surely it could confuse any fae looking for us from afar, especially with the entire cemetery's energies clouding us too.

Any regular dark fae. The Darkest One knew my soul and my king's too well. Once she arrived in this country, there'd be no hiding from her.

Darton set his sword down beside him. He rubbed that spot on his chest again.

"Are you all right?" I asked him.

"I've just been feeling a little... off, since the dark fae attacked us," he said. "I don't know how to describe it exactly. It feels as if there's a knot in my chest, that's...

twisting around? Every now and then. The feeling is stronger when I'm holding Excalibur. The fae didn't cast some other spell on me, did they? It's not really *painful* or anything—just strange."

He was keeping his voice calm, but his jaw clenched after he'd finished speaking. It might not be painful, but it was bothering him. Why wouldn't it? After what we'd been through, any strange sensation could be the beginning of a new catastrophe.

I completed my circuit of the room and set down the bag of powder. "Let me have a look." I sat down across from him and touched his chest where he had.

His body was as warm as ever against my palm. The glowing life energy pulsed through it—and a hint of something shadowy coiled around it at the edges of my awareness. A familiar motion.

"It's the dragon," I said. "Having all that dark magic thrown around nearby must have stirred it up."

"So your spell before to weaken it didn't work after all?" Darton said. He reached for his sword, as if he could fight the creature inside him with that.

"I'm sure it did," I said. "But that thing's been fed on generations of dark fae energy, and I can only sap away so much at a time. Weaker doesn't mean it's not still plenty strong. But we can keep working on that. I should do the ritual again. This is the perfect spot for it. I brought the supplies so we could. When I'm done, it'll probably have settled down again."

Darton paused and then inclined his head. "Fine." He glanced around the room, his eyebrows arching slightly. "At least this place should put a damper on any, ah, embarrassing and unnecessary reactions. Are you sure you've recovered enough from the last time? I mean, with the blood loss?"

My own cheeks flushed a little at the memory of how his body had responded to the ritual a few hours ago. "We had some rest in the car on the way here," I said. "I finally got my juice and cookies and a whole lot more of a meal on top of it. I'll be fine. You just get yourself ready."

He pulled his shirt over his head and folded it into a makeshift pillow. I reached for the powder again. I'd washed up when we'd made a quick pit stop at a gas station, but a fresh coating would do the job best anyway. I rubbed it between my hands, over my forearms, and all across my face. Around my neck, down my chest. A careful swirl of it around my mouth.

Darton had lain back when I turned toward him. My gaze shot to a purple-black blotch that marred his skin across the left side of his rib cage. Right where my hip had collided with him when the van had tipped. I winced.

"I'm sorry. I didn't realize I battered you that badly."

"Hmm?" Darton raised his head a few inches. He brushed his fingers over the bruise. "It's okay. I've had a hell of a lot worse after a football game."

"Maybe we should start having you wear that padding everywhere we go," I said.

He managed a chuckle and a smile, even though I could see the tension in his eyes. He rested his head back on his folded shirt. "A bruise shouldn't interfere with what you need to do, should it?"

I shook my head. "No problem. Just tell me if anything starts to hurt. More than it already does, I mean."

I set the bowl by my side and picked up the knife. I wasn't really sure I was in the best state for spilling out more blood. I hadn't exactly been keeping track of how much I'd lost during the fight with the dark fae. But there was nothing more important than weakening the dragon.

Nothing I had any hope might save us, anyway.

My palm stung as I sliced the cut open again. The pain was duller than it'd been before—I wasn't sure if that was a good thing or a bad thing. At least it still prickled over the urging of the oath.

I'm trying to fulfill the most important part of that promise, I thought at it. *Making sure nothing in my king poses any threat to anyone.*

The oath didn't seem to care about my explanations. I aimed a silent expletive in Cormag's direction and settled myself into the meditative state the ritual required. Slow, even breaths. Slow, even pulse. Drip, drip, drip of my blood into the bowl.

I bent over Darton as I had earlier that day. Inhale, dragging in those wisps of shadow clinging to his soul. Exhale, feel them flow through my veins to the bowl. Over and over, sinking deeper into the shimmer of his soul with each repetition. Sharper flickers whipped past my internal sight. The dragon's tail, lashing just ahead of me. A flap of constrained wings. The dark energy quivered through the glow with a restlessness I could taste.

No doubt the creature sensed that its master was approaching. Its time of freedom was almost at hand. And even bottled up in that concentrated form, the power the beast contained made me wince. I'd drained a little of that energy last time, definitely, but nowhere near enough. How many more blood-lettings would it take?

How many did we have time for? How many could my body handle?

I wet my lips and breathed in again, careful of my lips over the bruise on Darton's abdomen. Whatever it took, I could handle. If I drained myself dry while draining that beast, oh well. My life wouldn't matter much if I didn't.

The tender spot on the top of my head where I'd hit the van roof started to throb. My thoughts swam through my head. In and out. In and out. I could stay focused on that, even if my head was starting to feel as if it was going to float right off my body. A little more might make all the difference. I wasn't stopping until I had to.

Shadows wavered behind my eyes. It took me a moment to realize they reflected the clouding of my own mind, not the dragon's movements. My body had dipped farther, my lips brushing Darton's sternum. For a second, I felt as if I would tip right over into him, down into his soul, into that cavern of light where the dragon lurked.

I jerked myself upright. The granite walls around me spun. I closed my eyes and opened them again, willing the world to settle.

A thin ache crept up my arm from my still bleeding palm. The bowl was full of my blood.

"Em?" Darton said, sounding concerned.

"I'm all right," I said. I might have been more convincing to myself if my tongue hadn't felt detached from the rest of me. I shut my mouth and swallowed hard. "*Seal and stop,*" I mumbled to my palm. *More* bleeding definitely wasn't going to help.

Another wave of dizziness passed over me. I swayed and braced my hands against the floor. Breathe in, breathe out, like before. But this time for myself.

Darton pushed himself upright to grab the bag of supplies. He opened a bottle of apple juice and pushed it into my good hand. "Thanks," I managed. I tipped it to my lips and let the tart liquid flood my mouth. One swallow, another. Refill my body. Bring it back down to earth.

I fumbled for the cloth and water I'd set aside and wiped the powder from my skin. The light fae energy inside me pressed back toward the surface with a feeling like a sigh of relief. It still twisted away from the feel of death around us, but that was a more distant discomfort.

Darton passed me a granola bar next. I wolfed it down despite the clenching of my stomach. I needed that energy too. Because I'd be doing this all over again in the morning if I had any say in it.

My body still felt slightly insubstantial, but I managed to stand up without shaking like a leaf. With careful hands, I got out the funnel and glass jar I'd brought. The blood I'd collected was run through with dark fae energy. That energy could serve us now. Using it felt like thumbing my nose at the Darkest One and all her efforts.

I poured half of the bowl's contents into the jar and quickly sealed it. Then I walked the circuit of the room again, dribbling the rest of the blood alongside the line of ash powder. Even more darkness to cloak us in our hiding spot. The Darkest One could be here as soon as tomorrow night. We were going to need all the rest we could steal.

Darton watched me circle the room. "You took a lot," he said.

"We don't have a lot of time for spacing out attempts," I said. "I've got to drain as much of the dragon's energy as I can when I can. Look, I'm perfectly fine." Other than the fact that my head was still throbbing and also filled with that floaty feeling. But hey, the oath's urge had been completely drowned out by those combined sensations. I could look on the bright side. "How about you? That knot in your chest—is it still bothering you?"

He touched the spot over his sternum. "There's a bit of pressure there still," he said. "But that twisting feeling, like it's *moving*, is gone. That's a good thing, right?"

"I tired your dragon out," I said with half a smile.

Darton opened his mouth, looking like he was going to protest my use of *my* again, but then his expression settled into a resigned smile of his own. I set down the bowl, and he held out his arm to me. "Come here?"

I wasn't sure what he wanted, but I'd never been good at saying no to my king anyway. Besides, this standing up thing was definitely getting old. I sat, and he eased me down beside him so we were lying together on the hard floor. He tucked my head under his chin. I couldn't resist snuggling closer to him, letting him wrap me in his warmth. The musky, earthy smell of his bare skin filled my nose.

Darton made a pleased hum into my hair. He tugged me even closer to him with his arm around my back. Then his body tensed. "If this is too much... I just—" He swallowed audibly. "I'm not going to try anything. I just want to feel you."

He didn't have to explain any more than that. The same need was running through me. As if my old soul inside this young body wanted to reach right through both our skins to his. It couldn't, not exactly, but I could get us a little bit closer.

Without letting myself second-guess my decision, I squirmed away from him just enough to peel off my sweater. Darton let out a hitch of breath as I lay back down. Our bodies aligned, bare skin to bare skin, nothing covering me from the waist up except my bra. I draped the sweater over us to hold in the warmth. But there was nothing chilly about the heat that seemed to burn everywhere my skin touched his. A flame of desire shot down through my belly.

I shut my eyes against it. I didn't have to give in this time. I could simply enjoy the closeness without needing it to be something more. No, not more, just *else*. There wasn't any such thing as more when my king was already giving me everything he could offer.

Darton's hand brushed over my hair. His pulse, thudding against my ear, evened out. I rested my fingers on the soft curls of golden hair that ran down the middle of his chest and let my mind drift on the memories floating up.

The memories our close contact was waking in Darton would be even more potent, coming to him for the first time. His breath tickled my ear. "Do you know," he said, his voice gone distant but still affectionate, "the first time I met you—the first you—I thought you were so earnest and calm. All politeness and bows and waiting to see what I'd ask of you."

"You *thought*," I said. "Are you suggesting that impression was wrong?"

"Well, it obviously took you a while to get comfortable being yourself and let loose that sarcastic tongue of yours. And I definitely would never have imagined just how grouchy you could get."

I made a disgruntled sound. "Only after you put me through a long muddy ride in the rain or something equally horrific."

"Yes," Darton said lightly, "I probably deserved every spark of that temper." He tipped his head, lapsing into silence as another memory must have swept over him. When he spoke again, it was with a chuckle. "And you did have an odd sense of humor at times. Why did you enchant Lord Barimeld's clothes to smell like pickles?"

A snort escaped me. I'd almost forgotten that little act of revenge. I'd never told Arthur exactly why back then, because he hadn't been there for the conversation I'd overheard.

The sun danced over the forest floor between the shadows of the leaves. I settled myself in a patch of it, examining the patch of coltsfoot I'd found. The tiny yellow petals tickled my fingers as I snapped one of the flowers off.

The tramp of horse hooves carried through the woods. I went still, murmuring a quick concealing spell.

Two horses walked into view, one carrying a man I recognized as one of the lords currently visiting the castle, the other his servant. The lord was speaking in low, harsh tones.

'It really is ridiculous, all that running about from town to town, getting involved in every tiny peasant concern. You'd think he's a laborer, not a prince."

I bristled. The servant's head bobbed in automatic agreement, his gaze vague as if he was lost in his own thoughts and hardly listening. "Yes, m'lord."

"Someone should set him back a few paces. Remind him that he's as human as the rest of us. Trip him up in front of the other lords so they stop looking at him like he's some kind of hero, and not just a spoiled brat whose head's got too big."

"Yes, m'lord."

The lord tsked his tongue. "You're helping with the serving tonight, aren't you? I've still got some of that mushroom powder left.

Lace a little in his cup, and let's see how he talks when we've loosened his tongue."

"Yes, m'lord... M'lord?"

"Yes, that's the perfect plan. He won't know what hit him. Now the way you'll need to play it..."

His voice trailed off as the horses wove on through the forest. I glared at his retreating back, my hands balling into fists.

The lord had never gotten his chance to drug my prince, of course. I'd dashed straight back to the castle, snuck into his rooms, and found the packet of dried hallucinogenic mushroom in one of his trunks. I'd burned it to a crisp. And then I'd enchanted his entire wardrobe with a thick briny smell as if it'd all been pickled. With all the angry energy I'd put into that spell, I suspected the stink had stuck on for at least a month.

I started to formulate a vague excuse and caught myself. No. No more lying to spare my king the discomfort that would come with the truth. This might be a little thing, but I owed him my honesty after all the bigger truths I'd kept from him so long.

He was stronger than I was, when you came down to it. Maybe all this time it'd been my own discomfort I was trying to prevent. Wanting to feel I'd kept just one small weight off his back, with all the other responsibilities he'd had bearing down on him.

"Lord Barimeld was an ass," I said. "I overheard him scheming about how to undercut you. So I made sure he didn't and figured out a suitable punishment. And kept a close eye on him whenever he was at the castle again. It obviously worked, though, because he played nice after that incident."

"Ah," Darton said. "I remember wondering about his

sudden change in attitude. He must have thought I'd found out about his scheming and sent someone to undercut him myself."

"Almost the same thing," I said. "We were a united front."

"We were." He ducked his head closer, his lips grazing the top of my forehead. His voice dipped too. "You know, over the years a lot of people gave me a piece of their mind about how closely I worked with you. But I've never regretting trusting you, not for one moment, Merlin."

I smiled, my heart swelling with a glow to match the magic ball I'd conjured. Right then, skin to skin, warmth to warmth, I couldn't imagine a greater bliss than lying there in my king's arms. He needed me. I was here for him, like I always was. Like I always would be.

My eyes drifted closed. "Is it safe enough here for us to sleep?" Darton murmured.

I nodded against his shoulder. "I laid down a ring of salt just in case. If any dark fae *do* come out this way, we'll know. But all they should be able to see now is the darkness around us."

"That doesn't sound like it should be comforting, but somehow it is."

He managed to scoot even closer to me, his breath rising and falling in a deeper rhythm. But my eyes had blinked open. I stared past him at the wall, thinking of the lines of dark energy I'd drawn around us. Like a cage. Like a trap. A memory flashed through my mind of the fae hunters' electro-guns and their crackling light. My heart leapt.

"I think I know how we can stop the Darkest One."

17

Keevan looked over his shoulder three times as he eased the storage room door open.

"I don't think you need to be quite that nervous," I said under my breath. "You have a key. No one's going to think we're breaking in."

"A key I stole from my sister's apartment," Keevan whispered, and groaned. "Why do I always let you talk me into the craziest things?"

"Hey, don't put the blame for this on me," I said. "From the way I remember it, *you* volunteered."

"Okay, fair. But if I've developed an addiction to adventure, *that* is definitely your fault."

"Less talking, more checking out the inventory," Howard said. The third member of our party, a thirty-something guy with long black hair in a ponytail nearly as long as mine, was the fae hunters' local technology expert—the one who'd invented their electro-guns. And possibly the key to my plan for dealing with the Darkest One.

We slipped into the room and shut the door behind us. The still air had a slightly floral smell, as if someone wearing a strong perfume had recently walked between the stacks of equipment. Keevan flicked on the light.

The stainless steel shelving units that filled the room were piled with all sorts of lab supplies for the physics department's use. I poked at one box and peeked inside another, but I didn't know exactly what we were looking for. I'd come up with the concept, but the logistics of the mechanical arts were far from my specialty.

"Let me know if you see any spools of wire," Howard said. "I'll have to check to make sure the conductivity is appropriate."

"Roger that," Keevan said, giving him a salute.

"I don't want you to get into any trouble," I said to Darton's best friend. "If there was an easier way..."

He waved me off. "It's for Darton. Which means it's not a problem. The college has a crapload of stuff, obviously. And you've saved the place at least once, so you probably deserve some payback."

While that might be true, it was also true that the campus wouldn't have been in danger in the first place if Darton and I hadn't been here. But Keevan clearly had enough on his mind with this criminal turn. He paced the aisles with a slight jitter in his step.

Howard had drifted toward the back of the room. He picked up a metal tube with some sort of circuitry protruding from one end, frowned, put it down, and checked another. "None of these is an ideal voltage."

"Is there one close enough to what you think we'd need?" I asked. No, this was our one chance to overcome the Darkest One. We couldn't skimp. "Grab whatever you can make do with, but if there's something better you can't find here, make a list. I've got funds. We'll track down whatever you need."

At least, I hoped we would. We didn't have much time for searching out lab equipment suppliers and the like. It wasn't as if we could just waltz into a Wal-Mart to grab what we needed.

"Emma and her bottomless bank account," Keevan said. His tone was teasing, but my gut twisted.

I *had* saved an awful lot of money over the decades, across my most recent lives. Computerized banking had made keeping track of my funds between each death so much easier. I hadn't had much to spend it on, most of the time, so it'd just sat around accumulating interest. But the last couple months had put quite a dent in my savings, between replacing cars and custom building entire houses at a rush rate and last-minute international flights. If I kept going at this rate, I'd be penniless by next year.

But I had enough to get us through this, and that was all that mattered. It wasn't as if we were going to get another do-over. If I didn't spend that money keeping Darton and me alive now, then no one was ever going to spend it.

"How much electricity do you think we'll be able to keep flowing in a continuous circuit?" I asked Howard. "You said we should be able to flood the entire surface of the trap with it, and reduce the amount of energy lost to almost nothing. But there must be limits to what the materials can handle, right?"

"Oh, I can build something sturdy enough that the strongest dark creature out there couldn't stand the touch of," Howard said. He picked up a jointed metal rod, gave it an approving nod, and stuffed it into the duffel I'd lent him. "The trickiest part is going to be getting a natural source for the volume of current you want in the first place. The guns I rigged using static are only capable of a small fraction of that power. But I've got some ideas to tackle that difficulty."

"Ideas you can get working in less than twelve hours?" I said. I had no idea how long it would take the Darkest One to reach us even once she hit the east coast, but we couldn't count on her taking her time.

"I'll work as fast as I can work," Howard said. "Ah, these will be useful." He scooped up an entire box of something that clinked as he dropped it into his bag.

"Hey!" Keevan said from the other side of the room, where his restless feet had taken him. "I think these are the coils of wire you were asking about."

Howard hustled over, and I ambled along behind, wishing I had the knowledge base to be of more help. My studies had followed my light fae inclinations toward the sciences of life: biology and chemistry. Machines tended to be more the domain of the dark, with their orderly construction. But there were areas where mechanics and the chaos of light could interact. It just wasn't going to be as simple as calling down a lightning bolt this time.

Not that the lightning bolt had been simple. I rubbed my arms in memory of all that wild power coursing through me.

Howard started examining the coils of wire one by one, dismissing most of them. Keevan wandered over to join me. "So Darton didn't want to join our little field trip?" he said.

"Oh, he would have if I'd agreed to let him," I said. "But he's a heck of a lot safer back in the mausoleum."

Keevan raised his eyebrows at me. "That doesn't

sound like the Emma I know. You've always been pretty strict about keeping him right by your side."

That was before the itch of that deadly oath had started pricking at me. And before entire armies of full dark fae had gone on the attack. "There are too many fae looking for him now," I said. "The second he steps outside the barriers I set down, they might sense him. When we were just fighting glooms, that was one thing, but I'm no match for the average dark fae on my own."

"Right," Keevan said. He'd help me destroy the first—and only—full dark fae I'd ever killed, so he should know. But he still sounded doubtful.

The twist in my gut tugged tighter. I *didn't* like leaving Darton behind, and I knew he didn't like it either. Before she'd even set foot on this country's shores, the Darkest One was managing to tear us apart.

"I don't see you bringing Izzy along to make her a criminal accomplice," I pointed out, keeping my voice light. Keevan and I didn't always see eye to eye, but I did have sympathy for his crush—and his reluctance to reveal it. After all, it'd taken me fifteen hundred years to come clean about mine.

"The more people with us, the harder it'll be to avoid getting noticed on the way out," Keevan said. "I just didn't tell her. You think she'd listen to me if she decided she needed to be a part of this? I don't have any great wizardly knowledge to make my arguments convincing."

"*You've* never been very good at listening when other people tell you there's danger up ahead either."

"Fair." He rubbed his face. "That doesn't mean I'm not going to try to protect other people from danger when I can. Unlike you, we're not going to get to start over if this all goes wrong."

At that comment, my entire stomach balled into a knot. "Neither are we, this time," I said.

Keevan's head jerked around. "What? What happened to your special reincarnation spell?"

I hadn't realized he didn't know. We'd told him and the others about the Darkest One getting free. I'd assumed the other consequences were obvious.

"It was all part of the same magic that was keeping the Darkest One shut away," I said. "A big tangled mess of an enchantment. When she broke free, she broke the spell—all of it. We're just ordinary one-lived mortals now... who happen to have very old souls."

"Oh." Keevan looked vaguely ill. "I thought— You've got no more safety net, then."

"That's one way of putting it." Just thinking about it made me feel sick too. I turned back toward the shelves. "All the more reason we need to make sure this plan goes off without a hitch."

Howard strode over, hefting the now-bulging duffel bag. "I've gone through the whole place. I think I've collected everything here that we can use. I have some bits and pieces back home that we can add to the mix... We may just have enough."

That wasn't quite the level of confidence I'd have liked to hear. "Remember," I said. "Anything else you need, let me know what it is, we'll track it down as fast as we can." I had at least the rest of today. The Darkest One couldn't have caught a boat faster than that.

We ducked back out into the basement hallway. Keevan locked the door and shot a guilty look at the key before tucking it into his pocket. "Thanks," I told him. "If you want to dash right back to your sister's place to return that—"

He shook his head. "I'm coming along with you two. Darton must be going stir crazy, cooped up in a cemetery of all places. I don't have classes until the afternoon. I can keep him company while you all work on that crazy contraption."

A thread of worry ran through his usual playful tone. "Of course," I said. "I'm sure he'll appreciate that."

Neither of us wanted to say what we both knew: This might be Keevan's last chance to spend any time at all with his best friend. If my "crazy contraption" didn't work...

No, I wasn't going to think that.

We hurried through the hall and up the stairs to the doors leading to the parking lot. The fae hunter van we'd taken looked a lot like the one I'd borrowed from Jagger— the one that the dark fae had pretty much destroyed yesterday—only even bigger. Howard yanked open the back doors and scrambled into the workshop area he had set up behind the seats.

"You want this done fast," he said. "So I'll get right to work."

"Perfect," I said, with only a small twinge of relief. We still had so much to do. And I didn't even know yet if my imagined invention would work once we'd put the thing together.

I got into the driver's seat and turned on the ignition. As I drove toward the parking lot's exit, my gaze roamed over the buildings and green around us. This campus was where I'd spent most of my waking hours in the last few months. Where Darton had gone to school like a normal college guy for the last two and a half years.

All the uncomfortable feelings inside me condensed into one huge lump just below my heart. I'd told him—no, I'd *promised* him—that I'd give him as much of a normal life as I could. I'd wanted him to have at least a little more time to be Darton instead of a fae-hunted king. I'd barely given him a week before that plan had fallen apart.

But if my contraption did work, if I could contain the Darkest One like I had before, after that—

The handheld radio mounted on the dash crackled. Jagger's voice broke through the static. "Emma and crew, are you there?"

Keevan tugged the radio out of its holder. He glanced at me and I nodded, my hands tight on the steering wheel. "We're here," he said. "Heading to the cemetery now."

"Good," Jagger said. "Make it fast. The dark fae are on the move—and it looks like a bunch of them are heading this way."

18

A truck honked at me as I whipped the van into the lane ahead of it, but I didn't give a sow's ass. In normal circumstances, it was nearly an hour's drive from the campus to the cemetery where Darton was holed up. If I had my way, I'd cut that time in half.

"We're watching the energy readings on the ground here," Jagger was saying over the radio. "Our scanning system has picked up some major fluctuations moving toward the cemetery from a few different directions. They're still en route."

"Thanks for the update," I said, jerking the wheel to veer around a slower moving car. "If you can stay there, standing guard as well as you can, that would be great. And be ready to jump in the cars and take off. Now that they know we've holed up there, we can't stay. Darton is still in the mausoleum, right?"

"Hasn't left it for a second, though he looks like he'd like to take a chunk out of those fae with that sword of his."

I'd bet. My hands tightened around the steering wheel. If Darton hadn't stepped outside my ring of protections, I didn't think it was my king's soul that had led the dark fae to us. It was too convenient that they'd honed in on the cemetery only after I'd left.

They must have been watching for traces of my hybrid light fae energy too. Closely enough that they'd caught on so soon after I'd left that they'd been able to figure out where I'd been leaving from.

I'd led our enemies straight to my king.

I pressed the gas pedal even harder. The van lurched forward with a fresh burst of speed. Something clanked as it fell over in the back, but Howard didn't complain. Keevan gripped the inner door handle.

"I'm thinking we'll protect Art a lot more effectively if we get there in one piece," he said, shooting a plaintive look my way.

"Just keep your seatbelt on," I told him. My fae senses were alert to every movement around the van. I sensed every opening a second before the cars even turned their signals on. I wasn't letting us get into an accident, but I wasn't going to let traffic laws slow us down either. I'd already stretched my awareness ahead of us to confirm there were no cops patrolling along this stretch of highway.

The new pouch of salt I'd stuffed in my jeans pocket hadn't stirred. No dark fae or vermin had crossed the warning boundary I'd laid around the cemetery. I still had time.

A hill dotted with dark pines came into view up ahead. The cemetery was right on the other side. I swerved around another truck, ignoring the rude gesture the driver made, and tore along the open stretch of road ahead of me. Keevan let out a shaky breath.

"I guess if I ever need a getaway driver, I know who to call."

As we came up on the cemetery entrance, I saw a couple other cars pulling into the drive—cars mounted with the fae hunters' standard flood lamps. Jagger had summoned all of his colleagues to hold this ground.

I jerked my chin toward Keevan, and he pressed the talk button on the handheld radio. "We're almost there," I said. "Two minutes tops. Get Darton ready to run for the van. I'll get him out of here, and we can figure out where we're going after that once we're no longer surrounded."

"Sounds like a reasonable plan to me," Jagger says. "I'll let the guys with him know to be ready."

I took the turn into the cemetery so fast the van skidded, tipping onto one set of wheels just for an instant. Keevan made a face like he'd swallowed a frog. We roared down the lane, turning left at the split.

The cemetery's road only got us within a hundred feet of the mausoleum on the top of its grassy slope. Several fae hunter vehicles were already parked at the foot of the slope. I slammed on the brakes as soon as we reached the closest available spot and leapt out, snatching my wand from the cup holder as I went.

Jagger waved to me from the truck he was standing by. I nodded and started jogging up the slope.

Darton and a couple of fae hunters, one holding a flamethrower and the other an electro-gun, appeared at the entrance to the mausoleum. Cattle sod. I should have told Jagger that they needed to stay in the inner room, with all its barriers, until I reached him. The blood and ash I'd laid down wouldn't stop the dark fae from reaching Darton, but it might have prevented them from figuring out exactly where in the cemetery he was.

Too late to worry about that now. Darton eased a step ahead of his companions, Excalibur gleaming in one hand, our bag of supplies slung over his other shoulder. I felt the moment he spotted me, his gaze snagging on me like a thorn on a sleeve. He blinked. An expression I couldn't read crossed his face, his eyes widening and his jaw twitching as if he was somehow surprised to see me, but at the same time a faint flush crossed his cheeks.

I didn't have time to puzzle out what could be wrong. The pouch of salt shuddered so hard it nearly jumped out of my pocket. A wave of cold air washed over me, stealing my breath with its sharpness.

"Watch out!" I shouted, throwing myself up the slope faster.

Not fast enough. Shadowy bodies shot through the air toward my king so fast they were little more than streaks through the air. I drew in my breath to shout out a spell, and one of the dark fae had already slammed a fist writhing with dark magic into the face of the hunter holding the electro-gun. The other hunter raised his flamethrower, but two fae grabbed his arms, ripping the weapon out of them and hurling him down the slope toward me.

I dodged his tumbling body with a silent apology. "*Shining shield, fend off the shadows!*" I hollered, snapping my wand through the air. At the same moment, two of the dark fae threw a clot of churning darkness toward me. Our spells shattered against each other like a firework of light and shadow.

"Where did they come from?" someone was saying down by the cars. "How did they—"

Darton swung his sword. He caught the closest fae in the gut. A bolt of soul-driven light seared through the blade, and his attacker fell with a spasm. Darton whipped the sword to the other side, catching another. His arms moved with the weapon like they were one being, exactly the way he was meant to fight.

But even my king's valiant soul and an enchanted sword weren't enough to fend off a concentrated assault of dark fae. I shouted out another spell, and one of the fae still standing leapt in front of Darton to smash it. Another wrenched a shroud of shadow over Darton's head from behind.

Darton slammed back with his sword, but the fae rammed a knee into his elbow, hard enough that I heard a bone snap from twenty feet away. His fingers flinched apart. The sword fell.

No. My king's name caught in my throat. I spat out another spell, putting everything I had into the casting. A blaze of light swept forward from my wand. My nerves prickled with the life energy I'd expelled into it.

The wash of light careened toward the dark fae. In the instant it crashed into them, I could see nothing but searing white. Then several shadowy bodies reeling, two toppling with their heads between their hands... but no sign of Darton.

Panic rushed through my body, drowning out the thumping of footsteps on the slope behind me. I scrambled forward. My wand had burnt out with that last effort. I dropped its crumbling length and grabbed twigs from my sleeves.

As I snapped out spells to keep the dark fae disoriented, the fae hunters caught up. Flames and electricity blazed. The dark fae staggered away from our onslaught. With a series of faint *pops* that I felt in my eardrums, they vanished into the air.

Leaving nothing at all behind.

I stopped at the spot where my king's sword and our bag of supplies had fallen. Excalibur lay in the grass, looking far too dull without his soul's light guiding it. The ground was trampled with the indents of frantic feet. But there was no trace of Darton or the fae that had grabbed him.

The dark fae must have magically apparated away with him before my spell had hit. There was no way of telling where they'd jumped to.

My shoulders sagged. "Emma?" Jagger said, coming up beside me. I dragged a breath into my suddenly raw throat. The last of my twigs tumbled from my shaking fingers.

"He's gone," I said. "They took him. He's *gone*."

19

"We can tap into satellites all over the country," Yasmin was saying. "The level of energy dark fae give off when they're doing this amount of casting, we'll always pick it up. We'll narrow down their possible locations. I promise."

The fae hunter seemed to expect some sort of answer. I made myself nod. She was perched in the bed of a pickup truck, computer open on her lap, a swirling map that didn't mean anything to me filling its screen. I looked away from it across the cemetery. I couldn't concentrate on anything in front of me for more than a second.

Darton. Arthur. My king. The dark fae would be carting him off to the Darkest One right now. She might not have reached this country's shores yet, but light only knew how much of a head start they'd gotten on us. And we didn't even know where they were now, where they were going—anything that might have given us a direction.

I pushed away from the truck, paced to the other side of the road, spun myself around, and walked back. Keevan was standing near the van we'd arrived in, his arms folded over his chest, his eyes even darker than usual. Jagger watched me from where he was leaning against the hood of the truck. All the fae hunters were standing around, waiting to find out what we'd do next. Waiting on me. And I didn't have a clue.

I'd never lost my king to the fae before, not like this. And when the dark vermin had overwhelmed us in the past, that had always been the end. I'd never been able to do anything other than give up.

But I couldn't give up now. The fae would keep him alive. They *needed* him alive, for their lady's plan to work, whatever exactly she meant to do with that dragon inside him. I had to keep my head, stay grounded. Pull all these people around me together.

I dragged in a breath and propped my arms on the side of the truck. The swirls I'd seen on the laptop's screen before had condensed into several brighter dots speckling the western half of the country. Yasmin frowned, swiping her long bangs back from her narrow brown face.

"Those points of energy all formed at approximately the same time," she said. "It takes a lot of magic to teleport like you said those fae did, I guess?"

"Yeah," I said. "It's one of the most tiring spells there is."

"I don't understand why they'd be scattered all over the place."

I did. "The magic only works if you have an emotional tie to the place you're jumping to," I said. "Dark fae... they don't get emotionally attached very easily. Most of them probably couldn't magic themselves to anywhere except the place they consider their home ground. And the ones that attacked us had come from all over."

But all from this side of the country. It wasn't good,

but it could have been a little worse. Okay, maybe I was grasping at straws.

"The one that took Darton apparated maybe half a minute before the other ones," I said. "And it would have taken more energy for the fae to bring someone with him. Can you figure out where Darton ended up with that information?"

Yasmin made a face. "Unfortunately the readings only give us a general idea, nothing fine-tuned. We only just figured out how to detect magical activity at all in the last ten years. It's a work in progress. I'm sorry."

"Not your fault," I said. No, it was mine. I hadn't made it back here fast enough. I hadn't protected my king well enough. I'd failed, and this time there was no starting fresh.

This time, losing him might mean losing not just his life, but millions of others. I'd failed my oath too, or nearly so. Its itch scraped at the inside of my ribs, nagging me with a bitter pressure.

Jagger must have been listening in on our conversation. "We've got to come up with a plan of action somehow. Are there any other factors we could look at?"

I considered, tapping my fingers against the side of the truck bed. "Well, if they were being strategic, which dark fae tend to be, they'd have wanted Darton grabbed by the fae who could take him the farthest from here, so we'd have the most difficult time giving chase. But that's assuming the fae who grabbed him is the one they planned to have do it. He did take out a couple with his sword first."

Yasmin circled a few of the dots on her screen to highlight them. One at the farthest point south, another to the southeast, one almost due east from here, and one in the northeast near the border to Canada. "If they *were* following strategy, we'd bet on it being one of these."

"That sounds about right." Identifying those spots didn't narrow down our options in any very useful way. The northernmost dot and the southernmost were a couple thousand miles apart. "We can't split up to chase down all of those fae. Whoever finds Darton won't have the manpower to get him back."

"Let me look at overall patterns of movement across the last twenty-four hours," Yasmin said. "Maybe that will give us more of a clue. They'll be taking him to the lead dark fae you were talking about, won't they?"

"Probably."

She leaned forward to peer at the screen as her fingers raced over the keys. Several ripples creased the fainter swirls that still dappled the entire map. "Hmm." She pointed to a ring of darker ripples in the northwest. "This is the movement we saw this morning, toward the cemetery. But here"—she gestured toward the Midwest— "there's been a broader but fainter pattern of movement. It looks as if quite a few dark fae or creatures, or both, are gathering."

She typed in something else, and the ripples moved. At the sight of them shifting across the map like surf on the ocean, my stomach tightened. Why would they be converging around the general area of—oh. Sodding hell.

I didn't want to believe it. Maybe I'd read the map wrong. "Can you do some kind of analysis to see what point they're all heading toward?" I asked.

Yasmin nodded. "We can't predict perfect, of course, but with them coming from a few different angles, we can determine the general center point... Huh. Looks like they're coming in toward Chicago. That's an awfully populated area for fae to hang out."

"Yeah," I said, a rasp creeping into my voice. "That's why they want it. That's why the Darkest One wants it. It's not just people. That World Peace Summit that's been all over the news—it's happening in Chicago. Leaders from all different countries..."

She wanted to destroy them all. Release the dragon and rip apart any pretense of peace. Leave dozens of countries scrambling without their leaders. All the pain, all the fear. She'd just drink it up, wouldn't she?

She must be loving this modern world, where she could strike a blow to human life all across the globe in the snap of her fingers.

Keevan ambled over. "The Summit starts in two days," he said. "So that means we've got two days to get Darton back, right?"

I blinked at him, and he grimaced at me. "I do pay some attention to current events." At the sound of a car engine down the road, he raised his head. "Oh, hey. The rest of the gang is here."

What? I glanced past him, and my heart sank. A car I recognized as Keevan's parked behind the row of fae hunter vehicles. Izzy stepped out on the driver's side, clutching the key. Keevan must have given her a spare for emergencies. I guessed this qualified. But I didn't want to have to look her in the face and tell her I'd lost her friend and former boyfriend, the guy as far as I'd been able to tell she still carried a torch for.

Priya hopped out on the other side. The two of them strode over to us. "I called Izzy to tell her what was going on," Keevan said, his tone defensive even though I hadn't questioned him. My expression must have been tense enough to give away my discomfort. "I figured she'd want to know. And she was hanging out with Priya on campus."

"It's okay," I said. Not really. Not at all. But at the same time, all three of them had been through a lot with Darton and me. They did deserve to know.

"What's happening?" Priya asked as they reached us. "Have you figured out where the fae took Darton?"

"Not yet," Keevan piped up, to my sudden gratitude. "We're working on it. We have determined that this Darkest One lady is planning on blowing up Chicago while the World Peace Summit is on. And that's how my life goes these days."

Izzy rolled her eyes at him and turned her gaze on me. Her mouth was tight with worry, her hands balled in the folds of her flowing skirt. "Keevan said you don't think they'd hurt Darton. He should be okay as long as we get to him in time?"

"Definitely," I said. "The Darkest One needs Darton alive to use him the way she wants to." Which didn't mean her minions wouldn't do him any harm at all. They'd at very least broken his arm in the attack. But Izzy didn't need to hear that. The thought already weighed on me like a boulder on my back.

She raised her chin. "Okay. Okay. Let me know if there's anything I can do. I know you'll find him."

Her certainty sent a jab of guilt through my chest. I wouldn't have had to find him in the first place if I hadn't lost him. But apparently she wasn't blaming me.

"What have you got so far?" Priya asked. She sidled over to check out Yasmin's laptop.

The fae hunter pointed to the screen. "These points are our best guesses of which fae whisked your friend away. We're still considering other possibilities for narrowing it down."

Izzy and Priya's arrival had diverted my attention. I focused it back on the map. "If the Darkest One is meeting the rest of her minions in Chicago, they'll be bringing Darton there. So it wouldn't make much sense for them to have taken him south. One of these two points would be most likely." I motioned to the two points farthest east from us. "Unless they're trying to throw us off the trail."

"That doesn't sound like the usual dark fae M.O. to me," Jagger said. "Granted, you've got a lot more experience with them, but from what I've seen they tend to be awfully... direct."

"Absolutely." I pressed my hands together. "Okay. Let's not sit around talking anymore. We head east, staying about halfway in between those points in latitude. Yasmin, you can keep checking the data for other patterns that seem meaningful. If we haven't been able to—"

A chime sounded from the open van Keevan had left. It took me a second to recognize it. My new cell phone—a text alert. Who would be texting me? No one had my new number except the people standing around me...

And Darton.

I dashed to the van and hopped in to grab my purse. My hand shook as I pulled the phone from its pocket. Keevan, Izzy, and Priya hurried after me.

"Is it him?" Izzy asked. "Does he know where he is?"

"It's from his number," I said, my pulse hiccupping. "But it's not exactly coherent." He'd typed out *Em* followed by a short string of letters that didn't form a word in any language I was familiar with. Other than my name, it looked like a butt dial more than anything.

But maybe that made more sense than anything else. "The dark fae probably didn't think to check him for a phone. It's not like they're in the habit of kidnapping humans and having to worry about that. But he wouldn't want them to see him using it. He must have tried to type something blind."

They'd have him bound somehow too. He might not even be able to see his surroundings. I remembered the shadowy shroud his captor had pulled over his head. Even if he *had* been able to see, the dark fae's territory would be out in the wilderness somewhere. The chances he'd be able to tell us how to find him were slim.

But he was alive. And well enough to type something. Even though I'd known they wouldn't kill him, having that confirmation sent a flutter of warmth through my heart.

I couldn't let him down. We had to get to him.

"If he's still got his cell phone, and it's on, there are ways of tracking the phone's location," Priya said, her eyes lighting up. "At least, if those crime TV shows are accurate."

Yasmin perked up where she'd been watching us from the truck. "They are. I can tap into that network. Let me see your phone?"

I jogged over and handed it to her. She examined the text and Darton's listing in my contacts. Then she bent over her computer again. The keys clattered under her fingers. A different map popped onto the screen, this one dotted with what I guessed were cell phone towers.

"Let's see where he pinged," she murmured. She

typed in one last strand of data, and three of the dots shone red. She zoomed in and then flipped back to the map where she'd been tracking dark fae energy. "And now to compare..."

Darton's self defense must have thrown off the dark fae a little—or else they hadn't been quite as strategic as they could have been. The cell phone data put him at a dark fae arrival point that was a little closer to us than the two outliers to the east, smack in the middle of Wyoming.

Still a long haul from here. But now we knew where we were going. A spark of hope lit inside my heart.

I wasn't sure if I could say I'd found Darton, but he'd found me.

"There he is," I said. "Let's go get him."

20

"Here, this part isn't too difficult," Harold said, handing two metal rods to me. "Fit the joint on the end of this one into the middle of that one."

My hands closed around the smooth metal cylinders, warm from their many hours in the van's workshop space. The floor rattled under us with the roar of the engine.

We hadn't stopped since we'd taken off after Darton this morning, other than to fill up on gas when the tank got low. After a few hours spent checking my silent cell phone over and over, and probably driving Yasmin batty asking her over the radio if she'd seen any change in Darton's phone position or the dark fae energies, I'd decided my own energy was best spent working on my trap.

We still needed it, if we got Darton back. If I was going to believe this entire mission wasn't hopeless.

I twisted the joint to work it into the second rod. Keeping busy did distract me from my worries. There was something vaguely reassuring about having equipment to grasp with my hands. Equipment that I knew might end up trapping the Darkest One where she couldn't hurt a single soul. Howard was fiddling with a more delicate mechanism that he'd said he was designing to modulate the flow of electricity.

The work distracted a little, but not enough to completely avoid my thoughts. As I set the rods down, the memory floated up of Darton's reaction when I'd told him about my new plan.

So you're going to make a trap for the Darkest One... and I'm going to be the bait. This sounds a little too familiar. He'd shaken his head with a wry smile.

Hey, it worked last time, I'd pointed out. *And with a little luck, this time you won't have to cut open your arm to tempt her over.*

We'd been able to joke about it, as if our lives and light knew how many millions more didn't depend on it. The threat had still been distant enough then. But night had fallen outside the van's windows. If I'd peered through the glass closely enough, I'd have been able to make out stars. For all the speed limits we'd broken, we were only just coming up on Darton's last identified location.

I left Howard to his work and leaned between the front seats, where Jagger was driving and Izzy navigating, to grab the radio. "Hey, Yasmin," I said. "Still no movement?"

"Nothing recent that I can see," Yasmin said. "Just the same few miles of travel we saw before. They don't seem to be in any hurry."

"Better for us," Jagger said.

Izzy looked up from her phone. "Why do you think they're staying there? I thought you figured they wanted to get Darton to Chicago."

"If they can't jump all the way there, they'd have to haul him by normal means," I said. "Maybe he's making it difficult. Or maybe they decided it isn't worth expending the energy. They don't *need* him in the city until the day after tomorrow. My best guess would be they've got another fae coming to meet them who can apparate with him closer in one quick leap."

We just had to get to him first.

Izzy bit her lip and turned back to her phone. "Who are you texting?" I asked.

"Keevan. If he's not talking to me, he'll badger his driver so much I think they'll toss him out of the car."

Keevan and Priya were each riding in other vehicles. It hadn't made sense for us all to cram into the same one. But it didn't surprise me that they'd be getting restless.

"Darton wouldn't have expected you to come, you know," I said. "You're missing classes, you've got exams coming up... You didn't sign up for this."

Izzy lowered the phone to her lap. "Sure we did," she said. "We're his friends. He's in huge trouble. That's more important than exams."

"Taking on the dark fae—it's going to be harder than anything we've faced before."

She shrugged. "You didn't expect us to be able to help the first time around. But we did, didn't we? You couldn't have stopped the mercenary that was after him without us. Maybe that'll happen again."

I couldn't argue with that reasoning.

Another text alert popped up. Izzy glanced at it and laughed. She clapped her hand over her mouth as if she thought she shouldn't have let the sound out. But it was nice to hear it. Nice to know someone could laugh.

"He's just... You know how he is," she said, waving her hand vaguely. But her mouth was still curved in an affectionate smile. I watched her for a moment, gaze fixed on the screen as she replied.

Maybe Keevan's situation wasn't so hopeless. The guy really should speak up already. Or else Izzy should, if she was starting to catch feelings there too.

After all, there was no telling whether any of us were going to survive the next hour, let alone the next week.

"Emma," Howard called. "I think we're ready to test out the conductive functioning. I'll need a hand for that."

"Right," I said, swiveling. "Of course. Just tell me what I should be doing."

He'd fixed most of the poles I'd helped join together across the walls and ceiling. Several others crisscrossed the floor. In one corner, he'd built up a generator housed in a black box, four times the size of the chambers fixed to the electro-guns. Mounted on the opposite wall was a control panel with a row of buttons and switches.

"When it's completely ready, I'll have it automated," he said. "For now, I want to take things slow. I'm going to build up the current in the generator, and you release it through the framework as I tell you. We're working with the switches for now. One at a time."

"Got it." I positioned myself on a rectangle of bare floor between the rods. "Should I be worried about getting electrocuted?"

Howard chuckled. "Just stay right there and you'll be fine."

"Should *I* be worried about getting electrocuted?" Jagger said from the driver's seat. "I know what you mad scientist types are like."

Howard just smirked at that. "No need to worry. I've padded all the outer edges with insulation."

That wasn't especially comforting given that I was standing *inside* the framework, but he seemed to know what he was doing. I braced my feet in case the van rocked, setting my hand beside the panel for extra balance.

"Okay," Howard said. "Initiating the electrical cycle now."

He turned a dial on the black box. A hum, thinner than the rumble of the van's engine, carried from it. It rose in frequency until it tingled at the very edge of my hearing, a thready whine that probably would have made a dog whimper.

"First switch," he said.

I jabbed at it with my thumb. The whine rang louder. My body tensed, but nothing zapped me. Howard studied a tablet he'd hooked up to the system and nodded as if satisfied with what he saw.

"Second switch."

That one stuck a little when I pushed. I gave it a good poke, and it clicked over. The whine rose with it. I rubbed my ears. Earplugs would definitely have been useful right now.

The framework around me looked exactly the same as before. "Is it working?" I asked.

"Everything's proceeding as expected," Howard said. "It's not supposed to put on a show. You want to catch this fae, not entertain her, right?"

I glowered at him. "I was just asking."

He turned the dial on the box and tapped something on his tablet. The whine expanded to a piercing note that was almost a squeal. Izzy winced.

"I can smooth out the connections once we know the basic functioning is in order," Howard said, which I guessed meant we wouldn't be tormenting the Darkest One's ears while also imprisoning her with electrical energy. "Third switch."

I flipped it, and a quivering energy raced over my skin. Something was radiating through the rods by my feet now. I was starting to feel the power of it, fast and heady. And bright. No, the Darkest One wouldn't like this at all. We just had to amplify the electricity enough that she couldn't break through.

A faintly acrid smell tickled my nose. I turned my head, trying to place it. Was it just a bit of exhaust from outside?

"Fourth switch," Howard said. I nudged it up, and the squeal leapt into a screech. Izzy yelped and covered her ears. I flinched.

And the rods across the floor crackled, emitting a puff of smoke.

Howard swore and wrenched at the dial. The screech faded, and so did the crackle. I waved at the smoke to disperse it, my stomach knotting.

"I'm guessing *that* wasn't the reaction you were hoping for."

Howard shook his head. "I think I'll be able to build up the charge as intense as you need it, but the framework has to be able to carry it without frying. Maybe if I double up the wiring... We're going to need to take it apart so I can do a proper job of it. Why don't you start on that side? The rods shouldn't be too hot there."

Hog's balls. I gritted my teeth against a surge of disappointment and grasped the rods on the wall next to me. It was a little much to expect this experiment to pay off on the very first trial run, wasn't it?

But how many more trials would we have the chance for before we'd run out of time?

"How far off are we from Darton's location now?" I asked.

Izzy consulted her map app. "At the speed we're going right now, about half an hour."

Almost there. Almost to my king. I had to focus on that.

I twisted and detached the rods with an efficiency I'd built up through the day's practice. Howard pulled out one of the heavy coils of wiring he'd taken from the college supply room. When I finished my part of the job, I rolled my shoulders and suppressed a yawn. I couldn't afford to be tired right now. We had not one but two big battles ahead of us.

"Take a left at that intersection up ahead," Izzy told Jagger. He was just slowing when Yasmin's voice crackled from the radio.

"They've jumped again! The cell phone signal moved too."

Sod it. I dashed to the front. "What do you mean? Where have they gone now?"

"Looks like they took a leap to the west end of Iowa. I guess we're adding a bunch more hours to this trip."

I closed my eyes. Iowa. Damn it. We were going to have to drive right through the night. And that was assuming the fae didn't manage to teleport Darton even closer to Chicago—or right to the city—before we caught up with their new stopping point.

"I'm thinking we are going to need your help, at least with the driving," I said to Izzy.

"I can keep at it for a few hours longer," Jagger said.

"This won't even be the longest drive I've done."

"Yeah," I said. "But a few hours longer isn't going to get us there. We'd better sleep as well as we can so we're ready when you need to tap us in."

And ready to run into the first of those battles if we got our chance.

21

The electro-gun felt uncomfortably bulky in my grasp.

"You need to put harnesses on these like you've got for the flamethrowers," I said.

"That's coming soon," Howard said from the driver's seat. "You're lucky we've got those at all. I had to throw them together in less than a day."

He'd taken over the driving from me as dawn had crept up over the land around us. We'd crossed into Iowa forty minutes ago. Treed hillsides rose on either side of the road in the thin sunlight. To the best of Yasmin's detecting skills, Darton hadn't been apparated again. Of course, I'd seen how quickly the dark fae could slip from our grasp last night.

"You set the generator spinning by pushing this button here," Jagger said, adjusting my hand on the weapon. "And then when you press the trigger, you'll get your jolt of power. It's not the most elegant contraption I've ever seen, but it does send the dark varmints running."

"So I've seen." I handed the gun to Izzy, who'd joined us in the back. "Are you okay carrying one of these when we storm the dark fae camp?" If we were able to this time.

She took the weapon from me awkwardly, fitting her hands into the spots Jagger had demonstrated on me. "I think I can handle this. It's a little less scary than one of those flamethrowers. And anything that keeps the dark fae running *away* from me sounds good to me."

I couldn't argue with that sentiment. With nothing left to do with my hands, I re-checked the spread of wands I'd laid out for the seventh or so time. I'd propped Excalibur against the wall behind them. Light willing, I'd be putting it in my king's hands in fifteen minutes' time.

"Still no movement," Yasmin reported over the radio. I was pretty sure she'd slept sometime during the night, but every time I'd checked in for a report, she'd been there on the other end. "We're coming up on the location now—as close as we can get by car, at least. From satellite footage, it looks like they're hiding out in some caves about a mile off the nearest road."

Howard turned the van, following her directions. I tucked a wand into both of my sleeves, others into my pockets, and kept one in my hand. "We wouldn't want to drive too close anyway. We'll have a better chance if we can sneak up on them."

The dark fae wouldn't pay much mind if they sensed my human companions. They barely saw people as anything different from the animals of the forest. To mask my light fae essence, I'd smeared more of the willow ash over my skin. It itched at me, but not as much as my nervousness about the fight ahead of us. Or the prickle of my nearly broken oath, digging into my gut like a particularly vicious thorn.

I haven't gone back on my word yet, I thought at it. *The Darkest One doesn't have him.* We wouldn't get into how close she was to setting her hands on my king's soul.

Howard eased the van to a stop. He clambered into the back to grab his own electro-gun. I hefted the sword in my free hand. We slipped out the back in silence, congregating with the other fae hunters who'd parked along the road. They all stood solemn and quiet, watching me for direction. Even Keevan had the sense to keep his mouth shut.

I stretched my awareness over the uneven hillside. The wind hissed through the bare branches of the oaks and hickory trees, rustling the needles on the firs. To my senses, it was laced with a sharper cold than the regular autumn chill.

The dark fae were here. Only a small group, from the feel of them. And in their midst, the pulse of my king's soul came to me.

There. Darton was so close. My heart wrenched. Now that I was near enough to feel his presence, I could have jumped straight to him with my magic. But then we might both end up caught instead of just him. I needed my allies with me.

I motioned with the sword in the direction I could feel the cluster of dark fae. The others readied their weapons. Dragging in a breath, I stepped off the road and into the hillside forest.

It would have been a tiring walk even under regular circumstances, up and down the sloped terrain—and mostly up. Carrying a sword meant for a practiced fighter and going on no more than three hours sleep? My head was spinning by the time the fae energy grew strong enough ahead of us that I raised my wand to motion our company to a halt. I took a moment to catch my ragged breath. Sweat was trickling down my back under my sweater despite the chill in the air.

The dark fae were barely stirring in their caves. I didn't taste any concern or wariness in the air. They probably couldn't imagine that a group of mere humans could have figured out a way to trace their magic. The fae liked to think themselves so mighty compared to the rest of us, but if they'd paid more attention to what the human beings around them were doing, they'd have been a lot more prepared.

This once, it worked in our favor. We had the full element of surprise.

I waved the fae hunters and my friends closer to me. "I'm going to magic myself over to Darton," I murmured. "If he's conscious, we should be able to knock them back between the two of us and the sword. If he's not... I'll do the best I can on my own. Either way, we'll need the rest of you running in there to have our backs and scatter the fae. There are probably glooms and other dark vermin around too, so keep your eyes open."

Jagger and several of the others nodded. I turned back toward the vague shape of the cave openings I could make out through the trees. My king's presence, so much stronger now, wound through my chest. *I'm coming.*

"Here I go," I said, and switched to the old tongue. "*Wind carry me to the place of my heart.*" Darton might have looked at me strangely if I'd called him a "place" in his hearing, but the truth was he was the closest thing to a real home I had.

I twirled my wand. The wind whipped up around and through me. And with a lurch—much less disorienting than crossing an entire ocean, thank the light—I was stumbling on cold stone ground in the darkness of the cave.

One of the dark fae standing nearby gave a cry. Darton was slumped by my feet. I snapped out a lash of light, jerking the sword through the air at the same time. The five fae gathered around me staggered back a step, and the spell lit up my reborn king.

His hair was damp from the cave's moisture and matted at one temple with scabbing blood. A coil of shadow bound his wrists and ankles. The arm the fae had broken rested at an unnatural angle. But his eyes were open and bright.

"*Darkness begone,*" I spat, gesturing to his bonds. They fell away—and the dark fae charged at me, shouting spells of their own.

Darton shoved himself upright and grabbed Excalibur from me with his working hand. It lit up with an eager flash. He stabbed the blade into the bolt of dark magic blasting toward us and smashed the energy apart. I bent down to grasp his shoulder so he didn't have to try to stand just yet. He lifted the sword, already knowing what we needed to do.

"*Darkness begone, darkness fall! Light knock the sense from their darkened minds!*" I yelled. A thunderclap of light blazed through the cave. Two of the fae toppled. The other three had conjured shadowy shields around themselves. The light slammed into them, shattering the shields and throwing the fae backward, but not quite hitting them.

The three of them started to press forward again, but a crackling rang out on the other side of the cave. My allies had reached us. Flames leapt and electricity shot out all across the cave entrance. My grip on Darton's shoulder tightened.

"Again?" he said, his voice creaky. It pained me to hear it, even as his determination squeezed at my heart.

"Let's show them what they get when they mess with my king," I said.

He chuckled roughly and heaved himself onto his feet. I shifted my hand from his shoulder to the bare skin at the back of his neck.

"*Darkness begone, darkness fall!*" I hollered, my own voice hoarse. Darton sliced the sword through the air. Another wave of light crashed through the cave. It smashed into the remaining fae, sending them flying right out of the cave into the midst of the fae hunters.

Excalibur dipped in Darton's hand. He swayed. I caught him with an arm around his back. "Hey," he said, sounding slightly dazed. He leaned his head next to mine. "My wizard."

I laughed, but something about his tone made my throat constrict. It was so tender. How hard had they hit him in the head? I touched his cheek as I steadied him. His broken arm hung useless at his side. I bent over it and murmured a few words to knit the bone. It would still be too painful for him to swing the sword with it quite yet, but it was a step in the right direction.

"Your wizard, as always, sire," I said. "And right now I recommend we make sure these fae are well and truly beaten."

He carried his own weight walking to the cave's opening, mostly, but he moved stiffly after the many hours of lying bound. "You got my message?" he said. "I tried... I couldn't manage much. And then they saw me moving and tied my wrists tighter. Took the phone off me too."

"I got the message," I said, "inarticulate as it was. It gave us a better idea of how to find you. Apparently they held on to the phone, because it led us right to you. And here we are, back together."

"I tried to fight them off, in the cemetery."

"I know, my liege. You felled two of them, did you realize? It'd be a little much to expect you to conquer an entire dark fae army. You might be an excellent king, but you're not a god."

His mouth twitched with a hint of a smile, but his expression still looked pained. "It shouldn't always be you," he murmured.

I didn't know what he meant by that, but we'd reached the edge of the forest then. "Art!" Keevan hollered, and slapped his arm around his best friend. Izzy hurried over too. The fae hunters had spread out through the woods around the caves. They looked as though they were patrolling rather than actively fighting now.

"The fae?" I said.

Priya loped over to join us. "They took off when they saw what they had to contend with out here." She hefted her borrowed flamethrower with a grin. "I've never seen a fae look quite that disgruntled. It was really very satisfying."

They'd be more than disgruntled. They'd be furious—and panicked at the thought of the Darkest One's displeasure.

"They'll have been waiting for others to join them, to take Darton the rest of the way to Chicago," I said. "We should get moving before those reinforcements, or others, show up."

"Chicago?" Darton said as we headed down the

mountainside toward the road. His legs were steadier now, but he wavered a little on the rocky ground. "Why would they be taking me to Chicago? Where are we *now*? I haven't seen anything except shadows and trees for... however long it's been."

"The World Peace Summit," I said. "It looks like the dark fae are gathering around Chicago to meet the Darkest One." A shiver passed through me. They've probably *already* met her by now. She herself could be sweeping toward us at this very minute, ready to claim her long-awaited prize. "I think that's where she's planning on unleashing... her plan." I caught myself just shy of mentioning the dragon. He'd asked me not to tell his friends.

"Oh," Darton said. He swallowed audibly. Probably processing the thought that the monster lurking inside him could be poised to destroy one of the largest cities in the country. He wet his lips. "But we're going to stop her."

"Of course we are," Keevan said. "That's what we do."

"Emmaline has been working with one of the fae hunters on this trap for the Darkest One," Priya said, with a brightness that sounded a little forced. She knew it wasn't going to be easy. "Something to do with electrical currents and I don't know what else."

Darton lifted his head. "You got that thing working?"

Well... "It's getting closer," I said. "And, sorry, you're still the necessary bait."

He gave me a crooked smile. "That seems to be what I do best." He held my gaze for a beat longer than usual, his eyes searching mine. I didn't know what for.

Keevan cleared his throat. Izzy motioned to the

scabbed cut on Darton's forehead. "Did they hurt you anywhere else? I think the fae hunters have medical supplies. I guess they'd need to in their line of work..."

Darton touched the patch of dried blood and made a face. "They mostly just kept me tied up. Even this is really my fault. I hit my head on a rock while I was trying to break free after they first grabbed me. I think they added something to their magic after that, so I couldn't move at—"

A cry rang out through the forest from below. Most of the fae hunters had gone ahead of us. My pulse stuttered. I grasped Darton's hand, and we pushed faster through the forest.

I had my wand ready as we burst from the trees, but there was no battle to join when we emerged from the trees. The fae hunters were hustling around the line of parked vehicles with more sounds of dismay. My gaze caught on shattered glass glinting on the pavement.

Several of the flood lamps on the cars had been smashed. One had a gaping hole in its windshield. Another's hood was completely caved in. The dark fae had battered our transportation as they'd fled.

I turned, and a yelp escaped my own lips.

One of the van's back doors was hanging sideways from one hinge. The other was folded inward. Howard stood there, his hands shoved into his hair, his stance defeated.

22

I dashed to the van, dragging Darton with me. Even if I couldn't see any dark fae at the moment, I wasn't leaving him out of arm's reach. I wasn't giving them another chance to grab him.

As we came up on the back of the van, my heart sank all the way to the soles of my feet. A blast of dark magic had consumed most of the interior. The rods were crumbling, eaten away by a sudden rust. The black box that had housed Howard's generator lay strewn in little pieces across the floor. Wires had melted together into a shapeless blob.

Our trap looked like a pile of old junk.

Howard pawed through the mess, his mouth pressed tight. "Can you salvage *anything*?" I asked. My voice came out raw.

He shook his head. "I'll have to start over from scratch. I don't know where I'll get another conductor like the one I had in there... I constructed those at home. I've got other ones there..."

But his home was a day's drive away, he didn't need to say. We didn't have a day. We might not even have an hour.

I exhaled shakily. That trap had been our one shot. I didn't have any other plans left. We had Darton, but no real way to protect him. No way to stop the Darkest One from doing whatever the hell she wanted.

Jagger walked over. He studied the ruin of the van and folded his arms over his chest. "Is it still drivable?" he said.

Right. Because the only thing worse than having lost our chance at imprisoning the Darkest One again would be losing Darton again, right here, because we didn't have any means to escape her minions.

Izzy had already opened the driver's side door and hopped in. The engine rumbled and then sputtered out. Whatever magic the dark fae had thrown at the vehicle as they'd charged past, it had wrecked the van all the way through.

"How are we getting out of here then?" Keevan asked.

Jagger let out a huff of breath. "We'll manage. They didn't hit all the cars. They haven't knocked us down yet. But I'm thinking we should be getting out of here *fast?*"

He glanced at me. As if anything I'd contributed so far had gotten us closer to real safety. I swallowed a slightly hysterical laugh. "Yeah. Out of here and fast sounds good."

"All right. We've got people one state over we've been in contact with. They're already heading out to meet us. We'll pile into the cars that are still working and meet them halfway. I'll see if they can scrounge up a few extra vehicles while they're at it." He paused and gave my shoulder a quick squeeze. I had no idea how despondent I must have looked to provoke that gentle gesture from

Jagger of all people.

"We'll regroup," he said. "We're not beat, and we won't be."

He could say that, but from where I was standing, it sure as hell felt like we were. The Darkest One had no doubt already landed on America's shores. I'd barely managed to weaken the dragon in Darton. We were out of time and out of options.

But there was nothing to do but go forward and hope some other answer came to me on the way. Jagger motioned us toward the truck where I'd first met Yasmin. Darton and I climbed in the back with her and a couple of the other fae hunters. She'd already gotten out her laptop.

"Let's go!" she said. "I'm not liking the readings I'm seeing here."

Jagger waved his arm, and the truck and a few of the cars pulled onto the road. The driver gunned the engine. I watched the wrecked van until we turned the corner, leaving my last great plan behind for good.

* * *

We had our rendezvous with the local fae hunters at a farm near the state border. The windmill creaked as its tattered blades rocked back and forth in the breeze. Weeds choked the fields beyond wooden fences that were half collapsed. Not much chance of us being spotted here by anyone who'd find our activities suspicious, but the whole place had a deathly atmosphere that left my nerves prickling.

Only four new hunters joined us, but they'd managed to bring one vehicle apiece, partly thanks to a quick bank transfer I'd made through my phone. They'd picked up a couple of RVs for sale at a used dealership. "That'll make sleeping on the road a little less painful," Jagger said, as if he thought we could just keep driving and somehow that would fix everything.

But what else was there to do? As the hunters bustled between the vehicles, redistributing supplies and discussing routes, I took a bottle of water one of them had passed me and wiped the powder from my face and hands. Then I rinsed out my mouth. Between the aura of death and the literal poison in the ashy mix, I'd been feeling increasingly queasy. Painting myself in darkness definitely wasn't a permanent solution.

When I was done, I handed the bottle to Darton. He drained the third of water left in the bottom. I brushed past him to flick on the truck's radio.

After a few attempts, I found a station with a news show. The hosts chattered away about a political bribery scandal and a deli meat recall. Then the weather anchor came on.

"We're seeing quite a sudden cold front sweeping the east coast this morning," he said. "Temperatures have dropped to around fifteen degrees below the expected average at this time of year. It's not clear what caused this sudden shift, so meteorologists are having difficulty predicting when it might pass."

Darton rested his hand on the small of my back and leaned his head over my shoulder. "Do you figure that's because of the Darkest One? No storms this time?"

"I'd stake my life on it," I said. "She's here. And she can't resist strewing discomfort to lead up to the main event. But a full-out storm would mean planes can't fly in all those world leaders for tomorrow."

"If we can stay ahead of the dark fae until after that...

I guess there isn't much chance she'd give up?"

"No. Not much chance at all." I grimaced. "The summit is supposed to last for an entire week. I don't know if we even can stay ahead of all of her minions that long. And if by some miracle we did, she'll find some other way to use you. She's been waiting fifteen hundred years for this moment—more if you count the time before. A small delay isn't going to put her off."

As if on cue, the news show switched focus. "Anticipation is building for the massive World Peace Summit. Crowds gathered near the O'Hare Airport to watch the presidents from France, China, and Brazil arriving. The event will kick off with a public forum held in Lincoln Park tomorrow afternoon."

I shut off the radio. Hearing that news didn't help me. We couldn't outrun the Darkest One forever. We couldn't take her on with flamethrowers and electro-guns. Between Darton's sword and my magic, we couldn't do more than knock out regular dark fae, so we certainly weren't stopping their high lady with the tools we currently had. What was left? What was I missing?

Or maybe there wasn't anything.

The oath's itch crept up my fingers into my hands. I shoved them into my jacket pockets and turned away from the truck. I was exhausted. I hadn't eaten anything since yesterday. Maybe the newcomers had brought some food to give me the energy I needed to keep resisting.

I took one step toward the nearest RV, and an icy finger traced down my back.

My body stiffened. I held my breath, taking in the sensation, as the frigid tendril pierced deeper inside me. A hum of dark magic ran through it. A magic and a chill I knew better than I'd have liked to.

It was her. The Darkest One was searching me out. Because she knew she'd find Darton with me, of course. And she'd found me. Practically tapped me on the shoulder from afar.

I tried to grasp onto the thread of her magic with my own awareness, but it yanked away from me. I stretched my mind after it as it trailed into the distance. The chill vanished, leaving only the regular fall damp in the air around me.

From afar, yes. She wasn't close enough for my half-fae senses to find her. But that was a small comfort. She'd pinpointed my location. We had to get moving. I had to throw her off somehow. I had to—

In my panic, I lost my grip on my body. I swung around, my arms jerking toward Darton. He caught them by the elbows as if thinking I'd turned to him for an embrace. The heels of my hands rammed into his chest. Words sputtered off my tongue.

"*Break and bur—*"

No. I couldn't make my arms budge, but my neck moved. I smacked my face into the roof of the truck, cutting off the spell less than a syllable shy of rupturing Darton's heart. Pain jarred through my jaw and into my skull, snapping the oath's hold.

Darton grunted. My stomach lurching, I wrenched my arms back to my sides. He pressed his hand to his chest, just below where my palms had struck him. His mouth twisted.

A little of the spell had slipped out. I'd hurt him. My throat choked up. "I'm so sorry. Let me—"

I cut myself off, jerking my hands back from reaching

for him. As if he'd want me trying to help after I'd done the damage. But Darton blinked at me, and then his face fell. As if, somehow, he was more bothered by my pulling back than the fact that I'd almost killed him.

I touched his chest tentatively, digging the fingernails of my other hand into my palm to hold back the oath's urge. With a quick murmur, I found the problem. My fractured spell had cracked two of his ribs.

At least I could knit those back together. Ramming my nails deeper into the wound on my palm, I whispered a few words to seal the bones.

"Are you okay?" Keevan said, coming over. I dropped my hand from Darton's body and stepped back.

"Sure," Darton said. He prodded the spot without so much as a wince. "Em was just healing me up."

He didn't say I was the one who'd hurt him in the first place. Keevan wouldn't even guess, considering where we'd just found Darton. He'd assume it'd been the dark fae's doing.

But even his kidnapping had been *my* doing, hadn't it? I'd led them to the safe place we'd made, even if inadvertently. I'd taken the oath that was preventing me from being able to keep him by my side without risking him more. And now the Darkest One was using me as a target to track him down.

A different sort of chill passed through me, one that twisted my stomach with guilt. Maybe I'd been going at this problem all wrong. I'd been so focused on us getting through this *together*... But that didn't really serve my king, did it? By all evidence, he was safer without me. I'd been clinging to him for my own sake. For my own longings.

I'd taken another oath, all those centuries ago. I'd

sworn to protect him with my life. It hadn't been magically binding, but it meant more to me than the words I'd given Cormag and his light fae cronies. I'd followed Arthur across all those centuries and all over two continents meaning to fulfill it.

Now was the time. I couldn't think about how I felt, only what was best for him. What would keep him alive and away from the Darkest One.

"I have to go," I said.

Keevan cocked his head. "Yeah, I think Jagger's people are almost done strategizing. I'm supposed to tell you we'll be moving out in a couple minutes."

"No, *I* have to go. I can't stay with the rest of you."

Darton stared at me. "What are you talking about, Em? Do you really think we can handle it alone if—"

"Not *we*." My hands balled by my hips. "You'll stay with the fae hunters. I'll lay down some barriers that should make it hard for the dark fae to trace your energy before I go. It's me they can track the easiest, not you. They've used me to get to you before. I can feel the Darkest One herself trying to reach me already."

"No." He shook his head, his voice hard. "No, not a chance. We're in this together, Em. There has to be a way to rebuild your trap, or to keep ahead of the dark fae, or..."

He trailed off, because what other possibilities were there? I gave him a pained smile. "Even before the fae wrecked the trap, we couldn't tell if it was going to work. And we can't run for the rest of our lives. I came all this way, all the times before and now, to make sure you have a life. I'm not backing down from that mission now. I'll do whatever I have to do."

"So, what, you're going to take on the ruler of all the

dark faeries by yourself?" Keevan said. "I mean, I've got a lot of respect for you, Emma, but weren't *you* saying before how impossible that is?"

"Maybe I was thinking about it the wrong way." I'd been thinking like a light fae. But all the good moves I'd made in the last few days, I'd accomplished by letting darkness seep in. Maybe the way to defeat the Darkest One wasn't by clashing with her. Maybe there was some way I could sidle close and then yank the ground out from beneath her feet.

I had no idea how. But I did still have a little time. I could go, and watch, and hope the right strategy would come to me.

Jagger ambled over to us. "What's going on? It's time to head out."

"Emma says she isn't coming with us," Keevan said.

"What?" Izzy's head jerked around where she was standing farther down the lane. She marched over. "What are you talking about?"

Darton was still focused on me. "This is crazy," he said. "You can't— What if they find me anyway? You know we won't be able to fight them off without you here."

"I'll be where she'll be bringing you," I said. "If it comes to that." If I couldn't stop her first. The immensity of that task settled over me. I focused on my resolve, but my body betrayed me. My legs wobbled. I set my hand on the side of the truck to steady myself.

Jagger's eyebrows rose. "You don't look like you're in much condition to walk across the farm, forget battling dark fae queens."

"We can help," Izzy said. "If the problem is the dark

fae tracking you two... You should stay with Darton, Emma. Can't we use the same strategy as we did when you were going to the airport? Take some of your things and drive off in different directions to confuse them? That'll be better than you just taking off."

"Yeah!" Keevan said. "I'm totally up for that, and I'm sure Priya would be too."

I hesitated. That trick would muddy the trail at least a little bit. But it wouldn't solve our problems for long.

"Please." Darton touched the side of my face, so gently my heart started to melt. His voice dipped. "At least stay until you have a definite plan. Get some rest, make sure you're thinking straight. We'll talk it through. Please."

"You two can have first dibs on one of the RV bedrooms," Jagger said, but that last *Please* from Darton had already broken me. Was I kidding myself? My thoughts were too scattered in my exhaustion.

"Okay," I said. "I'll grab a few things that you three can take, Izzy. We'll get moving, and I'll sleep, and then we'll see where we're at. But if I'm going, I'm going soon."

23

The sliding door clicked shut behind Darton and me. I sank down onto the end of the narrow double bed. The RV's engine rumbled beneath us as the driver pulled out of the farm. I pulled the shade closed over the window. I'd insisted on marking the outside of the vehicle with my ash mixture before we'd left, but I didn't trust that to be enough of a shield. Not for very long.

We had a head start. None of the fae had been near us. Keevan and Izzy had taken off in his car, Priya in one a fae hunter had lent her, carrying the most meaningful items I could give them marked with our blood. And Yasmin could keep us away from any hot spots of dark fae activity. They shouldn't be able to catch us for at least a few hours. I could get that rest I'd promised I would.

But my nerves were humming way too loud for sleep to seem likely.

Darton laid his sword on the floor by the door and sat down beside me, leaving a few inches of space between us. My hands twitched. I swallowed hard.

"Maybe you should sleep on one of the bunks up front. I don't know how much control I can keep after I've drifted off."

"I want to stay with you until you're asleep," Darton said. "I want to make sure you *do* go to sleep."

"So you're my babysitter now?"

He narrowed his eyes at me. "If that's what you need. You're not going to be saving anyone if you're about to collapse on your feet."

He might have had a point there. I sighed and flopped back on the bed. A faintly spicy lavender smell rose off it. Apparently the previous owners had been potpourri fans. At least the mattress was decently firm.

Darton was watching me. His expression had gone odd again, that uncertain look I'd noticed when I'd been coming to him in the cemetery.

"What?" I said. "Are you waiting for me to ask you to tuck me in?"

A smile crossed his face, but it faded quickly. Okay, something was definitely bothering him. Before I had to pry it out of him, he dragged in a breath.

"I've been remembering a lot more over the last few days," he said. "From my first life. From being Arthur."

"Excalibur probably helped with that," I said. And moments like lying half naked in each other's arms. A flutter of warmth passed through me at that memory. I squirmed away from it, farther up the bed to where I could rest my head on one of the thin pillows. "And? Did a new great plan come to you?"

"No." He looked down at his hands and then turned to face me. There was something so haunted in his eyes that my heart started to ache. "But I need to tell you something. I don't know if it'll make things better or worse or— I don't know. But before you go making decisions about running off on your own, before the Darkest One maybe catches up with us, or anything... I think you need to hear it."

"Okay," I said, bracing myself.

His Adam's apple bobbed in his throat. "You told me not that long ago that—that you've always loved me, but I haven't felt the same way. I thought, from what I'd remembered so far, that had to be right. I wasn't ever going to bring it up again. I saw how hard it's been for you. But I—"

His voice faltered. He seemed to gather himself and pressed on. "The more the pieces come together, the more I see how it was for me in that first life. The more I *feel* it. Maybe your confession dragged that part of my past up, or maybe it's how intense the last few weeks have been, or... I really don't know. But I know what I remember. It couldn't be more clear."

My heart was thudding now. I shifted upright on the bed, drawing my knees in to my chest. "What are you talking about, Art?"

His fingers curled into the bedspread, but he held my gaze steadily. "I'm talking about flirting with a beautiful lady during a dance in the castle and finding myself thinking how much I'd rather be bantering with you. I'm talking about missing you when you left my chambers for the night. I'm talking about catching myself wondering how it would feel to really *touch* you, with more than a playful swat here and there. I'm talking about the dreams—gods, the *dreams*."

He shook his head. "Some part of me had to know it meant something. But it didn't fit how I'd expected to feel. It didn't fit anyone's expectations for me. So I kept squashing down those thoughts, those feelings. Telling myself it wasn't more than close friendship, telling myself my mind was playing tricks on me. Pushing you away when I couldn't convince myself quite enough." He lowered his gaze then and rubbed his brow. "I owe you so many apologies."

My chest had gone fizzy. I couldn't do anything more than gape at Darton for a long moment. My heart thumped dizzyingly on.

Had I already fallen asleep? Maybe *this* was a dream. Because what he was saying, it sounded like he meant—

No. I would have known, back then. I would have seen, surely...

"I don't understand," I said weakly.

He raised his head. I could have fallen forever into the deep blue of his eyes. "How was it you put it? I've heard *those* words echoing so many times in my head. Em. Merlin. I have loved you, utterly, always. I just had my head too far up my ass to admit it, even to myself. I didn't want it to be true, back then. As if it was something to be ashamed of." He winced.

"I wasn't interested in *men*," he went on. "I was in love with *you*. And you happened to be a man, at the time. I don't know why I found it so hard... And all the times after, all the rejections I've obviously subjected you to..."

"Arthur." His name fell from my mouth, soft and light as a petal. He smiled at me, as if hearing that was all he needed. The fizzing in my chest softened too, into a slow unfurling of emotion, like a flower blooming. I'd thought I'd loved this man, this soul, utterly, in every one of my lives, but I'd never loved him quite as much as I did in that moment.

"I don't know how I can apologize properly," he went on. "I'd understand if you still want to keep your distance, if you feel that you're better off—"

A laugh bubbled from my throat. I shot across the bed with one quick scoot to grasp the front of his shirt.

"Art," I said, "shut up."

And then I kissed him.

We'd never kissed like that before. Tender and gentle, hard and passionate, we'd pretty much covered the bases. But without entirely realizing it, I'd always been holding a piece of myself back at a distance. As if I could pretend that it was only Emma, or Martin, or any of the other lives before who was getting swept up in the moment, while some part of Merlin remained untouched. Unshaken.

Not that it had ever hurt less that way.

Now I felt as if I'd thrown my whole self into the meeting of our lips. All of me, offered up for however he wanted to make use of me. Although I could think of particular uses I'd especially approve of.

A hungry sound reverberated through Darton's chest. His fingers tangled in my hair as he kissed me deeper, unraveling my ponytail. His other arm wrapped around me, pulling my body flush against his. I ran my hand down his chest and then up under his shirt, reveling in his heat and the coiled strength of his muscles.

He pulled back an inch, but couldn't seem to resist planting his lips on my cheek, the corner of my jaw, before he managed to speak. "I'm sorry. If I hadn't been such an ass—"

"It's okay," I said. "I forgive you. Enough talking. Do you have any idea how long I've been waiting for you?"

He chuckled low in his throat. "About fifteen

hundred years?"

I growled at him and yanked him back to me. His hands slid up my torso as we fell back on the bed, his thumbs tracing the curve of my breasts. I gasped into his mouth.

It wasn't just okay. It was fantastic. It was perfect. There was no spell binding us. No doubt about who exactly he wanted. Just the two of us coming together, as if we'd always been meant to.

He pulled my sweater off over my head as he kissed his way down the middle of my chest. "Em," he murmured. "Merlin." A shaky breath stuttered out of me. I tugged at his shirt, and he peeled it off. But that wasn't enough. I wanted all of him, now, while I could have him. A thread of urgency thrummed through my pulse.

That was why he'd told me now, wasn't it? He might not get another chance. *We* might not get another chance to make something real out of the words he'd said.

He tossed my bra aside and dipped his head to take one nipple into his mouth. I swallowed a moan. That sliding door hadn't looked especially thick. My breath turned into pants as he teased his tongue from one of my breasts to the other.

I pulled him back up for another kiss. My thighs splayed around his hips. He rocked against me, and a shudder of pleasure shot through my body from between my legs.

"Merlin," he said, his nose brushing mine, his gaze locked on my eyes. "Tell me you want this. Just because I— We don't have to—"

His voice was so raw and desperate it only turned me on more. "I've never wanted anything more," I said.

"Don't you dare stop."

He kissed me hard, his tongue slipping into my mouth to caress mine. His hand slid down my side and along the waist of my jeans to navigate the button and the zipper. I squirmed and kicked them off as soon as they were loosened. My fingers grazed down over his sculpted body and curled around the rigid length pressing against the fly of his pants. He groaned into my hair.

"You have no idea how many times I've imagined being inside you."

His muttered words sent a fresh wave of heat through me. I yanked at his zipper. The sooner we made those imaginings a reality, the happier I'd be. He jerked off his pants and made short work of his boxers as well. The heel of his hand settled over my sex, rubbing me through the damp fabric of my panties. I bit my lip, arching to meet him.

"Off," I gasped out. He didn't wait to be asked twice. Then he leaned over me, his erection sliding over my wetness. I gripped his hip, and he took the hint. With a sharp exhale, he slid inside me, all the way to the hilt.

I couldn't bite back the moan that escaped me then. I burrowed my face in the crook of his neck as he found his rhythm. It felt as if every part of him were touching every part of me, outside and in, and I only wanted to somehow get closer. Memories from our first life together swam up in my head, but I ignored them. None of them could come close to the bliss of this moment.

Darton's thrusts quickened. Pleasure shuddered through my body. It built and built with every plunge of his hips, every caress of his hands. He lifted my hips, fitting us together even more tightly, and the sudden burst of pressure sent me over the edge. I clenched around him, my fingernails digging into his shoulders. My lips parted. "Arthur."

He groaned and rocked into me a few more times. Then he slumped over me with a satisfied quiver of breath.

Without a word, he rolled onto his side and gathered me against him, tucking my head under his chin the way he had in the mausoleum the other night. I nestled closer, my legs still entwined with his. His earthy scent filled my nose.

"I love you, Em," he said softly. "Merlin. I love you." As if he thought by saying it over and over, he could make up for all the years before. Well, maybe he could. The words set off a warm glow in my chest.

"And I love you, my liege. My king." I kissed the base of his throat. "My Arthur."

He tucked his arm around me, encasing me in warmth. His happy sigh tickled past my ear. That was the last sound I heard before exhaustion dragged me down into sleep.

"Is it only the fae who can do magic?" my prince said. "That doesn't really seem fair."

We were standing by one of the castle's parapets, looking out over the surrounding lands. The air still held that summer mugginess, but I could taste the dry cool of autumn at its edges. Fall was on the way.

"A hawk can fly," I pointed out. "A fish can breath underwater. Human beings can make tools with their hands. Why shouldn't we have our own special strengths? Believe me, there are plenty of weaknesses to go alongside them."

Arthur raised an eyebrow at me. "What, like a perpetually sharp tongue and an absolutely horrid track record with horses?"

"Those are just my weaknesses," I said. "And I happen to

think a sharp tongue is an asset."

"You would."

I ignored that remark. "Anyway, magic doesn't only belong to the fae. It's part of all life. It's just that the fae have by far the easiest time calling to that energy. But in extreme circumstances, any creature can be capable of more than their nature. Do you remember seeing that scrap of a woman lifting an entire cart to get at her child?"

My prince made a noise of agreement. "So that was magic?"

"Well, not exactly. But it was tapping into a strength she wouldn't normally have. The same thing can happen with magic. If a person's willing to give themselves over to it, to sacrifice their own life, there's no power that can compare."

24

Whatever noise woke me, it was already over by the time I was awake enough to think. All I heard was dull silence around me.

Silence. That was wrong. Why wasn't the RV moving?

Darton's hand had slipped down my side to my hip as we'd slept. He was still out like a log, slow breaths drifting over his slightly parted lips. I eased myself away from him and off the bed, grabbing pieces of clothing as I went.

From the glow seeping past the window blind, it was still daytime, and not late in the day either. Voices filtered faintly through the wall from outside. I couldn't make out the words, but their tone was harried. My stomach knotted. I picked up the wand I'd left by the bedroom door and slid aside the door as quietly as I could.

The RV was empty. Worrisome sign number two. I padded down the length of it and nudged opened the door. Cool air and bright mid-day sun greeted me outside.

I understood part of what was going on right away. We'd pulled into a rest area to refuel. The other fae hunter cars and trucks were scattered around the two RVs. I guessed everyone had gotten off to grab some food and use the restrooms. But that didn't explain why a bunch of them were clustered at the far end of the parking lot. A couple of the hunters were gesturing with sharp jabs of their hands. Jagger made a sweeping motion toward something in the distance.

Then Yasmin noticed me hurrying over and said something that made them all fall silent. They turned to watch me approach. My heart sank as I drew to a stop in front of them. Something was wrong. So wrong it prickled up through my consciousness and stole my breath.

"What's going on?" I said.

Jagger swiped his hand over his mouth. "Your friends," he started, and hesitated. I'd never seen him look so downcast.

My friends. "Keevan? Izzy? Priya? *What?* Just tell me."

Howard piped up. "Dark fae took them. The damned creatures used one of their phones to text a message and a photograph to Jagger as proof."

My heart stopped. Like the video a dark fae had sent Darton of his sister. But then the fae had only been following Audrey. He hadn't touched her. "Why would they— What would they want—"

No. I didn't need to ask. The dark fae didn't pay a lot of attention to human activities, but they understood the basics of human nature well enough.

They'd threatened our families before, when they'd wanted to shift Darton and me to their will. That hadn't worked. So they'd gone for the only other people around we cared about. Easy targets, who wouldn't have been carrying weapons, who would have expected any fae that followed them to step back when they realized Darton and I weren't around. A lot easier targets than attacking the king with his wizard standing guard.

The Darkest One figured there was an easier answer than sending her minions chasing after us across the country. She'd found the perfect way to make us come right to her. As soon as Darton heard Keevan and Izzy had been taken—

My hands clenched. No. I couldn't let that happen. There would be no reasoning with him. There'd be no stopping him. These weren't just vague threats—our friends were literally in dark fae hands. He'd go after them. The king in him wouldn't allow him to do anything else.

Unless he never got the chance.

My body went still. There was my answer. The thought of him waking up and finding himself alone sent a twinge through my gut. But he'd understand, eventually. He'd know I'd done it for him.

That hadn't just been a memory that had tickled past the edges of my sleep. It'd been a reminder. Sacrifice was the most powerful magic. The fae mercenary had used it. Rhedyn had used it. It had always been there within my reach, except I hadn't been willing to face the consequences. I hadn't been willing to leave my king.

Better to leave than to see him killed. Better that than killing him myself. The itch this morning's bliss had subdued crept up through my arms again. I rubbed my hands over them.

"The fae have taken them to Chicago," Yasmin said. "It's obviously a trap."

"Obviously," I agreed. "But we can't just leave our friends trapped there. I was already planning on going."

Jagger started to speak, and I shot him a hard look. "I've rested. My head is clear. I know what I've got to do. Darton's friends and mine were my responsibility. *He* is my responsibility."

Jagger frowned, but he inclined his head. "You have to do what you have to do, Emma."

"Thank you." I sucked in a breath. "What I need all of you to do is not tell him. And don't let him leave that room on the RV. Someone can bring him food. He can pee in a bottle. Whatever. I'm going to lay down all the cloaking magic I can. If you can keep him there, they won't find him before I've ended this."

"Do you really think he's just going to accept you disappearing and us not telling him anything?" Jagger said.

"I think doors have locks and he doesn't have any magic to get past them," I said grimly.

The pickup truck had been carrying my main duffel. I stalked over, dug into it, pulled out the jar of shadow-tinged blood from the last time I'd worked on my king's dragon. With the jar in one hand and my wand in the other, I slunk back onto the RV.

Darton was still deep asleep. I couldn't help stopping for a moment to look at him, his arms and legs spread akimbo on the bed, his face gentled by sleep. Even with the blinds closed, the faint light that crept into the room sparked in his gold-blond hair. He had a lot of rest to catch up on after the horror of that day and night in dark fae hands. I hoped he'd sleep a long while yet, for his benefit as well as mine.

He was going to be angry with me. I was absolutely sure of that. But he'd also be alive, and after a while hopefully he'd be able to see that mattered more.

I opened the jar, dipped the end of my wand into the collected blood, and drew a streak of it along the bedroom wall. "*Darkness stretch and darkness hide*," I murmured. A splinter of pain shot up my arm at the shadow-working, but my magic complied. The dark energy I'd drained from the dragon shimmered up to the ceiling and down to the floor. I dipped the wand back in and drew the line longer, repeating the chant.

The hardest part was tackling the stretch of wall over the bed. I leaned over Darton, reaching my wand across, and he shifted onto his side with a murmur. I froze in place. He hugged the bedspread to him, his brow knitting, but his eyelids didn't even flutter. After a long minute, I finished my reach and slipped around to the other side.

When I connected the line to its tail, the dark shimmer snapped into place around the entire room. A crackling discomfort had spread all through my nerves. Sweat dampened my forehead and the back of my neck. I swiped at it with my sleeve. Then I gave myself one last look at the man my heart had always belonged to.

"Live long and well," I whispered. If I could have made that a spell, I would have.

Jagger was waiting for me outside the RV doors. He took in my weary state with only a crook of his lips.

"This is for you," he said, holding up a key. He motioned to a navy blue sports car parked on the other side of the rest area's lot. "It's full of gas, and it's one of our guy's private vehicles, so you won't stick out like a sore thumb in one all covered with lamps and solar panels. I figured you'd want to get where you're going as fast as possible."

I hadn't even started to think about how I was going

to get to Chicago. My throat tightened. "Thank you," I said. "I mean, not just for this—for everything—"

He cleared his throat to cut me off. Were his eyes looking a little misty? "Don't get started with that," he said gruffly. "You know we're good. And I think you'll also be wanting this." He hefted an electro-gun and handed it to me. "I know your magic gets you pretty far, but there's nothing wrong with having backup."

The tightness became a full-out lump. It took me a second to speak. "Thank you, again. You take good care of my king, all right?"

He smiled properly then. "You know I'll do my best. Blew up my house for the two of you already, didn't I? And hey, I'll tell you what. If you can manage to do what you've got to do and still make it back, you can have the story of my scars the next time I see you."

A grin touched my lips despite myself. "Sounds like a deal."

I stopped at the truck again to grab my duffel. I checked the side pocket quickly to confirm my spell-worked knife was still there. Then I tossed everything into the back seat of the sports car—other than the electro-gun and a fresh wand, which I decided to keep in easy reach up front.

Okay. I had everything I needed.

Most of the fae hunters had gotten back into their vehicles now, but they were all watching me. Light only knew what they were thinking of this plan. I gave them a quick wave, because some acknowledgement seemed only polite, and then I slid into the driver's seat. The engine hummed on with a buttery smoothness.

I wasn't going to kid myself. There was almost no

chance I'd get to take Jagger up on his offer. I wasn't coming back. But this sacrifice was what my life had been meant for. All my lives. How lucky was I that I'd gotten to have so many of them, frustrating as they'd often been, in the first place? How lucky was I that I'd gotten to know my king over and over, despite the lonely parts in between?

Darton had told me days ago that maybe I should let him go. He'd been right, just not in the way he'd thought. I had to stop clinging to my time with him and go to meet my proper fate.

I hit the gas and turned the car onto the highway toward Chicago.

25

Even if the fae hunters' data readings hadn't pointed us toward Chicago, I'd have known the dark fae had gathered around this place before I even hit the city limits. A supernatural cold stretched across the state for dozens of miles around, too thin for the steel shell of the car to keep out. I shuddered as I slowed into the urban traffic, wishing I could murmur a few words to warm the space. But any light fae magic might bring my enemies running right to me.

The first part of this plan required stealth. The second part... I hadn't quite figured out yet. I was hoping the first part would give me the pieces I needed.

The cold wasn't only in the fae energy saturating the air. A real, physical chill had settled over the city with the deepening night as well. The pedestrians on the sidewalks hurried along with coat collars high and hats pulled low. Frost dappled the edges of the windows. A bitter wind warbled past the car as I drove through the suburbs toward the city core.

From what I was hearing on the radio, the situation on the east coast was even worse. All the major lakes had frozen solid. It had hailed in New York City, chunks of ice big enough to shatter windshields and store windows. But the Darkest One didn't want to make this city too inhospitable. She wouldn't want to scare off the world leaders or the audience she wanted her dragon to devour.

The chill sank deeper into my body until I couldn't stop shivering. I parked on a downtown street, my senses alert for any fae physically nearby, and got out of the car. Walking got my natural energies flowing through my limbs a little more, keeping the cold at bay. And I didn't want to come up on the dark fae's urban enclave too fast.

I wandered the streets until I had a clear sense of it: The dark fae had taken over a section of parkland down by the lake. It looked like a recent installation: a series of neatly winding hedges stretching across a broad span of stone tiles. Just the sort of orderly lines that would appeal to dark fae sensibilities.

I watched from a few blocks away as people ambled toward the hedge garden as if meaning to take a stroll along the paths—and then veered away without a change in expression. A magical barrier like the ones the light fae put up in their woods was "encouraging" the locals to take other routes.

Figures stirred among the hedges, but I couldn't make out any of them clearly. If the Darkest One was there right now, she was out of my view. I'd have been able to sense her essence at the briefest glance. But I could feel her presence in the city in the sharpest jabs of the frigid air against my cheeks and hands.

The fae probably already had some idea I was in the area. All their previous actions suggested they'd been keeping an eye on my movements. But the Darkest One wanted me and my king to come *to* her. If I didn't push the matter, I could hope she'd be content to wait for my next move.

And *she* might have been, but a few minutes later, it became clear not all of her minions were of the same mind. Three figures shrouded in shadow, two male and one female from what I could make out of their features, slipped away from the hedge garden and headed my way.

My back stiffened. I wasn't ready for a confrontation. And how the hell was I ever going to get close enough to take on the Darkest One if the other fae perked up before I was near enough to even see her? I'd used up almost all of my willow ash—

Oh. The thought struck me like a zap of electricity. There was the inspiration I'd been looking for.

Instead of trying to paint myself into a dark fae, I could simply step right inside one, couldn't I? There'd be no better disguising my true nature than that.

The dark fae were approaching steadily. I faded back down the street, making for my car. If this was going to work, I needed to do it as far from the other dark fae as possible. No one could suspect the switch.

My fae senses tingled as the three followed me. They were only half a block away when I hopped into the car. I pulled onto the road and drove away from them as if I meant to flee. But I didn't challenge the speed limits even a little. I wanted them behind me but keeping up.

They fell back in the first minute, but after that they kept pace. They must have been tracing my energies the way I followed theirs at the edge of my awareness. I led them on a winding path through the city core and south into an industrial area that was even darker and nearly vacant this late at night.

When I hadn't seen or sensed another being in five minutes, I pulled over outside an abandoned warehouse. I picked up my wand and the electro-gun. Then I got out of the car and leaned against the hood to wait.

My followers emerged from the shadows by the street corner a moment later. They fanned out, the woman coming straight at me and the two men moving to circle around me. I held the electro-gun down by my side where it wasn't quite as noticeable. These ones might not have been in the groups that had engaged the fae hunters before. They might not even know what the weapon I held could do. Surprise would always work in my favor.

"What are you doing, fae-in-a-human-suit?" the woman said in a hiss of a voice. "Where is your pet king?"

"Do you really think I'm going to answer that question?" I said. "How stupid do you think I am?"

The dark fae sneered, which meant pretty darn stupid. "I'm sorry to disappoint," I said. "If you want any info from me, you're going to have to drag it out of me."

"A process I suspect I'll enjoy," the woman said, and lunged. Her lips moved at the same time, spitting out a spell. I jerked my wand to dispel it, snapping a line of my own at the same time. The man at my right whipped a lash of dark magic toward me too. As I whirled to meet it, the third fae joined in.

I wanted them closer. I had to hold on before I showed my entire hand. I cast a bolt of light in one direction and dodged the other spell. It clipped me in the shoulder, sending a searing chill down my arm. The electro-gun slipped an inch in my grasp before I caught it. But the fae were closing in on me, exactly the way I wanted. I bit back a whimper and swung the weapon into the air.

"*Darkness fall and darkness dull*," I shouted, gripping my wand and pressing the gun's trigger at the same time. As I spun around, a stream of electricity slammed out all across the street, urged on by my spell. It smacked all three fae across the head. They crumpled to the ground. Not dead—I wasn't using my one hope at producing that level of power on these lackeys—but unconscious, and hopefully for a while.

The exertion had left me panting. The wand had turned dark and brittle. I tossed it aside and grabbed a fresh one from the trunk.

I was getting low again. And this was the last of my supply anywhere. But then, I didn't expect to be needing them again after tonight.

I walked to each of the fae, keeping the electro-gun and the wand pointed at them. Over the two men, I cast a binding spell across their arms and mouths with a little zap from the gun for extra oomph. If they woke up sooner than I hoped, it would take them some time to break free from that spell.

Then I chucked the weapon in the car and bent down beside the dark fae woman. "I can promise you I'm not going to enjoy *this* at all," I said to her limp form.

Gritting my teeth, I dragged her to the car and pushed her into the back. To give this plan the best possible chance, I couldn't be finishing it here at the scene of this crime against dark fae kind.

I drove farther into the industrial district until I came across an alley so narrow I could only just squeeze the car into it and so dark I couldn't see more than a few feet inside. I pulled in until the darkness closed around the car. Then I flipped on the overhead light so I could see what I was doing.

The dark fae woman lay motionless as I dug a stick of incense and the knife out of my bag. With a snap of my fingers, I lit the incense and set it, burning, on the dashboard. Then I tipped the driver's seat back as far as it would go and held up my left arm.

I'd studied human anatomy for enough years that the spread of muscles, tendons, and bones beneath the skin were more familiar to me than my current face was in the mirror. I knew exactly where and how deeply to cut.

A slow bleed, that was what I wanted. I didn't know how long it would take me to get to the Darkest One. If this body died too soon, I might not be able to use the sacrifice against her to full effect. Eight hours—that should be enough.

I dug the blade into my skin. My breath hitched at the sting. A thin line down the wrist, just enough to let the blood start seeping out.

"*I give my life to take another's,*" I murmured, putting all my conviction into the words. "*I give my light to squash the greatest darkness. Lend me the power to shatter her shadows.*"

A tremor ran through me. I couldn't tell whether it was the magic's acceptance of my sacrifice or just my body objecting to its death. Maybe both.

I sagged back in the seat and closed my eyes. As I inhaled, the herbal smoke of the incense filled my lungs. My soul loosened within its shell of flesh. I cast myself up—and into the sprawled body behind me.

My spirit cringed the second I dipped into the dark fae's shadowy body. Every inch of her being made my consciousness burn. But that was why I needed her. All that dark essence would disguise my small soul hiding inside her.

Her own awareness stirred faintly as I settled into her mind. I could control her body easily, if not comfortably, while she stayed unconscious. If my knock-out spell faded before I'd done my job here, my sight-riding was going to become a lot more difficult.

So I'd better get going.

I opened her eyes. There was Emma's body, slumped in the driver's seat, dribbling blood onto the car floor. Nausea trickled through my spirit without reaching the dark fae's stomach. *Her* essence approved of that sight.

Testing the woman's limbs, I eased myself onto my feet. The sunroof opened when I gave it a sharp yank. I climbed out, slid down the back window, and walked out of the alley.

I had an appointment with the Darkest One to keep, even if she didn't know it yet.

26

Even with my new dark fae suit, as the woman I was wearing had so poetically referred to my human form, it would have been stupid to go charging into the middle of a crowd of dark fae. I ambled up the sidewalk across from the park slowly, watching the activity in that makeshift enclave.

The walk from where I'd stashed my car had given me plenty of time to familiarize myself with this body and its reflexes. The dark burn still nagged at my spirit, prickling through all my thoughts, but dully enough that I managed to ignore it. I could appreciate the fact that the wind's chill seemed to brush right past my dark fae shell. No wonder she hadn't thought anything of walking around with nothing more than a thin trench coat over her old-fashioned blouse and slacks.

My hand drifted to the trench coat's lower right pocket. My fingers ran over the hard line of the narrow shard of glass I'd picked up on my way. I couldn't have brought my light fae enchanted knife with me and expected no one to notice, but that temporary blade would work just as well.

I passed a few dark fae who'd wandered farther

across the park's lawns. None of them gave me a second glance—or even a first, in most cases. The dark fae liked order, and they usually found it much easier to maintain if they kept to themselves,—unlike the light fae, who preferred to live in groups with all the chaos that came with clashing wants and personalities.

In my original time, the dark fae had all given respect to the Darkest One, but they hadn't banded together in anywhere near these numbers. She must have called on every dark fae that could reach this end of the country in time for her grand act of destruction.

As I approached the hedge garden, a dark fae elder who was more shadow than figure stepped out to meet me. My host's heart jumped in response to my apprehension, but the man merely looked me over with a curl of his lips and said, "Straighten your shirt. Our lady wants to see us at our best."

Ah. My host's blouse had gotten a little rumpled in our fight. I smoothed her hands over the cool silk, and the elder nodded approvingly. There was no hint at all in his expression that he'd sensed anything off. No wonder. The dark energy encasing me felt as if it was outright gnawing away at the edges of my soul.

That didn't mean the Darkest One wouldn't notice. A little more time for my soul to settle in before I sought her out would work in my favor. Especially because I had another concern to address first.

"Has the king come looking for his friends yet?" I asked.

The elder frowned. "Have you not eyes? If he were here, our lady would make no secret of it."

I could also appreciate the dark fae tendency toward

speaking their minds instead of rambling off into vague poetics. I clasped the fae woman's hands in front of me, resisting the urge to twist my fingers together. A dark fae wouldn't fidget. "Perhaps if we caused them more distress, he might feel the urgency of the situation."

"Humans don't sense feelings that way," the elder said. "They are duller than most animals. He's barely fit to hold our lady's conjuring. But he will come. They also have no self-control."

He drifted away without giving me a chance to ask any more questions. Well, he hadn't been all that helpful anyway. I drifted along the fringes of the park, looking for another opportunity.

Maybe a fae a little less mature, a little more eager to please. The body around me wasn't *that* young. I'd guess, from the gritty tingling of the energy around me, she had at least five hundred years. Who could I exert a little authority over here?

Ah ha. A slip of a fae man with only the thinnest shadow clinging to his skin was entertaining himself by blackening the leaves on the side of a hedge, one by one. He smirked to himself in delight as he killed another. My light fae sensibilities shuddered, but I made myself walk up to him.

"You there," I said in a firm, even voice. "I heard we're holding humans at our lady's request. I have a taste for fear tonight. Where are they tucked away?"

The young fae blinked at me, looking startled that anyone had bothered to so much as talk to him. Then an even more wicked grin split his narrow face. "I saw them brought in," he bragged. "They're in the basement of the boarded-up bar down the way." He pointed, and then raised a careful eyebrow at me. "Perhaps I could join you."

I gave him my best darkly imperious stare. "I prefer to indulge alone."

The young fae deflated. Then he turned right back to his hobby of murdering leaves, so I left him to it without the slightest bit of guilt. Other than maybe over my inability to rescue the hedge.

A few blocks down the street, I spotted a bar that indeed had plywood boards nailed across its windows. Someone had spray-painted various swear words and a comically large penis on the wall. Lovely. I ducked around back to the alley there.

Glooms coated the bar's back door and windows, but they parted when I stepped toward them. Apparently this dark fae body got me full access. I knelt down to peer through the barred window that gave a view into the basement. If our friends already had dark fae company, I'd have to strategize around that.

It appeared the dark fae hadn't thought a full guard was necessary. The glooms and whatever magic they'd cast around this place would keep any wandering human beings away for the time being, and probably would have stopped me from tracing the three figures inside if I'd been trying to by my usual means. All the full fae wanted to be on hand for when the big show started, no doubt. Keevan, Izzy, and Priya were alone in the dim concrete room.

They'd been locked up in separate cages like the kind you might have crated a large dog in, a foot of space between them. Shadow magic coiled around the locks and the borders of the room. Priya was huddled in the corner of her cage, hugging her knees, but her eyes were open and wary. Keevan and Izzy had pressed up against the sides of their cages closest to each other.

When I first looked in, they had their arms stretched between the bars, hands clasped in the space between them. As I watched, Keevan murmured something to Izzy. She nodded, and he raised his hand to caress her cheek. She leaned into his touch, her lips forming a tight smile.

My heart squeezed. Maybe that was just friendly comfort. Or maybe Keevan had finally found the courage to tell Izzy how much he cared about her. Either way, I was torn between gladness for them and a pang that I was never going to have another moment like that with Darton.

I couldn't afford to waste time on mourning what was done, though. If our friends were still prisoners when I took down the Darkest One, there'd be nothing stopping her minions from killing them—in light knew what sort of torment—as revenge.

I eased open the back door and crept down the steps to the basement. All three of my friends tensed as I reached the bottom of the stairs. Keevan and Izzy pulled apart. Keevan shifted forward in his cage, as if he thought he could somehow defend her from behind those bars.

The less I said, the better. I started with Priya's cage, closest to me. She stared at me as I dipped my hands into the shadows binding the lock. They wisped eagerly around my host's dark fae hands, and my spirit winced. Ignoring the deeper jab of discomfort, I twisted the dark energy to my will. It fit into the lock—and clicked the mechanism over.

Priya's eyes grew even wider when I tugged the door open. She braced herself against the back of the cage, but I left her and moved to Keevan's. As I bent those shadows, an acid chill hazed over my thoughts. I gritted my teeth against the burn and moved on to Izzy's cage.

By the time I'd unlocked it and swung the door open, my mind was reeling. It took all my energy to pull myself stiffly upright.

"Go," I said, pointing to the stairs. "Get out of here, as far as you can."

Priya had already edged out of the cage. Keevan and Izzy followed suit, looking bewildered. Priya's forehead furrowed. My former roommate took a step closer to me, her eyes narrowing.

"Emmaline?" she said. "You're in there, aren't you? It's got to be you. This doesn't make any sense otherwise."

Swine crud. "Do I look like an Emmaline to you?" I said, motioning to myself. "Weren't you listening? You have to get out of here before anyone else comes."

My refusal to admit who I was didn't stop Priya from beaming. Keevan's expression relaxed too. Izzy grabbed his hand.

"What can we do now that we're out?" she said. "How can we help stop them from getting to Darton?"

Sodding hell, his friends were stubborn. "If you want to help Darton, the best thing you can do is make a run for it," I said, dropping most of the pretense. "You're the bait. You're the only reason he'd come here. Find him and the fae hunters, and show you're okay so he'll stay put."

Keevan made a scoffing sound. "While you're running around here in someone else's body with who knows what kind of crazy plan? I don't think so. If you're here, then Darton will be coming too."

I didn't intend to be here much longer, but if I told them that part of my plan, I had the feeling they'd insist on sticking around too, while trying to talk me out of it. Instead I motioned to the stairs again. "It doesn't matter. Just get going. I don't know how often the dark fae have been checking on you."

Finally, they started moving. Keevan and Izzy hurried up the stairs. Priya paused for a second to bob her head to me.

"Whatever you're doing, good luck with it, Emmaline," she said in her bright voice. Then she darted up after the others.

I looked around the room, but I couldn't see any way of hiding their escape, not without using my light fae powers and drawing so much more attention to this spot. As soon as anyone came by, they'd realize someone had let the prisoners out. I'd just have to hope that fact would work in my favor. If the dark fae were busy trying to figure out where their hostages had gotten to, they'd be less likely to notice me making a move on their "lady."

My friends were already out of sight when I emerged from the bar's basement. I wandered down the alley, which ran behind the backs of several stores, and meandered around the next few blocks. Gradually, I made my way back to the park. The roundabout route both gave my soul time to recover from the dark magic work and should have prevented anyone who saw me return from realizing where I was coming from.

I ambled by the hedge garden again. None of the dark fae drifting between them looked at me with any suspicion. Time to work my way closer and figure out where exactly my ultimate target was lurking.

I headed down one of the walkways between the hedges—and my host's pulse hiccupped. Panic flashed through my mind. Her spirit was twitching, deep in her head beneath my awareness. I hadn't managed to knock her out for anywhere near long enough.

The sense of her soul, like a fizzing thundercloud beneath my mind, stabbed up at me with a sudden blow. I pressed down at her with all of my will, but that left my control over her body shaky.

Her feet stumbled. She fell against the side of the hedge. I wrenched her upright while still grappling with the angry spirit trying to unseat me.

If I'd been alone, I could have risked a quick spell to silence her, even for just a little longer. I staggered around and found two older dark fae studying me.

"You seem unwell," one said with a frown. "Is something the matter?"

My tongue tangled before I manage to wrestle back full control over it. I stomped down on the fae woman's spirit with all the strength in my soul.

"I'm fine," I said. "Completely fine. Just not used to being in such a large crowd. I think I'd better step aside for a few minutes to clear my head."

The excuse might have worked if my host's soul had been just a little weaker. I made to stride past the two fae and their apparent concern, and she smacked my consciousness with a punch of energy that threw my coordination off all over again. I jammed my will back down on her, but at the same time her body swayed. It fell to one knee.

The other fae grasped my arm to help me up. "You look more than just overwhelmed to me," she said. "We'll take you to our lady. Whatever's wrong with you, she'll know how to cure it."

27

Take you to our lady. The words echoed through my mind with an even deeper cold than that brought on by the dark fae presence around me.

The older fae ignored my hasty attempts at humbleness—"Really, I'll be all right. She has so much to occupy her without bothering with me."—and ushered me farther down the paved paths between the hedges. There was no way I could protest more, not without giving away that I wasn't supposed to be there at all. Any real dark fae would have seen a chance to be attended to by the Darkest One as the highest possible honor.

The chill in the air, both supernatural and physical, thickened as we went. It seemed to enliven my host's soul. She shoved at me, and I shoved back, only just managed to keep my feet moving one step after another at the same time. Her eyelids stuttered. Her mouth opened and closed as she tried to speak. I snapped back control at the last second.

I could still do this. Maybe I hadn't meant my plan to proceed quite like this, but I'd wanted to reach the Darkest One. I'd just have to make do with the circumstances I'd been given. All that mattered was keeping my head—my host's head, really—long enough to see my intention through.

We came around the end of a hedge. A wind whipped over me that jittered through my host's nerves and nearly froze my spirit solid. Breath caught in my host's lungs with both her awe and my horror.

The Darkest One had fashioned herself a throne of sorts out of dead, twisted branches from the hedges. Its jagged form sat by the edge of the stone tile dais that overlooked the lake.

My greatest enemy perched on it, her narrow eyes glinting as dark as the water beyond her. They were the sharpest part of her body. The rest of her ancient figure seeped like living shadow over and between the brambles in the hazy shape of a tall, elegant woman. Her gray hair drifted around her wavering face like a storm cloud on the verge of bursting. Power thrummed off her even as she sat completely still.

"What's this you've brought me?" she said in an arch tone. Her voice was as cool and dry as autumn leaves long fallen.

"Apologies for disturbing you, great one," one of my supposed helpers said with a tip of his head. "This young one appears to be experiencing some strange distress. We hoped you could find the cause and see it gone."

The Darkest One shifted forward, tendrils of shadow streaming off her body as they clung to her throne. Her hazy lips pursed. My host's soul squirmed beneath me, wriggling and jabbing to try to break free. I rammed her down with a mental pummel, and her body stumbled forward. But that was okay, because I still had enough coordination to dig my hand into her coat's right pocket.

My fingers closed around the long shard of glass.

"I bring a gift," I gasped out. "For my lady. *Shatter this body, shatter her darkness!*"

As the words spilled from my lips, I whipped the blade of glass out of the pocket and stabbed it at my host's throat. A surge of magical energy swelled through my mind—

And the dark fae spirit hurled herself at me in the last moment. Her arm jerked just an inch to the side. The glass sliced across the side of her neck. Pain lanced through the flesh, but I'd missed the killing blow.

"*Halt,*" the Darkest One said before I could regain control. A magical vice locked around my host's body. My host's lips froze, parted. Freezing air tickled over her tongue. My soul shuddered, and the Darkest One's magic clamped around it too.

I couldn't even attempt a leap back to my own body if I'd wanted to. I couldn't do anything except hold there, staring. Together, my host's spirit and mine watched the Darkest One approach us through unblinking eyes.

I wanted to cringe back from that dark, fathomless gaze, but I couldn't so much as shiver. My greatest enemy stopped a few paces from where my host stood like a statue. She cocked her head, shadows trickling to the side with the movement. Her lips curled into a smirk. She let out a low chuckle.

"My dear Merlin. You've finally shown your face. Well, not your real face, but it's your soul that matters the most, isn't it? The same soul that sealed me away for all those wretched centuries. But what *have* you done with that ridiculous human body you've been inhabiting?"

Her gaze fell to the shard still clenched in my host's

hand. The edge of it had broken the skin of the fae woman's palm. Blood was beading along it and dripping down its length, untethered by the spell that had frozen the rest of her body.

"Ah," the Darkest One said. "Even you would know better than to try to make a sacrifice solely with someone else's life, wouldn't you? We can't have any of that mischief here. You won't be dying until I say it's time, little halfling abomination."

She drifted forward, reaching out her hand. Every ounce of my being screamed to pull away from her, but her spell held my host's body and my soul fast. The Darkest One's fingers grazed my host's thick bangs and settled against the fae woman's forehead. She murmured a few words under her breath.

A pinching sensation ran through my spirit. I'd have flinched if I could move. The Darkest One massaged her fingertips against my host's forehead as if drawing something loose from the skin.

I felt, with a shiver of understanding, what she was doing. She was tracing the thin cord of belonging that kept my soul connected to my body even at this distance, the one that would have pulled me back to it if I'd been able to let it.

After a moment, the Darkest One stepped back. Her shadows coiled around her gauzy limbs. She looked at the two fae who'd brought me to her, who were now standing nearly as motionless as my host in their shock.

"I need you to retrieve something for me," she said, and rattled off an address that I had no doubt was that of one of the buildings I'd parked the blue sports car in between. "Find the body, bring it here quickly. I want it alive."

The fae nodded with nervous jerks of their heads and swept off into the shadows around the hedges. The Darkest One turned back to me. We were alone now— well, the two of us and the dark fae woman whose soul was as frozen as mine.

"You do seem to have some sort of obsession with trying to be what you're not, halfling," she said, waggling a filmy finger. "It'll never lead you to anything good."

I'd done all right with that approach for fifteen hundred years before now, but I couldn't open my host's mouth to point that out.

"Uncomfortable, isn't it?" she went on, her near-black eyes peering into my host's as if she could see the shimmer of my spirit through them. "Being trapped, unable to move, unable to speak, cut off from the world and from your magic? It's only been a few minutes, and you're already hating it. Imagine spending fifteen centuries in that state, little wizard. Imagine how much you'd hate the one who did that to you by the end of it."

Her voice had stayed cool, but a crackle like breaking ice crept into the last sentence. Oh, light save me. I could imagine, and whatever she felt was probably a hundred times worse even than that. And now she was going to take it out not just on me, but as many living things as she could.

She had me. I couldn't see any way out of this. I had no magic without a voice, without the ability to even move. My enemy wasn't likely to accidentally let me out of these bindings. What could I even hope for?

"So I think I'll keep you in this state for a good long while," the Darkest One said. "You might as well get to witness my greatest work, which I'll be putting on even greater display now that there are so many more humans in such a small space." She grinned. Placing a chilly hand on my host's shoulder, she turned us toward the other end of the dais where it ended at a grassy field. A temporary stage had already been set up at the far end of the broad lawn.

"That's where so many of this world's human leaders will be gathering tomorrow," she said. "And all the other humans who wish to catch a glimpse. I'll crack open your king and watch all those mortals swallowed up, and you will watch it too. What a triumph. And it'll only be the beginning."

She'd given herself a front row seat with that throne. But she wouldn't get my king. *That* was the best I could hope for. The fae hunters would keep him far away from here... long enough for her attention to waver and for me to get another chance?

I wasn't sure that would happen in another fifteen hundred years.

The Darkest One stood gazing over the field in silence for what felt like a long time. The wind stirred the shadows so they rippled around her. That horrible grin stayed on her face. Was she picturing her triumph, playing it out in her head?

Fabric hissed against the ground behind me. The Darkest One shifted my host's body as she moved to meet the arriving fae.

The two she'd sent after my body had returned victorious. They were dragging my limp figure by the arms. One of them had bound my left wrist with a strip of cloth. Drying blood stained the hand below it. But not enough.

Not enough to have transformed my life's energy into a killing blow.

"Excellent," the Darkest One said. She motioned for them to prop my body against the nearest hedge. My head lolled. She jerked it upright and spoke a few magic-tinged words to freeze it in place the way she had my host's.

"All right, halfling. Time for you to take your proper place."

She spat out a phrase and whipped her hand between my host's body and my own. With a lurch, my soul shot back into its home. The world outside swam before my eyes as the sensations of my body came into focus. Stiffened limbs, thumping heart. The acid taste of panic in my mouth. An ache on my wrist. I was just as frozen as before.

"*Free,*" the Darkest One said, and the fae woman I'd been riding jerked back to life like a puppet whose strings had been abruptly grabbed. She stumbled and caught her balance. Then she dropped to her knees in front of her lady.

"Greatest one, I fought her, I stopped her. I—"

"You let her take your body and use it as a weapon against me," the Darkest One snapped.

Her hands shot out, so quickly I couldn't tell whether they actually touched the fae woman or merely cast magic around her. The woman's head wrenched sideways with a sickening crack of her neck. Her body tumbled over like it had when I'd flung my spell at her—except not. Because this time she wasn't waking up.

The Darkest One swept her arm through the air. The wind rushed over the fae woman's body and flung it over the edge of the dais into the lake. My stomach roiled.

The Darkest One wiped her hands together. "That's done now. All we have left to do is wait. I've gotten a lot of practice at that. You couldn't stop me, could you, Merlin? Not forever. Every delay comes to an end. Light fades, and darkness remains."

No, I wanted to scream at her. My voice was locked in my throat. Was this what my efforts to protect the world from her darkness would come to? It might have been better for everyone if I'd let her draw forth her dragon all those centuries ago. One ruler destroyed, one country in chaos, instead of dozens.

But she couldn't know the outcome for sure. The light hadn't faded yet. She didn't have my king.

As if she could read my thoughts, the dark fae chuckled. "Do you doubt me? Don't you worry, halfling. The king you've made a fool of yourself over is coming. He's already on his way."

28

The sun rose unbearably slowly, and yet far too fast. With its first gleam over the horizon on the lake, it woke me from the uneasy doze I'd managed to fall into. As its beams stretched across the park, spectators spilled into the field around the stage where the World Peace Summit would open its series of talks. The Darkest One lounged on her throne, watching them with a languid smile.

Darton hadn't come. She didn't look concerned, but that might be a front. Or maybe it didn't matter to her that much when exactly she dealt out her wave of destruction.

I could hope that she'd been bluffing when she'd said he was on his way. She'd wanted to torment me, of course. She'd known that was the best way.

Or she'd been telling the truth, and he just hadn't gotten here quite yet.

If I could have stretched my awareness beyond my body, I might have been able to determine the answer. But the spell that kept my body frozen also made a prison for my mind. I couldn't feel anything with my fae senses beyond the boundaries of my skin.

Posh black cars started to park along the road beside the park, down near the stage. Presidents and prime ministers followed a path marked through the swelling crowd, flanked by security officers. Cameras flashed. The murmurs rose.

No one in the audience paid any mind to the swarm of dark fae just a couple hundred feet away from them. The Darkest One's magic and their excitement for the event were working together to keep them distracted. She probably could have been setting off fireworks over here and they'd barely have heard a sound.

When all of the seats on the stage had been filled, the World Peace Summit's host stepped up to its edge with a microphone. His cheerful voice rang across the field, totally at odds with the apprehension that filled my body. He grinned at the crowd, said something about appreciating their enthusiasm despite the chilly weather, stirred up a few laughs. Then he presented the first topic of conversation, and the various national leaders started to say their bit one by one.

The audience pressed closer to the stage as more people trickled into the park to join them. No Darton. No triumph. The sun shone bright and clear in the stark blue sky. Cold as I was, its beams managed to bring me a small warmth. Just for a minute, the dread that was twisted inside me began to relax.

Then the Darkest One stood up. Her head turned away from the stage, toward the downtown buildings visible over the hedges behind me. I'd have followed her gaze, but my head was still locked by her spell. All I knew was that the smile that curled her thin lips squeezed the air from my lungs.

A few of her underlings hustled over to consult with her in low voices. Their lady never stopped smiling. She motioned them away with a flick of her shadowy hand.

"Let them try. They cannot enter. When you see the one I need, bring him to me. We will keep this neat and tidy."

A neat and tidy reign of destruction. How typically dark fae.

Every nerve urged me to move, to leap at her, to race to find my king, but of course I couldn't move so much as the tip of my finger. The Darkest One turned her smirk on me.

"And now you see exactly what your king is made of, halfling. Or should I say, what I have made inside him. I expect all those centuries of stewing have only made it more—"

The air seemed to hiccup. A shock of electricity smacked into me with the zap of a static charge. Yelps and grunts burst out all through the hedge garden. The Darkest One merely twitched, her lips pursing. My body flinched.

It flinched—it moved! I didn't know where that electric jolt had come from, but it had shocked me free from the dark magic that had bound me. The Darkest One's gaze jerked to me. Before she could spit out the words to renew her spell, I threw myself down the path between the hedges.

The muscles in my legs ached from holding the same position for hours. The dark fae amid the hedges were running this way and that. I staggered among them, snatching at the sides of the hedge. The brambles bit into my hands, but twigs snapped off in my grasp.

The air had filled with a familiar hiss and crackle. The

fae hunters' weapons. They were somewhere to my right—they'd managed to launch an attack.

And Darton had to be over there with them. That thought filled my entire mind. I had to get to him before the Darkest One did.

One of the frantic dark fae noticed me running past. He hurled a bolt of dark magic at me. I dodged it, stumbling into the hedge. The chill of it seared past my temple. Ears ringing, I ducked and shouted a spell back at him. One of my twigs crumbled into a blast of light. It sent the fae reeling backward, and I dashed onward.

The sweep of electricity through the hedge garden must have dissolved the spells warding people away too. Human voices carried over the hedges. A fae hunter I recognize but couldn't name charged into my view, zapping the dark fae in front of her with an electro-gun.

Another fae sprang at her from behind. She whirled around, only just managing to catch the spell he was whipping at her before it caught her with full force. It shattered around the stream of electricity, but the shadowy shards cut across her face. She cried out.

The three fae around her closed in. "*Darkness begone!*" I yelled, grasping another handful of twigs. A wave of light rocked the fae, giving the hunter time to whirl with her gun. I couldn't stay to make sure she could keep holding her own. My king needed me more. Wishing her luck and speed, I scrambled down the next path.

Voices were hollering all around me now, human and fae mingling together. Another wave of expelled static electricity rushed over us, leaving my nerves jittering and the fae flinching backward. But it wasn't enough to stop them. I darted around another bend in the path to see a fae hunter sprawled on the ground, his eyes deathly wide, a clot of shadow clogging his mouth.

My stomach turned. I had to find Darton. Where the hell was my king?

As if in answer, the warble of a sword singing through the air—the song of a blade in harmony with the soul that held it—reached my ears. Excalibur. And it would only sound like that when one specific person wielded it.

A cluster of dark fae appeared behind me. They propelled a surge of dark energy my way. I plunged my hands into the hedge. "*Let me fly!*"

My magic tossed me up and over the brambles. I landed on my hands and knees, the swing of a gleaming blade bouncing sunlight into my eyes. Darton was standing some ten feet down the path, Jagger at his left and Yasmin at his right. A stunned dark fae lay at my kings feet, but more pressed close to them.

Darton slashed out with his sword while Jagger blasted their attackers with flames and Yasmin sent out a bolt of electricity. It wasn't quite enough. One of the dark fae's spells smacked Jagger in the head. He squeezed the trigger of his flamethrower for one last spurt of fire, but he was already staggering backward.

I threw myself forward. "*Shield him, save him,*" I said, my fingers closing around my handful of twigs. A flare of light arced over Jagger's falling body. He crumpled—unconscious or dead, I couldn't tell—but the next bolt of darkness aimed at him shattered against the shield. The bubble of light wavered. It wouldn't hold very long against a dark fae onslaught.

"Em!" Darton dodged one spell and smashed another

with a swipe of his sword. He sidestepped closer to me. "You're all right."

"Only relatively speaking," I muttered, and barked out another flash of light to fend off a dark fae's attack. "*You* won't be. You're not supposed to be here. I told them—"

I had to stop talking to cast up another temporary shield of light. Darton jabbed at a dark fae who pushed too close, and the fae flinched away, clutching her chest.

"I'm the *only* one who's supposed to be here," he said, breathless from the exertion. "I remembered—I know what I need to do. This is my battle, Merlin. It always was."

What in light's name was he talking about? "You don't understand," I said. "You can't fight her. You have no idea how much power she holds."

Darton let out a raw chuckle. "But I do. I've got it inside me. Where is she?"

"No. You're not doing this. I'm getting you out of here."

I reached for him, ready to pull him to me and shout the words to apparate us away like I had before. Darton pushed me back, gently but firmly. "No. I refuse. I have to do this, Em."

"You *can't*—"

Another electric sizzle washed over us and rattled the words from my mouth. Thankfully, it rattled the dark fae that were rushing at us even more. They faltered, and Yasmin took the opportunity to blast them with a much more concentrated jolt.

I gripped Darton's arm as he swung Excalibur. My magic sent a scythe of light spiraling through the air in the wake of his attack. It smacked into the dark fae and tossed them over the hedge.

"What *is* that electric pulse thing?" I said, rubbing my arms. The hairs were standing up all over them.

"That thing that just hit us?" Darton whirled to face a few fae that were springing at us from the other side of the path. "Howard came up with that. It takes a while to generate enough power for the electrical field to hit the whole area even briefly. Otherwise he'd just keep it going the whole time. But it's handy, isn't it?"

"It might be the only reason we're not already dead." I snatched up more twigs and called my magic into Darton's next strike of his blade. I couldn't give him enough power. The dark fae stumbled backward, but they were already shouting out more spells. I shoved my hand deep into the hedge, clasping my fingers around one of the thicker branches.

"We've got to hit them with everything we have," I said. If we could knock out all the lesser dark fae, maybe I could get Darton out of here before the Darkest One descended on us. I didn't want to abandon the fae hunters to be slaughtered. But if he could see we had a real opening to escape—

"Ready," Darton said, bracing himself with his sword raised. I clamped my other hand onto his shoulder. I opened my mouth.

And a wave of darkness burst over us with a shuddering force. The shadow's thrust wrenched me away from the hedge and from Darton. He tripped, clutching Excalibur as he caught his balance.

The hedges in front of us crumbled into ash as the Darkest One drifted down to stand before us.

"*Halt*," she said. Her magic snapped into place around me again, holding my body rigid. Darton froze too. The Darkest One smiled and stepped toward him.

29

"Oh, ambitious human king," the Darkest One cooed.

"I've waited so long for this moment. And you've so kindly come right to me. Did you really think you stood a chance? Look at you and your wizard. You've got nothing that's a match for my power."

It was difficult to argue with that while her magic bound us, helpless, but Darton somehow managed to glare. The Darkest One snickered, amused by his anger. My lungs seized as she brushed her shadow-laced hand over his gold-blond hair in a gesture that could almost have passed for affectionate. Affection for the monster she'd grown inside him, maybe.

When her magic had thrown me away from the hedge, the branch I'd been gripping had snapped off with me. I still had it clenched in my rigid hand. Its green pulse of living energy tingled against my palm. If I could just break free long enough to say a few words of a spell...

I pleaded with my nerves, but I couldn't convince a single twitch of a muscle.

The Darkest One spun around with a sweeping gesture. All of the hedges between us and her throne crumbled away. Bodies lay scattered on the ground between the ruined brambles. Most of them were human forms. The dark fae edged closer, watching eagerly.

The Darkest One waved her arm again, without even looking at us. Her magic propelled our frozen bodies forward. We drifted along behind her as she stalked back to her throne. She stopped us with a sharp gesture when she was standing in front of it. Then she turned, her fathomless eyes glittering amid the shadows that formed her face.

"Watch and know how useless you are, little wizard," she sneered. She stepped right up to Darton. My heart wrenched so hard it might as well have burst out of my chest. The Darkest One raised her hands—

And another wave of static electricity shot across the hedge garden.

The spell binding us shivered apart. I leapt at the Darkest One, my muscles coiled, the branch clutched in my hand. Darton brandished his sword. I whipped my arm around, ready to dredge up every shred of magic I could find in my body. But my hand jerked toward Darton.

In my panic, I'd forgotten the oath. The itch of it surged up through my arms and clawed over my tongue. *Kill him, kill him before she takes him.* A spell sputtered over my lips. My fingers clenched tighter around the branch as they jabbed it at his chest.

I closed my eyes and jammed my teeth down into my tongue. My feet tangled under me. The taste of blood, sharp and metallic, flooded my mouth. My body kept hurtling toward my king—until the Darkest One smacked her fist into my skull.

I staggered backward, reeling from the blow. Pain

filled with dark sparks of magic radiated through my head. The oath dulled, but so did my mind.

The Darkest One loomed over Darton again. He backed up, holding Excalibur between them. She flicked the tip of the sword's blade with fingers trailing shadow and laughed.

"You think too highly of your halfling abomination's work, soon-to-be-fallen king. Do you really think this little sword can hurt *me*?"

Darton hefted the sword over his head. Just as he had all those centuries ago when he'd faced our greatest enemy for the first time. When I'd given him that memory through my eyes a week ago, he'd commented that the angle had looked odd. Now, seeing it as I struggled to set my thoughts back in order, the shape of his stance suddenly made sense. Oh. No. *No.*

I opened my mouth to form that protest out loud, to throw whatever spell my addled mind could produce between the two of them. But right then Darton glanced at me. My king's soul shone back at me through his eyes. The way he'd looked at me yesterday when he'd told me he'd loved me. Utterly.

Always.

I stopped, understanding washing over me. This was his battle. I'd tried so hard to fight it for him, but he'd seen the full picture for what it was.

Darton shifted his gaze back to the Darkest One. "No, I don't," he said. "But the sword isn't for you. It's for me. Me and *my* dragon."

Confusion stuttered across the Darkest One's expression. Then her eyes widened.

My king heaved his sword in a downward arc and

plunged it into his chest.

The Darkest One shrieked. She snatched at Darton's body as it crumpled, as if she thought she could catch his life before it left him. And maybe she could have, if all my king had meant to do was end that life.

But it wasn't. A shadow plumed around the blade where it protruded from his chest. The wind whipped up over the dais, shoving me back. It whirled the shadow larger, faster, wings spreading, claws extending.

The dragon swelled over the entire hedge garden, casting its darkness across the lake and field as well. The icy chill of its presence pierced my skin. The audience around the platform scattered. Screams and frantic babbling filled the air.

The Darkest One threw her hands toward her creation. "You are *mine*," she hollered. "Mine! You will obey my commands. Destroy them!"

She pointed at the field, but the dragon born of my king's sacrifice swung its massive head toward her. Its eyes glowed like hot coals in its vicious face as they fixed on the fae woman who had once been its master. Its jaws yawned open, revealing a row of gleaming fangs.

The shadows clinging to the Darkest One shuddered with what looked like panic, but she refused to believe she'd lost even that close to her end. Words in the dark fae tongue spilled over her lips. She whipped her arm, and a wave of shadow careened from her into the beast. The power of it rasped frigid over my skin.

The dark magic washed right through the dragon's enormous form without so much as a quiver. The beast flapped its wings with a gush of cold wind and slammed its jaws down over its creator.

The Darkest One's last screech vanished with her into the beast's mouth. Nothing but a few wisps of shadow remained, settling like dust on the dais.

The dragon roared, a thundering sound that reverberated right through to my bones. It swept around toward the Darkest One's underlings, who were standing around us motionless and gaping. As it dove toward them, they snapped out of their daze. The dark fae rushed away in its wake. But the dragon was too fast and huge to outrun. It snatched up one here, two there, in its fanged maw.

I heaved myself toward Darton. My king lay slumped on his side, blood pooling beneath him. I clutched his shirt, tears burning in my eyes. Not a hint of breath stirred his chest. Grief surged up from my gut to my throat, choking me.

"You stupid sodding idiot," I told him. The tears spilled out, streaking down my cheeks. I moved to bury my face against his body, but a sudden heightening of the screams across the park made me raise my head instead.

The dragon had finished with the dark fae in the hedge garden. With no more of our enemies left to devour, it appeared to have reverted back to the Darkest One's whims. It was soaring toward the stage and the fleeing crowd beyond it. Smoke streamed from its nostrils. A flap of its enormous wings shook the walls of the stage.

My work here wasn't done. I swallowed down my grief and shoved myself to my feet. I had to finish what my king had started. It hadn't been only my battle, but it wasn't only his either.

I picked up the branch I'd dropped in the chaos. It wasn't going to be nearly enough. Gripping it with both hands, I reached inside me to the thrum of life energy flowing through my veins. All of it, all of it, if I needed to. What did it matter if I lost decades? I'd been granted plenty of life already. The people the dragon meant to consume had barely gotten one.

"Creature of darkness!" I called out. The energy I was gathering inside me pitched my voice high and hard. It split the air.

The dragon veered toward me. A quiver of recognition rolled off of it. Of course it knew me. We'd met more than once in Darton's soul. We might as well be old friends.

"Darkness must be consumed," I said. *"The only darkness that remains here is you. Swallow yourself, swallow it all. Fulfill the purpose you were tasked with."*

With those words, I flung all the magic I could gather toward the beast. It tore from my limbs and chest like an uprooted tree. Pain lanced down the center of my body. I staggered, barely able to breathe. Yeah, that had been at least a couple decades right there.

The spell hit the dragon. It shuddered and lashed its tail. As I sagged to my knees beside my king, my gut clenched. Had my effort been enough? I reached down into myself again, right to the core, ready to pour every last shred into my next casting.

The dragon whipped its tail back and forth again—and caught the tip in its jaws.

My own jaw went slack as I watched the creature chomp down. It tugged and snapped, pulling even more of its own body into its maw. The wind whirled around it, pulling tighter. Its glowing eyes flared. It started to spin with the wind, coiling in on itself. Its mouth opened and caught its hind legs with its fangs.

It wrenched itself even more sharply around, until it looked like little more than a blurred ball of shadow. I lost sight of its limbs and wings in the haze. Its body undulated and contracted. It whirled faster and faster, shrinking so fast now that the air shrieked. Then, with an awful sucking sound and a wallop of wind that made my ears pop, it was gone.

I sagged over Darton's body, all my strength having fled my own. His face was still warm under my hand. I gazed dizzily down at the wound on his chest, the blood streaking the blade I'd enchanted fifteen hundred years past. One thought broke through the roar in my head.

He wasn't the only one who could be a stupid sodding idiot. I'd sworn I'd save him, and damn it, I would, with whatever life I had left.

I wrapped my arms around his still form and kissed his cheek. "*I love you,*" I murmured in the first language we'd ever spoken to each other, the first language I should have said those words to him in. But there wasn't any time left to regret that. I closed my fingers around Excalibur's hilt and dragged it from Darton's chest, wincing at the renewed gush of blood. Then I rolled him onto his back and pressed my lips to his self-inflicted wound.

"*Live long and well,*" I ordered him. With the last bit of energy in my limbs, I pushed myself to the edge of the dais. The lake's water lapped the shore beneath me.

"*For my king,*" I said, and tipped myself over the edge.

My body plunged into the frigid water. Some distant part of my brain woke up with an urge to save myself, but my body was already too exhausted to fight.

The water closed over me. My vision hazed. As the

liquid seeped into my lungs, my awareness drifted away from me to the body still lying on the dais. To flesh knitting and sealing. To a breath rasping down Darton's throat. I'd given my sacrifice, and the light had accepted it for my king. A smile crossed my face.

Then the blackness took me.

30

Pain. Hard and heavy, slamming through my chest. Air choking my throat.

My lungs heaved. Water spewed out of them, searing up my throat and over my tongue. I coughed in short, hacking bursts, and wretched again.

Everything hurt. My muscles ached. My rib cage throbbed around my still-stuttering lungs. A sharp jab of a headache needled my temples.

My eyes blinked open of their own accord. A face loomed over mine, blurring and then coming into focus. Darton's. Flushed with exertion, his shoulders tensed. Blue sky above him. My fingers clenched and found soft grass between them. The breeze shifted, and a shiver rippled over me. Wet fabric clung to my chilled skin from shoulders to feet.

"Where's that blanket?" Darton said, his hand jerking toward someone behind him. His blue eyes never left mine. A second later, he was spreading a stretch of knitted wool someone must have handed him over my shaking body.

"Em," he said, touching my cheek. "Em, can you talk

to me? Do you understand what I'm saying?"

I dragged in a shudder of a breath. My lungs protested at being put to use, but the fog in my head cleared slightly. "Yes." My voice seemed to scrape my already raw throat. I winced and tried again. "What happened?"

Another face appeared beyond Darton's. Jagger. He was holding his arm at an unnatural angle, his expression tight with pain, but he was alive. "What happened is Darton dragged you out of the lake and gave you the most impressive performance of CPR I've ever seen. How you ended up in the lake in the first place, I'm not so sure."

CPR. "He has a badge for that," I said inanely. "Boy Scouts." Jagger just gave me a puzzled look, but a smile flickered across Darton's face.

"If you remember that, you mustn't have been too far gone."

"Enough to make sure *you* weren't a goner," I muttered. I squirmed but failed to maneuver my body well enough to push myself upright. Darton eased his arm around me and helped me sit up.

People were milling around the field in apparent confusion. As you'd expect when a massive magic dragon had just terrorized a major city park and then eaten itself. A few of the other fae hunters were standing nearby, patching up wounds and eyeing Darton and I cautiously.

I was alive. The fact of it hit me out of the blue, as if it hadn't already been obvious. I'd sacrificed my life for my king, and he'd brought me back in turn, in his own way.

"You know," I said, tugging the blanket tighter around me, "I'm pretty sure we can only get away with something like this the once. No second chances."

"I think I'm okay with that," Darton said. "As long as there aren't any *other* hugely powerful fae enemies you've just forgotten to tell me about."

"Enemies, no. People I've generally irritated... Let's not start counting."

Darton chuckled, with an abruptness that seemed to surprise him. He snapped his mouth shut, but his smile remained. He traced his fingers over my forehead, brushing damp strands of hair back from my face. His gaze softened.

"You know," he said, "when your hair's wet, you really do look like him—like you. The first you."

When he'd made that observation before, it hadn't led to quite the reaction I'd been looking for. But the same question tumbled from my mouth anyway.

"Do you like that?"

Darton's smile tightened. My pulse skittered in a sudden panic. Then I saw him blink his eyes, hard. It wasn't a lack of emotion that was making him pause. It was too much of it.

"I do," he said roughly. "I like you every way you could possibly look. As long as you're looking back at me."

The tension seeped out of me. In that moment, I'd have been perfectly happy to snuggle into his warmth for the rest of the day. But I had the feeling this wasn't quite the place for it. Still, I could sneak in a quick cuddle before we had to haul ass back toward home.

I leaned into him, nestling my head against his shoulder. "I don't think you need to worry about that. You're my king, and I'm your wizard. You're stuck with me whether you like it or not."

31

THREE MONTHS LATER

My saber glanced off my sparring partner's blade. He parried it to the side and jabbed his saber toward me. I dodged the blow, distracted him with a quick feint, and landed a tap in the middle of his chest.

"Point!"

He chuckled. "You're too fast for me."

"Hmm. Maybe you just got too used to having a magical sword that did half the work for you."

Darton pulled off his fencing mask with a grin. "I suppose that's possible. You'll just have to beat proper discipline back into me. Some other day. Lucky for me, practice is pretty much over."

I rolled my eyes at him, and then lifted my own mask and did it again so he could see me this time. The gesture didn't stop Darton from stepping closer and leaning in for a kiss. The brush of his mouth against mine sent a rush of heat through me, still as potent as the first time we'd locked lips last fall.

Coach cleared his throat. Darton pulled back with a sheepish smile that provoked just as much of a flutter in my chest as his cocky grin before. Seeing Coach's expression, I decided not to give in to the urge to kiss that smile too. We had plenty of time for kissing—and whatever else we felt like getting up to—outside of practice.

Darton caught my hand to squeeze it, and we parted ways to our respective change rooms.

When I emerged from mine a few minutes later after a hasty change into street clothes, I found Keevan and Izzy waiting in the hall. They were talking to each other, their heads leaned close in conversation.

Izzy gave me a little wave when she saw me. Her hand stayed tucked around Keevan's elbow. He beamed at me. He'd been beaming at pretty much everyone and everything since they'd gone on their first date back in December.

"What's up?" I said as they strolled over.

"Oh, I borrowed a book from Darton that he said he needed back for some assignment." Keevan held up the book in question, which from the title was some sort of legal text. "Figured I'd stop by now. Ah, there's the man I'm looking for."

"Hey!" Darton said, coming out of the change room. Keevan gave a little bow as he handed over the book, and Darton accepted it with a grimace. "Don't you start."

"Just giving you the respect you're due, Your Highness," Keevan said with a wink. I had a feeling it was going to be years before he ran out of king-related humor.

"We were going to grab some dinner at that new Italian place just off campus," Izzy said. "Did you two want to come with?"

"Not tonight," Darton said. "Priya's coming over so she and Em can have their weekly cooking extravaganza."

"And I've got about a million assignments to get through." I made a face. "I'm still getting back in my professors' good graces after skipping out for all those weeks. Maybe we can hang out sometime this weekend?"

"Definitely," Izzy said. "I'll text you."

Keevan slung his arm around Izzy's waist as they ambled away. Darton and I set off in the opposite direction. He shook his head. "I've got to say, I never saw that coming. The two of them getting together, I mean."

I nudged him with my elbow. "It took you fifteen hundred years to figure out your own feelings. I'm going to have to say picking up on chemistry is maybe not your forte."

Darton made a non-committal grumbling sound and took my hand, twining his fingers through mine. "I figured it out in the end. That's got to count for something. I just don't see why he told *you* and not me."

"Ah, well, that's where you have to realize that he didn't so much tell me as I dragged it out of him. But it wasn't that hard to see."

As we crossed the courtyard, my gaze caught on a scrap of floating darkness that *would* be hard to see, for anyone on campus but me with my fae-touched sight. I tugged Darton to a halt and palmed one of the few twigs I tucked into my pockets every morning.

The dark fae had left us alone since we'd bested the Darkest One. Now that the dragon was gone from my king, Darton wasn't useful to them as a tool. Without their mistress urging them on, I suspected they valued keeping their own lives over seeking possible vengeance. Few of them had lived long enough to have met her more than a couple days before her demise anyway. And since the spell that had bound her to our lives was broken, the glooms didn't have any interest in Arthur's soul either.

But it didn't hurt to be prepared. And there was no point in letting dark vermin wander around, potentially stirring up minor mischief.

"*Darkness begone,*" I murmured. The gloom wisped away. Darton squeezed my hand a little tighter when we started walking again.

"Our lives are never going to be completely normal, are they?" he said.

The words sent a pang through my chest. I'd tried so hard to give him *normal* before. But when you were a reincarnated wizard attending to your reincarnated king...

"No," I said. "Probably not."

He shrugged and gave me a smile that melted my regret. "I'm okay with that. Normal *all* the time would get kind of boring."

We crunched through the thin layer of snow on the campus green and turned onto the street leading to the apartment he and I had moved into right after Thanksgiving.

"I've started thinking," Darton said, with a hint of hesitation that told me my opinion was going to carry some weight. "Instead of going all-out with the law thing as a career... I might like to try my hand at politics. I mean, I do have a little experience, even if it's not very recent. And, well, the idea just appeals to me."

I rubbed my thumb over the back of his hand. "That sounds great." He'd never seemed all that enthusiastic about becoming a lawyer—he'd picked it to follow in his dad's footsteps, not out of any real passion. "Maybe you won't end up with a castle, but I'd bet you can make a meaningful impact, just like back then."

"I might as well try, at least."

Priya was waiting for us in the building's lobby, where it looked like she'd just stomped the snow off her boots. She hefted a bulging grocery store bag. "I found the *perfect* recipe," she told me. "You are going to totally chemistry-geek out over it, Emmaline."

I laughed. "I can't wait."

In the apartment, we headed straight for the kitchen. Priya pulled out her phone and brought up one of the most complicated curry recipes I'd ever seen. The thought of the challenge set my thoughts buzzing.

Darton leaned against the counter next to me. "Is there anything I can do to help?"

My mind flashed back through the centuries to my king's attempts at cooking stew over a fire while we were on the road. "Nope. Definitely not."

"Hey," he said, holding up his hands in mock-offense. "I can handle a pot and a spoon. I *did* kill the greatest dark fae ever, in case you've forgotten."

"Right. By killing yourself. Not the sort of strategy you can replicate on the regular. Also, cooking is a *slightly* different skill set from combat."

"Fine, fine," he said, grinning. "I'll just provide the moral support, then."

I grabbed the spices we needed off the rack and started grinding them with a pestle. Priya got to work chopping the veggies. Darton stayed there next to me, his arm grazing mine when I shifted a little closer. The warmth of his presence spread through my body with a glow that felt almost like magic.

This was our life now. This apartment, those classes, fencing practice and hanging out with friends. I couldn't remember the last time I'd felt actually... content. Maybe I never had, even in that first life. The looming threat of the dark fae had always been there in the back of my mind.

We only had this one life left. I had no idea where it was going to take us. But all that mattered to me was that this time, we were going to get to really *live* it.

ABOUT THE AUTHOR

Eva Chase lives in Canada with her family. She loves stories both swoony and supernatural, and strong women and the men who appreciate them. Along with the Legends Reborn series, she is also the author of the Demons of Fame paranormal romance series, beginning with *Caught in the Glow*. You can visit her online at **www.evachase.com**.

www.ingramcontent.com/pod-product-compliance
Lightning Source LLC
Chambersburg PA
CBHW030243200626
46816CB00002BA/490